BRING ME SUNSHINE

ALEX BROWN

Boldwood

First published in Great Britain in 2024 by Boldwood Books Ltd.

Copyright © Alex Brown, 2024

Cover Design by Lizzie Gardiner

Cover Images: Shutterstock and Adobe Stock

Every effort has been made to obtain the necessary permissions with reference to copyright material, both illustrative and quoted. We apologise for any omissions in this respect and will be pleased to make the appropriate acknowledgements in any future edition.

A CIP catalogue record for this book is available from the British Library.

Paperback ISBN 978-1-83603-078-2

Large Print ISBN 978-1-83603-077-5

Hardback ISBN 978-1-83603-076-8

Ebook ISBN 978-1-83603-079-9

Kindle ISBN 978-1-83603-080-5

Audio CD ISBN 978-1-83603-072-0

MP3 CD ISBN 978-1-83603-071-3

Digital audio download ISBN 978-1-83603-074-4

Boldwood Books Ltd
23 Bowerdean Street
London SW6 3TN
www.boldwoodbooks.com

For Rowan, the best agent in town, thank you for everything.

Queenager
noun / kwen, ajer/

A woman with experience who still knows how to have fun.

PROLOGUE
KALOSIROS, GREECE, 1990

Sinking her toes into the sand, she savoured the soft sensation as the plump, peach sun streaked the sky amber, bathing the sea with its shaft of shimmering gold. Leaning into him, she rested her head on his shoulder as they sat together on a large rock at the water's edge listening to the waves tumbling over the sand. The holiday was almost over – two blissful weeks of snorkelling, sketching the gorgeous Greek island sights, shell collecting, horse riding on wet sand at low tide and hanging out together drinking cans of Fanta Orange and eating homemade houmous with warm pitta bread – before they'd each go back to their respective lives, him in Athens and her in London.

She touched a finger to the beaded friendship bracelets they had exchanged and smiled as she remembered the piece of paper tucked inside the pocket of her jean shorts. His address. Even though she already knew where his grandparents' whitewashed sugar cube house was, where he stayed in the summer, near his family's beach taverna, this was different. He had given her the piece of paper with his Athens address on, which meant things had changed between them now. This was the start of something special, a proper romance, she just knew it. She would put his address in her diary for safekeeping and, as soon as she got back home to England, she could write to him and cross off the days until they could be together again next summer. Her lips still tingled from the touch of his mouth on hers. Her first real kiss. And her heart had fizzed, sending butterflies swirling around inside her. She felt on top of the world. Back home she kept a Jackie Collins library book in her school bag to read in the privacy of her bedroom and now she finally understood how Lucky Santangelo felt when she was in love.

As the sun melted away, turning the night sky into a canopy of twinkling stars, she curled her fingers around his before tracing a heart on the back of his hand, whispering the first line from *their* song... '"Bring Me Sunshine".' The swirling sensation soared inside her again as she moved her head and he turned to face her, singing softly, '"In your smile",' as he rested his forehead on hers, the sweet tang of Fanta still there on his lips as they kissed again, making her wish she could stay in this moment forever.

1

TINDLEDALE, RURAL ENGLAND, PRESENT DAY

In the hall of the grand, gated residence on a hilltop overlooking undulating fields full of sheep where she was working, Gina hummed happily to herself as she packed her cleaning products into the laundry basket that she used to transport them from her clients' houses to the boot of her car. Checking that nothing had been left behind, she hitched the basket onto her left hip and pulled the heavy front door closed before making the trek all the way down the steep, million-mile-long driveway, or so it seemed, to the lane where she now had to park. Mr and Mrs Hawton-Jones were very particular about the honey-coloured stone brickwork on their driveway and, since that time last month when Gina's clapped-out old Clio had leaked sticky black oil all over the place, they had asked her to park on the grassy verge by the side of the road. She had apologised profusely at the time of course, willing her face to stop flaming, and inwardly cursing her top lip for choosing to flick on the sweat sprinkler at the worst possible moment, as she and Mrs Hawton-Jones watched the oil slick become a rivulet of rainbow-coloured liquid when the rain started. The oil had snaked and smeared all over the driveway, pooling at the toes of Gina's canvas slip-on trainers that had definitely seen better days. She wished she had been able to run away from her shame, but it had been impossible as she still needed the money from this cleaning job to go towards the last instalment due on her holiday – a whole two weeks away on the Greek island of Kalosiros.

Gina had been dreaming and cleaning and humming songs to herself for years as she thought about going back to the idyllic Greek island full of happy childhood holiday memories there with her single parent mum, Shirley. She fondly remembered the cylindrical windmills and winding white cobbled lanes and rock-lined beaches, the rays from the hot Mediterranean sun dazzling on the crystalline azure waves. Especially the summer she had turned fifteen and shared her first kiss – then more kisses in the summers after too – with Nico, the boy from the beach taverna. The holidays had stopped when Shirley became ill and then when she died, those good times had faded to a distant memory. Gina had met her husband, Colin, soon after, but all these years later she found herself wondering if Nico still lived on the tiny island and if he remembered her, because she'd never forgotten about him. Not that this was her reason for wanting to go back to the Kalosiros. It was more that she had never forgotten the happy, carefree feeling of her youth, or the romance and sense of escape she had felt when she was there and that she dreamed of recapturing once more. Then, after seeing her absolute favourite film, *Mamma Mia!*, a few years ago, having missed it the first time around, Gina had started working as a cleaner and had been saving up ever since. She had visions of frolicking across a moonlit beach in a floaty kaftan with a warm wind in her hair and the rousing strum of Abba's 'Fernando' playing somewhere in the background. And to be honest, it was the thought of doing this that had kept her going throughout all those times she'd snapped on her sunshine yellow marigolds ready to get elbow-deep in scrubbing somebody else's loo.

Reaching the Clio, Gina stowed the basket in the boot and fished her phone out from the front pocket of her pink tabard to switch it back on. The phone made a tweeting bird sound immediately to signify the arrival of another message. She closed her eyes momentarily and let out a long fortifying breath before looking at the screen. She knew the symphony of message alerts chirping one after the other would be from Colin, her husband of twenty-seven years. He was the only person who insisted on sending her streams of messages when she was out working. His first message had chirped on her phone over two hours ago just as she had arrived at Mr and Mrs Hawton-Joneses' house and was carefully putting the laundry basket down on the 'Welcome Home' mat outside their front door. She'd had her index finger poised to press the doorbell that chimed like a herd of mountain goats with bells on their collars, knowing that Mrs Hawton-Jones would do that impatient, sighing smile thing if Gina was looking at her phone when the door opened, so she had swiftly switched it off and shoved it in her pocket. But there was no ignoring him now, Colin would only keep on, calling or badgering her with more messages until she answered him. So after listening to a partial voice message before it cut out, she tapped through all the messages to get the gist of what he was actually saying, her eyes homing in on the key words that made her scrolling index finger start to tremble in disbelief and disappointment.

Sorry love... Can't be helped... Make it up to you... Never mind... Why don't you go with a mate or my mum instead?

Gina let it sink in, intending on counting to ten first, but she only made it to three before a rage reared up inside her and she pressed call, willing herself to try to keep calm, but no matter how hard she tried, it felt impossible to suppress the feeling. It'd been happening more and more for the best part of a year now – a horrible tension, a rage that seemed to descend on her from absolutely nowhere and often without reason. But right now, right here, there was a reason, and even if her frustration felt scarily disproportionate, it didn't change the fact that she didn't want to go on a romantic holiday of a lifetime with a mate! Not that she really had any mates, certainly not one she was close enough with to go on holiday for two weeks. Yes, there were a few women she chatted to over at the allotment she tended to on a Saturday morning, but she had lost touch with her real best friends from school when she had started going out with Colin all those years ago. He always said that they were enough for each other and didn't need other friends and it had felt sweet in the beginning, but not so much now. And her much older mother-in-law, Pam, who lived with her and Colin, hated everything 'foreign'. Pam would refuse to even try a chicken ball from a Friday night Chinese takeaway, already convinced 'it won't agree with me and then I'll have one of my turns and be up all night with heartburn'. Gina was tired of hearing stuff like this all the time. It sucked the little bit of joy, that she still felt from time to time, right out of her life. She did love Pam, in her own way, but there was no way she was about to test this love by spending two weeks with her, twenty-four-seven, in a foreign country. No, Gina had no desire to end up in a Greek jail charged with throttling her own mother-in-law.

'Are you on your way back now?' Colin said as a conversation opener, seemingly without a care in the world and oblivious to having trampled all over his wife's long-held dream holiday plans that she had worked incredibly hard to save for. Gina pulled the phone away from her ear in an exaggerated fashion like they do in slapstick movies when words literally fail the person holding the phone, his nonchalance further stoking the bubbling furnace inside her.

'No. Colin. I am not on my way back now!'

'But you're usually finished by now and I've made you a cup of tea. My treat. Thought you could do with it after all that cleaning, love.' She could actually hear the smile of satisfaction in his voice as he gave himself a proverbial pat on the back. A cup of tea – give the man a medal. The beat of silence that followed was deafening as Gina focused on the pumping sound of her own blood throbbing in her ears and turning her clarity of thought into a head full of cotton wool.

'Is that all you have to say?' Gina quickly shook her head and took a big breath as she tried to garner some focus. She got in the car and closed the door, figuring it probably wasn't a good idea to lose her flaming temper within earshot of her employers. Mind you, if the holiday was off, then she wouldn't need to clean for them any more in any case. Colin covered the household expenses but wouldn't pay for extras, which was why she had got the cleaning job in the first place, so she could save up for their holiday. The disappointment was crushing and for a moment she thought she might cry. Tears made her vision filmy as she pulled the seatbelt over her shoulder and clicked it into place, flipped her phone to hands-free and put it in the cradle on the dashboard. She turned the key in the ignition, and, as if on autopilot, she prayed for the car to start the first time, as she always did. Nothing. Just the hollow sound of grinding metal as if the car had finally decided to give up for good, much like Gina was feeling like doing in that moment.

Catching a glimpse of herself in the rear-view mirror, Gina wondered when she got so tired-looking. Weary and worn down. Her grey roots in stark contrast to the box-dyed brown curls of the rest of her hair. She let out a long sigh, swiped the cuff of a sleeve across her cheeks to stem the tears and sat back in the seat. She was in no fit state to drive home safely anyway, and to be honest, home was the last place she wanted to be right now. Not with Colin being all nonchalant about having let her down, no doubt, and Pam complaining about something or another.

'I did say in one of my messages that I'll make it up to you, love. We could use the money you've saved to go to that caravan place you like for a long weekend—'

'Colin, please, don't...' she said quietly, seemingly now resigned to the fact they wouldn't be going on holiday after all. The chance of rekindling a romantic connection and revitalising her lacklustre marriage completely shattered.

'Well, I'm only trying to help... What would you rather I do? Lose my job? Because that's what will happen if I don't go on the away-day,' Colin piped up, and Gina's heart sank even further. She had heard enough. He just didn't get it. She wondered if he ever had.

'If you really wanted to help then surely you would have put our holiday plans before a team-building away-day!' she snapped. 'Where did you say it was again?' That part of Colin's voice message had been full of crackling static and so it had been impossible to hear what he had been saying.

'Oh, somewhere near Slough, I think. I can get all the details for you if you don't believe me...' he offered keenly. A little too keenly, it suddenly struck Gina. 'You know, the hotel where we're all staying...' Gina inhaled again, his vagueness making her uneasy, but she didn't have the energy to ask more right now. The top and bottom of it was that Colin had clearly never even booked the time off work, because surely if he had, then they wouldn't expect him to cancel a foreign holiday that had been well over two years in the planning, to attend a team-building day somewhere near Slough?

A sudden tapping on the window startled Gina and she instinctively told Colin, 'I've got to go,' and ended the call. Mrs Hawton-Jones was standing at the door of the car. Just what she needed.

Gina gingerly cranked down the window.

'Is everything alright, dear? Only you've been sitting here for quite some time now,' Mrs Hawton-Jones said, fingering the heirloom gold locket on a chain at her neck before folding her arms and rearranging her face into one of concern.

'Yes, yes, thank you, sorry, I was about to leave, I just had a bit of trouble with starting the car and then my husband called to tell me we can't go on the holiday I have been dreaming of forever and —' Gina stopped talking, conscious that she was babbling and massively oversharing and that Mrs Hawton-Jones now had her head tilted to one side in sympathy – the last thing she wanted. She could feel tears stinging in the corners of her eyes again. *Please don't feel sorry for me. Please don't feel sorry for me.* Gina said it over and over like a calming mantra inside her head, willing herself not to cry as she always did when someone was being nice to her.

'Oh dear.' Mrs Hawton-Jones studied Gina for a few seconds and then to her horror, surprise, or utter disbelief... she wasn't sure which exactly, her employer swung open the car door and took Gina's hand off the steering wheel, holding it firmly and reassuringly in hers. 'Come on now, let's get you a strong, sweet cup of tea and see if we can sort this out together. Harold can take a look at the car while you tell me about this holiday you can't go on.' Gina stumbled out of the car. 'That's it, there you go,' and she couldn't hold back the tears any longer as Mrs Hawton-Jones put her arm around her shoulders and chivvied her back up the million-mile-long driveway towards the house.

* * *

A few weeks later, and Gina was still thanking her lucky stars for making the sensible decision when booking the holiday all that time ago to sign up for the special, fully comprehensive insurance policy. Mrs Hawton-Jones, or Anne – as she had said Gina was to call her now – had explained it all. And, being a consumer rights solicitor, Gina knew right away that Anne meant business, as she sipped her tea and listened while Gina told her all about Colin and his team-building away-day. So after a few phone calls, Gina, with Anne telling her what to say, had managed to get a refund on Colin's ticket and was going to use the unexpected windfall to have the time of her life, on her own, in her dream holiday destination. Including an upgrade to a deluxe room with a sea view in the brand-new boutique Hotel Mirabelle, that she was able to afford now she'd be travelling on her own. Anne had insisted on it, horrified on hearing that Gina had contemplated even for a second that she wasn't going on the holiday just because Colin couldn't or wouldn't.

'Oh no dear, you mustn't let a little blip send you off course,' Anne had told her. 'You are a woman of substance! Come on, say it after me. "I am a woman of substance; I will not be deterred, and I am perfectly capable of going on holiday by myself and having a jolly good time!"' Gina had felt a bit daft saying all that, especially when Anne had stood up into a power pose, with fisted hands on hips, chanting the motivational mantra in a very loud Margaret Thatcher voice and motioning for Gina to do the same. But Gina had managed it and had been surprised to discover that she did actually feel stronger and a little bit more like her old self – the woman she had been in her late teens and early twenties, when she had much more confidence and didn't take anywhere near as much crap as she did these days. Although Colin hadn't been impressed by her 'behaving oddly', as he'd said when she had told him she was still going on the holiday, and she mooted the idea of them needing some time apart. But then seemingly wanting to have the upper hand he had swiftly followed it up with some 'odd behaviour' of his own, saying, 'I can't believe you're still going. It's like you don't even want to be married any more if you're gallivanting like a single woman. Perhaps you want to leave me. Well, if it's what you *really* want, Gina, then it would be very selfish of me to stand in your way. Let's call it a trial separation, a chance for you to see if you can manage without me.' And she had felt strangely calm at the prospect of doing just that.

Now, as she walked down the aisle of the aeroplane looking for her seat, dragging a wheelie cabin bag behind her and struggling to stop it swerving at a right angle on account of one of the wheels being broken, Gina wondered if she should have shaved her legs, waxed her top lip and flipped open the pop-up tent she kept in the garage to give herself an all over spray tan inside it, like she would have done years ago, before her libido started ghosting her and she still liked having sex with Colin. Thinking of her now estranged husband, she wondered if he had spotted the note she'd left on the fridge yet? *Gone to Greece.* But on second thoughts, sod it, she couldn't be bothered with all that palaver, and besides, she had every intention of getting a real tan in the Greek sunshine as soon as she arrived, in about four hours' time. The rousing strum of the opening chords of 'Fernando' were playing once again as the internal soundtrack to the exciting adventure she was going on. She was kaftan ready – hairy legs, top lip and all – and she could not wait for her holiday to begin.

2

The landing gear touched down and Gina braced backwards in her seat to savour the thrilling sensation as the aeroplane rushed along the runway. Through the oval window to her left, the majestic rise of the granite mountains in the distance took her breath away. As did the creamy curve of sand and sparkling, lapis blue sea, still rippling in the backdraft breeze from the aeroplane flying over the coastline before the sharp descent needed to get a head start on making sure they didn't miss the end of the island's tiny runway and end up in the water. It had nearly happened the summer she turned sixteen, when the pilot left it too late and had to do a sudden ascent, circle several times, before attempting the landing again. Thankfully she had brought them to a successful halt amidst a spontaneous round of very relieved applause from all the passengers. Gina had often thought about that moment over the years, the way her mum, Shirley, had patted the top of her hand and calmy told her, 'It'll be OK, love, and if it isn't, then at least we are together.'

Gina wished they were together now, with Shirley here by her side, excited and looking forward to all the things they used to love doing here on the island. She had also wondered over the years what Shirley would have made of Colin and knew deep down that she would probably have liked him in the beginning. He had seemed kind and caring when they first met, not long after Shirley had died from the breast cancer that had returned with a vengeance after a long remission. Gina had been at such a low ebb back then, having lost contact with her friends from art college after taking a break, and so she had been feeling lonely and like the spark had gone right out of her life. Then after meeting Colin, he convinced her there was no need to go back to college, that the studying was too much for her so soon after losing her mum.

Grief. Looking back, she knew that's what it was now. As an only child, she had always been very close to her mum, and then when she was a teenager, they had become even closer, more like best friends, sisters even, and so when Shirley died, the void had been unbearable at times. Isolating and lonely. Meeting Colin had given her a lift. A proper boost! He had brought the laughter back in to her life and she had fallen in love with him fast, his smooth charm and desire for her hard to resist. Gina hadn't felt lonely or isolated any more. Being with Colin had softened things, and then when he proposed and they got married a year or so later, she had felt secure again too; it had given her a sense of belonging. She was determined to make her marriage work, knowing the heartbreak of her own parents' marriage having fallen apart when she was a little girl. And she had loved getting married, with visions of creating a new family and having babies with her husband and living happily-ever-after – the whole fairy tale she had still believed in back then. But it hadn't worked out that way.

Colin hadn't really been interested in having children but reluctantly said they could try. Still, it never happened, and he wouldn't engage in pursuing fertility treatment. Gina often wondered too how different her life might have been if she had stayed at college and pursued her passion for painting and sketching. If she had ignored Colin when he had laughed that time after she persuaded him to sit for a portrait to celebrate their wedding anniversary. She had been toying with the idea of taking up an art course again, but he hadn't liked the shape of his eyes, or nose, ears, or... well, any of it to be precise. The canvas had ended up on the bonfire with 'the rest of the rubbish' she had heard him muttering as he pushed it under his arm and pulled open the back door to go out into the garden. They had argued about it after she told him how hurtful his words had been to hear, and he had apologised and pacified her, saying it was 'just a joke' and that he had only been trying to help her by getting rid of it because she seemed upset with the way the painting had turned out. And then the whole matter had been forgotten about. But deep down, Gina knew this was when the cracks in her marriage really set in and they had been mostly plastering over them ever since.

Oh well, she had spent the best part of the last four hours or so of the flight with her headphones on, listening to music and thinking about the shambolic state of her marriage and didn't want to dwell on it any longer and let thoughts of regret spoil her holiday. She couldn't turn back time, so what was the point of picking over it all. She had to look forward because she had dreamed of this holiday and worked very hard for a very long time to pay for it, and so she was going to blooming well enjoy every second of the next fortnight. Smiling to herself, she took off her headphones and nodded as if to underline her thoughts. An air steward made an announcement.

'Ladies and gentlemen, British Airways welcomes you to Kalosiros, the local time is 5.30 p.m., and the weather is a glorious twenty-seven degrees...'

A collective 'oooooh' sound circuited the aircraft cabin.

'Oh, thank goodness for that, I can't wait to get off and find a nice taverna to eat moussaka in, and finish off with a small glass of that delicious Greek liqueur, mastika,' an older woman with pink-framed glasses sitting next to Gina said, then quickly followed it with, 'Sorry, did I say all that out loud?' Gina nodded politely at the woman. 'I'm not sure I can handle another minute of my husband's complaining, you probably didn't hear him going on about it being too cold, too hot, too many people, not enough food, beer or what-ever with your headphones on, which I have to say are a very good idea and I wish I'd had the foresight to get myself a pair,' she added in a covert voice. 'It's been non-stop, and the holiday hasn't even started properly yet.' The woman rolled her eyes towards the man in the aisle seat, her husband presumably, and Gina smiled, unsure of what to say, but didn't need to respond as the woman carried on obliviously. 'It's OK, he can't hear me... deaf as a post and he refuses to wear the hearing aids that we paid a fortune for, which is part of the problem as he gets frustrated and then yells at me, convinced I'm doing it on purpose... talking too quietly, that is.' The woman shook her head in exasperation. 'Are you travelling alone?'

'Yes, my husband,' Gina paused before explaining, 'my err... we are trialling a separation.' The words felt funny, unfamiliar coming out of her mouth, and she wobbled momentarily but quickly took a big breath and carried on talking. 'Yes, he was supposed to be coming too, but couldn't make it in the end.' Gina flicked her eyes downwards. It was all well and good her being maverick, a woman of substance or whatever it was she had chanted with Anne in her drawing room that day, but she'd be lying if she didn't admit to feeling a bit weird as well now that it was actually happening and she was here on the Greek island of Kalosiros, completely alone. She had looked around the aero-plane during the flight and seen so many happy couples, the woman sitting next to her included, or so she had assumed, which was ironic really when the woman didn't sound happy at all.

'That's a shame,' the woman said, the tone of her voice sympathetic now. 'How long are you here for?'

'Two weeks.'

'Well good for you coming on your own! And if you want my advice, which you may not do of course, but I have a feeling it may help you... just make the most of it, dear. There's been so many times over the years when I wish I'd had the courage to go it alone, but well... I never did. And don't suppose I ever will now.' The woman's eyes clouded with a sadness that made Gina want to step forward and give her an enormous hug. 'Anyway, cheerio and I hope you have a fabulous time.'

'Thank you. And I hope you find that nice taverna and enjoy your moussaka and mastika.' Gina gave the woman a warm, kindly smile.

'Oh I will! And if you see a woman sitting on the beach all by herself, it will be me... having bumped off my husband so I can have a wonderful Shirley Valentine moment in peace,' she laughed, but Gina spotted the fleeting glimmer of sorrow that passed across the woman's face.

As she unbuckled her seatbelt, Gina closed her eyes momentarily, inhaled deeply and smiled as if to bank the giddy feeling of anticipation into her memory forever, just as she had as a teenager all those years ago on arriving here with her mum for their annual summer holiday. Two whole weeks of sunshine and bliss. Time to potter along the harbour arm, mingling with the pelicans that roamed freely, time to wander around the open-air market, time to sit in the sun with her romance book without Colin coming out with his usual jibe about her wasting time reading such rubbish, time to swim in the sea, time to enjoy a long, lazy lunch with a glass of chilled wine, time to *just be*, and to do whatever she pleased. What a treat! Although she'd be fooling herself to think she wasn't a little bit nervous about being here alone for fourteen days.

It was going to be a first for her, having never even lived on her own. Colin had moved into her house soon after they started dating and then Pam too, a week after the wedding, supposedly on a temporary basis while she recovered from a hysterectomy, but then she never moved back out. Gina hadn't minded though as she felt sorry for Pam, who suffered with rheumatoid arthritis too, and so looked after her; it had reminded her of when she had looked after Shirley when she was ill. And Pam was fairly easy-going and kind enough, when she wasn't complaining, although did have a tendency to think the sun shone out of her only child, Colin's, backside. But it did mean that Gina never had a moment to herself, apart from when she was out doing one of her cleaning jobs or helping out at the allotment, and even then, Colin would be messaging her, with a variety of requests, usually along the lines of 'what's for dinner?', closely followed by 'when will you be home?', or his favourite 'where are you?' Even though he could easily find out for himself by looking on the Life360 app the three of them had installed on their phones – not in a weird stalkerish way, but because there had been a special promo on the 'family bundle' and Colin loved nothing more than a bargain. So Gina, Colin and Pam now had their own family 'bubble' with a special button to press for emergency assistance, like if they were ever taken hostage and couldn't use their voice to communicate, Colin had explained.

Then, when she did get home, Pam was always ensconced in the big cuddle armchair by the window in the lounge, the one that Gina and Shirley used to sit in as they shared a bucket of popcorn and watched a favourite film or TV series together. *Grease, Pretty Woman, An Officer and a Gentleman* or old episodes of *Bewitched* were their go-to favourites for a full-on binge-fest packed with romance, laughter, highs, lows, and lots of nostalgia.

Gina had certainly never been on a holiday by herself before, not even a day trip or a spa day. She wasn't even sure if she liked her own company but supposed now was as good a time as any to find out, as what better place to do so than on a gorgeous Greek island? Plus, with a bit of luck the mobile signal on the island would be patchy and she could give herself a digital detox – a proper break from Colin and his million-messages-a-day habit. And yes, even though they had sort of agreed on a trial separation, Colin had continued contacting her for the entirety of the taxi ride to the airport with twenty-three unread messages, which Gina had seen on the screen when she had switched off her phone as the aeroplane had been waiting on the runway shortly before take-off.

3

Gathering herself and the glossy magazine she had treated herself to at the airport, Gina stood up and politely waited for the woman with the pink glasses and her husband to leave before moving into the aisle. After retrieving her wheelie cabin bag from the overhead locker, she slipped the magazine into the big, reusable bag for life that she was carrying in the crook of her elbow and made her way to the exit door.

'Wow! This place looks incredible and isn't the weather wonderful?' a woman with curly blonde hair styled into a chic, bouncy bob said to Gina as they moved down the mobile steps leading to the runway. As both women made it to the rustic, sun-bleached tarmac, the perimeter lined with tufty mounds of grass and wildflowers, they smiled at each other and adjusted the handles of their respective wheelie cabin bags.

'It sure is,' Gina replied shyly, not used to being noticed by a complete stranger, but liking it that two women had spoken to her now. And it briefly crossed her mind that they may not have talked to her if she had been travelling with Colin, people rarely did on the odd occasion they went out together. But then Colin could be a bit frosty with people he didn't know, often suspecting they had an ulterior motive or were out to take advantage. Like the time he'd been very offhand with a man on the next table in a restaurant when he had asked if they'd mind keeping an eye on his young daughter while he popped to the loo. Colin had then bemoaned the entire time that the guy had a flaming cheek expecting them to be unpaid babysitters, even though the girl had sat quietly reading a book for the five minutes or so that her dad wasn't there. Gina, on the other hand, had loved looking after the little girl, having a taste of what being a mum might have felt like, if only for a short while.

Walking on, with the perfect blue sky and the gorgeous Greek air scented with jasmine, oregano, pine and sea salt cocooning her like a cashmere blanket, Gina discreetly studied the woman who was in front of her now. She looked about the same age as Gina and seemed to be travelling on her own too. But that's as far as the similarity went, as the other woman was impeccably dressed; stylish and fashionable in a very classic way, reminding Gina of Charlotte from *Sex and the City*. She was wearing a candy pink and white gingham full skirt with a wide belt, a sleeveless white blouse, cork-heeled wedge sandals and a silk scarf tied at a jaunty angle around her neck, and she smelled divine too, of very expensive perfume. Gina gave her own crumpled cotton skirt and matching pink Primark T-shirt a surreptitious glance and made a mental note to shower off the musty 'travelling scent' that was lingering on her body as soon as she got to the hotel. Admiring the chic, floppy straw hat the woman pulled from a designer tote bag looped over her arm, and popped on her head, Gina made another mental note to see if she might find a similar hat for herself somewhere. And a tote bag too, so she could ditch the bloody awful big bag for life she'd had to bring on holiday after discovering at the last minute – as she pulled the front door closed behind her and walked to the taxi waiting by the kerb to take her to the airport – that the lovely looking, but cheap, raffia beach bag she had bought especially for the holiday had a hole in the bottom. She had got all the way to the end of her front path before noticing the trail of bag paraphernalia scattered across the crazy paving slabs. She wondered if she might find what she was looking for here on the island – in the market near the harbour arm perhaps? Then she wondered too if the market was actually still here and felt a bubble of anticipatory fizz at the prospect of exploring the island, retracing her teenage footsteps to find out. From memory, there had been a weekly market, every Wednesday afternoon and into the evening when traditional Greek music would then play, and street food would be served. White canopied stalls sold fresh fruit and vegetables, fish from the sea lapping mere metres away, and freshly baked bread too. Plus handcrafted, traditional pottery and plates, trinkets, and occasional items for travellers like her, who had forgotten to bring the essentials... a sun hat and factor 50 sun cream, she realised, as her pale, freckly skin was already beginning to prickle in the heat.

The Charlotte-styled woman with the sun hat put a pair of designer shades on too and headed towards the ramshackle hut where a group of handsome, tanned and toned Greek men in uniforms were smiling and checking passports with a cursory, laidback glance before ushering everyone towards the luggage retrieval area inside the small, single-storey whitewashed airport building. Having managed to pack all her clothes inside the wheelie cabin bag – Gina didn't have very many summer dresses, and just a couple of bikinis with matching wraps and a kaftan, in any case – she left the airport and went straight to a waiting queue of taxis to find one to take her to the hotel.

Twenty minutes of very narrow, winding, rustic, cliffside roads with hairpin bends driven at breakneck speeds later, and the taxi came to a halt at the end of a long driveway on the top of a hill. She paid the driver and waved goodbye with a cheery, but very relieved, *efcharisto* in thanks as she took a deep breath and willed her racing heart to slow to a more normal rhythm. Smoothing down her crumpled skirt and tidying her curls into place, she exhaled and adopted a serene smile to create how she imagined a breezy, chic, well-travelled woman would present, and pulled her cabin bag towards the honey-coloured converted farmhouse nestling among vineyards, citrus and olive trees. The setting was stunning and looked even better in real life than it had in the online luxury travel brochure Anne had popped up on the laptop screen during that phone call to get the refund on Colin's ticket and give her holiday the ultimate glow up.

'Welcome to the Hotel Mirabelle.' A man in jeans and a white polo shirt with the hotel's logo on, opened the glass and brass furnished entrance door and took her suitcase in one swift, effortless movement.

'Thank you.' Gina followed him to the reception desk, the cool, citrus-scented air-conditioned breeze refreshing on her hot body, that had chosen this precise moment to flare up like a flaming bush fire. Typical. Grabbing a crumpled-up tissue from her bag for life, Gina swiftly used it to dab at the beads of sweat she could feel forming on her top lip. The man parked her suitcase by the reception desk where an exceedingly attractive bearded guy with curly hair the colour of chestnuts glossed in sunshine, and matching, melting brown eyes took over.

'Hello, I am Cristos, and welcome! May I have your name please?' he asked, with a sexy Greek accent, locking eye contact and holding it for a second or two longer than necessary, smiling warmly, charismatically, intimately almost, as if she were the only woman in the world. And it felt unnerving but mingled with a thread of thrill too. It sounded daft, but Gina swore she could feel a sort of awakening, something inside her, like a switch flicking back on and she wasn't complaining about it. It felt good to be seen by a very hot man, and not feel as invisible as she often did, when minding her own business back home in England doing her cleaning jobs and fielding Colin's constant messages.

'Oh, um...' she started, but the words wouldn't come out properly, so she swallowed and willed her cheeks – that she just knew would be resembling a pair of plum tomatoes by now – to dial themselves down. 'Err, yes of course, it's Gina,' she squeaked, fiddling with her hair. *So much for my breezy, chic, well-seasoned travelling type woman persona.* She was instantly back to a bumbling, foggy-headed version of herself. And to be honest, she didn't like it one bit. But it was happening more and more these days. She never used to be this unassured and lacking in confidence – yes, she'd always been a bit self-conscious and introverted, but at least she used to know how to walk into a hotel lobby and say her own name to possibly the hottest man she had seen in a very long time! Ever, in fact. Nowadays, it was as if the last drop of confidence flowing through her veins had done a U-turn and taken off to be somewhere else far more appealing, like birds do in the wintertime when they've had enough of the cold weather and want a more exotic climate. Plus, her confidence going AWOL often happened without warning, not so much at a moment's notice, which just made her feel even more unanchored and like she couldn't even trust herself, never knowing from one moment to the next if her properly functioning adult life skills were going to show up. And it was annoying. Rude. She thought her brain would have got the hang of what it needed to do by now after forty-nine years of practice. She was going to be fifty next year. FIFTY. And always imagined that she would have got her life together by now. Sussed it all out and knew how to behave with poise and purpose.

Resting the big bag for life on the desk, next to an exquisite arrangement of vivid fuchsia pink bougainvillea in a large white ceramic pot, Gina immediately changed her mind when the pot wobbled precariously, and so dumped the bag on the floor by her feet instead.

'Welcome, Gina.' Cristos smiled and tilted his head slightly to the side before gently adding, 'and your surname, please?'

'Err, yes... it's—' And she froze, a sudden swirling feeling surrounding her. Her mind had gone completely blank. She couldn't remember her own full name! Panicking, she pursed her lips and absent-mindedly touched one of the bougainvillaea's pink petals to buy herself some time. The pumping sound of her blood pulsing in her ears was intense. But then overwhelming relief flooded through her when a nanosecond or two later the synapses of her brain kicked in and she knew it; 'Bennett. Two n's and two t's,' she hurriedly explained on autopilot as she usually did, to be helpful, as people always asked how her surname was spelt. She wreathed her face in a big smile and folded her arms to cover the momentary memory loss... and sweat-drenched cleavage she could feel, trickling in rivulets down between her boobs and pooling across her midriff. She didn't even dare glance down to see if the sweat had gathered into a pattern that looked like a mini map of Australia across the front of her T-shirt. It had happened a few weeks before, in a cafe when she had gone in to treat herself to a frothy coffee and a cake, when she'd become overwhelmed with indecision on seeing a menu board full of things that she had never heard of before. The barista had patiently talked her through every option like she was some kind of doddery old lady who had escaped from her care home, all the while the perky young girl behind her in the queue had huffed and puffed and chewed her bubble gum with ever increasing intensity so Gina was left in no doubt whatsoever as to just how annoying she actually was.

'Gina Bennett,' Cristos confirmed, his Greek accent making her name sound far more evocative than it ever did back home in England. 'And your passport, please?' he added, stroking a tanned index finger across the screen of an iPad on the desk. Tasting salt from the sweat pooling on her top lip, Gina ducked down and hid her head in the bag for life to buy herself a moment to dab with the tissue again before popping back up like a meerkat with her passport in her hand.

'Here it is!' she exclaimed, a little too enthusiastically, the relief palpable now the 'episode' or whatever it was that had just happened seemed to be over. Her body temperature was working its way back to some semblance of normal.

'Thank you.' He took the passport and was about to check it with the booking details on the screen, she presumed, when he paused, placed his stroking finger to his top lip which he tapped a couple of times and motioned to her with his head inclined and one eyebrow raised. It took a moment for her to realise. The tissue. He was telling her she had a clod of dried-up old tissue stuck to her top lip. *Kill me now.* Using the palm of her hand, Gina swiped at the whole section surrounding her mouth. Satisfied that she had it all, she ducked down again and flicked the flakes of sweat-stained tissue inside the bag for life, silently willing the tiled floor to crack right open and drag her down under. This was not how she had envisaged her dream holiday would begin.

'Sorry,' she said, swiftly followed by, 'I didn't, um... realise, thank you,' and promptly stopped talking, wondering why on earth she was apologising.

'It's no problem,' Cristos shrugged easily, before running through the arrangements for breakfast (on the terrace outside with the breathtakingly beautiful view of the sea in the distance, or delivered to her room if she preferred), telling her where the lounge bar was, the roster of hotel events and activities available to guests, and about the outside infinity swimming pool too, before adding, 'And here is your room number and key card. You like me to come with you and bring your luggage?' He lifted an eyebrow, the delicious scent of his cologne – sandalwood and sea salt – permeating the air between them.

She took the little envelope with the number on and key card inside and pushed it into her skirt pocket, quickly replying, 'Um, no, thanks, I'll be fine, err... thank you very much.' Grabbing up the bloody awful big bag for life and her wheelie cabin bag with the wonky wheel, she dashed away as fast as her new Hermes dupe sandals could carry her, vowing right away to add one of those mini battery-operated handheld fans to her market shopping list. And it would have been OK, just about, if she hadn't then tripped on something or another and stepped right out of her left sandal and ended up doing one of those absolutely cringy comedy staggers before pivoting and slapping her foot back inside the offending sandal to slink away towards the lift. Dying all over again inside as the lift doors slid together, she caught sight of her face in the mirror to see fine flakes of white tissue still clinging to the row of dark hairs above her top lip. And instantly wished that she had taken the time to do a thorough waxing session after all...

4

Gina pushed open the door to her deluxe hotel room and gasped, letting the bag for life slip from her fingers and drop onto the marble floor in a daze. The sight before her was beautiful and tranquil and scented with honeysuckle, vanilla and holiday happiness and completely exceeded all of her expectations. The main feature of the room was a giant-sized, sumptuous 'princess and the pea' style bed with a hand-embroidered white cotton cover and a mountain of pillows and cushions so high that she was sure she was going to need to do a running leap just to launch herself onto the top of the bed every night. On a stand beside the bed was a large gold lamp and a proper leather writing set which she opened, and then smiled in sheer joy on seeing a selection of postcards with exquisite photographic island sights on. In the little lounge area, there was a snack station stocked with bottles of water, foil pods of coffee to pop into the Nespresso machine and a large wooden box with an assortment of teabags and biscuits. Next to it was a platter of fresh figs and homemade sticky baclava sprinkled with pistachios on top and a little silver fork on the side so she wouldn't even need to use her fingers to eat, although she probably would, wasn't that part of the pleasure from eating such delicious food?

Gina tucked her hands up underneath her chin in glee as she sat on the blue and white tapestry print covered chaise longue, next to it a real olive tree in a big terracotta pot and a coffee table with an enormous cellophane-covered white wicker hamper packed with all kinds of treats. Expensive sun cream, face masks, body spray, bubble bath, a trio of votive candles, glossy magazines, a couple of paperbacks, chocolate, fruit, wine, and towelling slippers with a matching robe just like the ones she saw people wearing in the Champneys spa brochure she had dusted underneath on the hall table in Mr and Mrs Hawton-Joneses' house. There was a little white envelope tied with a blue ribbon taped to the top of the basket. Leaning forward, Gina carefully removed the card and smiled, wondering if perhaps Colin hadn't lost that loving feeling after all! He had been very attentive on the day before she left, peering over her shoulder as she had checked all of the holiday itinerary on the PC they shared – it sat on the console table in the alcove underneath the stairs. *Mind you, he's never pushed the boat out this far, the hamper must have cost a small fortune and looks like it's been personally curated, handpicked especially for me, there's even my name embroidered on the robe, for crying out loud!* Gina had read about this sort of thing happening in the magazine she'd bought for the flight but had no idea you could then have the personalised gift delivered to someone's hotel room on a small Greek island. And the hamper, the whole experience would definitely have cost at least ten times the amount of the bunch of chrysanthemums that Colin had presented to her on her birthday two years ago. He had forgotten her most recent birthday, blaming the supermarket for closing early on the day before as being the reason why. But perhaps he had been thinking about her 'Gone to Greece' note on the fridge and decided to make much more of an effort, the trial separation having galvanised him into action at last. Because right until the moment she left, Gina had got the impression that Colin thought she wouldn't actually go through with it.

Smiling, she quickly opened the envelope, vowing to find out the password for the hotel's guest Wi-Fi so his messages could be delivered, figuring it wouldn't hurt to see what he had to say at least, and wondering if there might be a possibility of resurrecting their marriage after all. Because it had been good in the early days, really good. They'd had fun together, liked each other and laughed together, and the sex had been brilliant at times... it was just the rest of it that had run out of steam somehow over the last few years. A slip of paper that looked like a voucher of some kind, fell out of the card, and landed on the floor. Gina picked it up, seeing a picture of a cocktail on the corner and some words written in Greek. She tucked the voucher back inside the envelope and read the card.

Dear Gina

I hope you have the most marvellous holiday and enjoy the hamper, and the raspberry ouzo cocktail too that will be waiting for you in the bar on exchange of the voucher enclosed. They really are quite delicious!

With warmest wishes, your friend,

Anne x

Silence followed. Stunned, Gina didn't know whether to laugh or cry. It was so kind and thoughtful of Anne to organise such a wonderful gift for her, and she was touched that someone like Anne, posh and elegant and living her life in a different league to Gina, would want to be her friend. But then another part of Gina felt deflated, foolish even, for letting herself have hope, for thinking, if only momentarily, that her husband might have organised such a lovely, thoughtful gift as this hamper delivery to the hotel room, just for her. Of course he hadn't, and she had known him long enough to know that it wasn't something he would do. She should have realised. Why would he? When he'd forgotten her last birthday and never remembered their wedding anniversary, or made much of an effort at Christmas, sometimes giving her a twenty-pound note on the big day and telling her to treat herself to something nice in the sales, like they were living in the 1950s or something, because let's face it... a decent dress or a pretty pair of shoes cost more than twenty quid these days! Even in the sales. They had argued about this kind of thing in more recent years and Colin had retorted with, 'Well you know me, I've never been one for making a fuss,' and now looking back in hindsight, which was always a very wonderful thing, she supposed he was absolutely right about that. She certainly did know him. And also knew that she should have spoken up years ago, instead of letting it slide on year after year and never saying what she really wanted. Which was just a *bit* of effort, some thought would be nice, even a wrapped present or two like the pile she always put underneath the tree for him. It was funny how putting a bit of distance between them was already giving her some crystal clarity. She'd had four hours on the flight to contemplate and could see it now and felt like a fool for settling all these years. Well, no more, she was going to have her lovely holiday and then make a decision about her marriage, and the way she felt right now in this moment, there was a high chance her future wouldn't include Colin. Their 'time-apart' trial separation or whatever this was, could very well become a permanent thing.

Gina helped herself to a hunk of baclava, mulling over the mixture of emotions as she took a big bite and gave herself a moment to thoroughly enjoy the gooey, chewy, flaky pastry, honeyed delight and then found herself laughing on thinking how huffy and puffy Pam would be right now on seeing her eat something so 'foreign'. And so Gina took another big bite, and another and another until she had polished off the whole hunk and thoroughly enjoyed it *on purpose* just to annoy Pam in her mind. Ha! Gina already felt a million times better. After licking the last of the honey from her fingertips and then wiping them clean on a napkin, she carefully opened the cellophane around the hamper and took out the robe and slippers, sinking into the softness of the lightweight waffle cotton material as she slipped the robe around her shoulders, having quickly discarded her T-shirt and skirt. Pushing her feet into the matching slippers, she sauntered over to the white, floaty floor-length chiffon curtains covering the window where she could feel a warm breeze floating into the room. Gina moved the material aside and took a sharp intake of breath all over again on discovering two open wooden shuttered doors leading out to her very own private balcony.

The view was magnificent, and Gina thought it well worth the extra she had paid as she stepped outside and immersed herself in the evocative citrus scent from the lemon tree orchards all around the hotel, the mountains in the distance wreathed in hazy mist against the vivid, turquoise sky. Her gaze meandered over more vineyards to her right, then to her left, winding cobbled streets of whitewashed sugar cube shaped houses with shuttered windows, pretty pink or pastel blue front doors, purple and red geraniums tumbling from rooftops. At the bottom she could see the hotel's very own beautiful beach, the white-capped waves lapping gently back and forth as if greeting her, welcoming her home, to come and sit on the rocks that sparkled in the sunshine, just as she had all those years ago as a teenager.

Giving herself a moment to just be, to listen to the cicadas buzzing in the breeze and to soak up the atmosphere, Gina rested her elbows on top of the wooden safety panel that wrapped around the balcony and allowed herself to breathe. In for four and out for four. Or something like that – there had been a whole article about calming techniques in the magazine she had read on the flight, but she reckoned they had missed a trick by not including 'stand on a balcony with quite possibly the best view in the world set out before you'. Because for the first time in a very long time, Gina felt completely calm in the current moment. It was as if all the tension and sudden ragey surges she had been putting up with had vanished and she felt lighter, even her shoulders were no longer tensed up somewhere around her ear lobes and had moved down a good couple of inches. It made her feel light and lifted. In fact, she actually felt a bit like her old self, the girl she was when she was last here, full of optimism and exciting energy, and it was a lovely feeling: exactly what she had been dreaming of for the last few years while planning and saving up to come back here. And she couldn't wait to explore the island, to wander through the lemon orchards and walk on the sandy beach below. But first she wanted to say thank you to Anne, so went back inside her room and over to where the writing set was, figuring a proper, old fashioned hand-written postcard was far more meaningful than a text message.

Then, after showering off the 'travel scent' and selecting one of her floaty maxi dresses, Gina slid on her sandals, applied some make-up – more than she usually wore, but then she had all the time in the world now to treat herself to the full works with a nour-ishing moisturiser, concealer and highlighter and properly blended eye shadow – and scrunch dried her hair. She had dyed her grey roots brown to match the rest of her hair last night so felt happier with the way it looked now, her natural curls falling loose to her shoulders and not scraped back in a scrunchie as it usually was when out doing her cleaning jobs. With her purse and the room key card in one hand, she automatically went to pick up her phone, but hesitated, and then decided that Colin and his million-messages-a-day habit could go cold turkey tonight, and so she stowed the phone inside the safe in the bottom of the wardrobe instead. Gina closed the door behind her, took a deep, fortifying breath and made her way to the lounge bar downstairs to try a raspberry ouzo cocktail for the first time.

5

On arriving in the reception area and wanting to hold on to her newly found feeling of calm and optimism, Gina quietly hummed the rousing strum of Abba's 'Fernando' as a kind of power anthem to spur her on as she made a beeline for the bar. She was hoping to avoid Cristos, in case he was still there in charge of the front desk, which she had to walk past in order to get to the bar. She didn't want any more mishaps before her holiday had even properly started, certainly not a reminder of that 'tissue issue', as she had filed the memory under and relegated to the cringe corner of her brain.

'Gina.' Too late. She stopped walking and spun around. Cristos appeared from behind her with a smile and his arms open wide in greeting. 'How are you?'

'Oh, erm... I'm good. Thank you. And you?' Gina said, avoiding eye contact, and tentatively touching her top lip just in case.

'I am good too,' he smiled. 'You look very beautiful tonight,' he added, his Greek accent seeming stronger than ever as he moved a little closer to her, his sandalwood and sea salt cologne lingering and teasing her nostrils. Gina blushed and willed her body's thermostat not to crank up the dial again, wishing she was one of those women who instinctively knew how to handle this kind of fake flirtiness, because let's face it, she knew that he was just being kind and probably felt sorry for her holidaying here all alone. She opened her mouth to speak, hoping to say something semi-normal, but when the words, 'Thanks, I just put on some make-up and washed my hair and...' came out, it sounded like she had sucked on a helium balloon and dialled the pitch of her voice up to an embarrassingly high octave. She stopped talking and fiddled with her purse instead. Forgetting the key card was in her hand, it suddenly slipped from her fingers, making a horrible clattering sound that reverberated around the marble pillared atrium before skidding across the super shiny tiled floor.

'Sorry, I forgot it was ther—'

'It's OK,' Cristos said, gently touching her arm, which felt like an electric charge as she immediately went to move off in search of the key card. Holding his hand in place as if to calm her and stop her from going, he added, 'Let me get it for you,' and walked over to a cluster of wicker egg chairs next to a window where the key card had slid to a halt. He returned a moment later.

'Thank you.' She took the key card from his outstretched hand, her fingers accidentally brushing against his. 'Sorry,' she said, swiftly pulling her hand away.

'Please, there's no need to be sorry, I like to do this for you.' She dipped her head, pretending to be busy slotting the key card inside her purse, desperately wishing she could be more poised and, well... smart and together and not feel as though she was unravelling all the time. 'Come, I take you for a drink.'

Gina jerked her head up and blinked. What did he mean? Admittedly it was a very long time since she had been single and navigating her way through the dating scene and all of that... And even then, there had only ever been Colin, if you didn't count her teenage romance with Nico. But was this really how it was these days? Maybe it was. She wasn't sure, but she had heard about the apps where you could see if someone you fancied was close by and then simply swipe them to hook up for sex if you felt like it. Or maybe her knowledge was out of date and there was none of that messing around with an app. Oh no, just a case of walking up to a complete stranger and telling them they looked 'very beautiful tonight' and that you were taking them for a drink. Straight to the point. Bam! Or should that be bang! She swallowed hard and could hear her heart beating in her ears.

Seeing her hesitation, Cristos quickly clarified, 'The bar! I take you to the bar so you can have a cocktail perhaps and relax after your journey here. I show you where to go.' And she was sure she saw a flicker of confusion, or was it fear, flash across his handsome face as he ran a hand over his beard.

'Oh, yes, yes of course.' So, he didn't want to *take* her for a drink as in a *drink drink*, as in a date... no, he was just doing his job and wanted to show her where the bar was. Of course he was, and how silly of her to think for even a second that someone as hot as him would be interested in a woman like her. Memory of that time she had overheard her mother-in-law telling Colin his wife was 'getting frumpy and needs to be careful she doesn't let herself go completely' flooded her thoughts. Smarting momentarily all over again, Gina instantly shoved the negative voice aside and stuck the 'Fernando' song back on inside her head instead, because what had hurt most about the criticism was that Colin hadn't said a single word to defend her or disagree with his mother. And then later, when they were alone in their bedroom and she had tried to talk to him about how his mother's comments had made her feel, he had told her off for being oversensitive. In fact, according to him, Pam was actually doing her a favour by mentioning it as she might not have even realised otherwise.

'That would be lovely. Thank you,' she said to Cristos, relieved to be back in familiar territory. She knew where she was when someone was simply showing her the way. But then she wanted to shrivel up and evaporate when she absent-mindedly squeaked, 'I've got a voucher!' in a far louder voice than she intended as she waggled the square of paper up in the air to show him like some kind of proof and they were in the local Lidl and not a lovely, luxury, five-star hotel on an idyllic Greek island. Plus, as she walked, she found herself doing some kind of weird show-pony prance alongside him, struggling to keep up as her freshly moisturised feet were all sweaty from the heat and slip-sliding all over the place inside her Hermes dupes that she now knew were definitely not real leather as they claimed to be.

Later, and safely seated at the last vacant table outside on the busy terrace shaded by grapevines, having gathered herself and got all the way to the end of 'Fernando' several times over by now, Gina took a sip from the sugar-dipped cocktail glass and just about managed to refrain from making an oohing sound in pleasure, when the deliciously sweet and tart raspberry flavour mixture teased and tingled on her tongue.

Sitting back, she admired the view from the hotel's vantage point on top of undulating hills of lemon and olive groves and savoured the warming sensation as the cocktail slipped down her throat and radiated across the inside of her chest and straight into her bloodstream like a shot of adrenaline, giving her a giddy feeling. Gina wasn't used to drinking strong alcohol, certainly not the enormously generous shots of ouzo she had watched the bartender pour before shaking it all up for her like he was Tom Cruise starring in that *Cocktail* movie.

'Ooh, that looks interesting. Do you mind me asking what it is?' commented an effortlessly glamorous older woman as she walked out onto the terrace looking for an empty table and gesturing at

Gina's cocktail. She had zhuzhy, silvery-blonde hair, and was wearing a gorgeous orange silk trouser suit and real Hermes sandals, by the looks of them with the extra padded sole and properly centred logo.

'They call it a raspbouzo,' Gina told the woman, remembering what it had said on the voucher. 'My first time trying one and it's very nice indeed.' She lifted the glass slightly, her confidence boosted by the alcohol rush.

'In that case, I'll have one too. I'll try anything once.' The woman winked, giving Gina a warm, but very wicked smile. 'I'm Diana, by the way, or Deedee, as I prefer. Are you travelling solo too?'

'Solo?' Gina repeated vaguely, before quickly realising what this meant. 'Oh, yes… yes I am,' she added, her shyness returning, but after taking another quick mouthful of the cocktail, she grinned and did something she hadn't ever done before. She gestured to one of the other empty seats at her table. 'You can sit here, with me… if you like. I'm Gina.' She politely held out her hand.

'Well, great to meet you, Gina. Thanks for sharing your table. Love your hair by the way… Are those natural curls?' Deedee asked, giving Gina's outstretched hand an enthusiastic squeeze as she shook it.

'Yes.' Gina felt her cheeks flush. 'Thank you,' she smiled tentatively, taking another sip of her cocktail, feeling pleased with herself for politely accepting the compliment and not immediately going into some sort of dull deflection or explanation about having washed her hair and having had time to scrunch dry it naturally or whatever.

'Fabulous. OK, I'll pop to the bar and put an order in… Same again?' Deedee asked, pointing to Gina's drink. But before she could decide and reply, Deedee added, 'My treat – a thank you for inviting me to join you,' and disappeared, leaving a plume of heady, summery, coconut-scented perfume in her trail. Gina smiled as she realised that since coming on her solo holiday, three women now had started chatting to her like they were old friends. She liked it. And she admired the women's boldness too. It was empowering, lifting, and she wanted some of it too and supposed this was why she had asked Deedee to join her.

Twiddling the straw in her glass, Gina looked around while she waited for Deedee to return, enjoying the buzzy but laid-back atmosphere with all the happy holidaymakers mingling with local multigenerational Greek families gathered around tables chatting and laughing and enjoying each other's company. For a moment she felt a pang of nostalgia for all those happy holidays from her past that she had loved so much. The balmy, summer evenings with her mum sitting at tables outside the beach taverna that Nico's grandparents owned, enjoying the traditional Greek menu, before the music would start and they'd sing and dance on the sand until well past sundown and on into the night. She wondered if the restaurant was still there, Toula's it had been called, after Nico's grandmother, Gina recalled. Maybe she would take a look while she was here and remember the wonderful times they all had together. And the little complex of holiday apartments where they always used to stay, not far from the taverna. She remembered walking back from the beach feeling happy and fulfilled from a day spent swimming in the sea and soaking up the restorative Greek sun's rays. With her towel slung over her shoulder, and her bare, sand-covered feet, they would make their way up the steep, winding, cobblestone-paved street lined with pretty whitewashed, higgledy-piggledy houses where cats dozed in the sun-dappled courtyards, and old ladies in flowery dresses and headscarves sat in the shade chatting and giving her gummy smiles as she went by. Wicker baskets, leather belts and bunches of cinnamon sticks hung from hooks on the walls ready to be taken to the market. Gina had found it fascinating and now, all these years later, she really wanted to do that walk again, to feel the same way she had then... happy and fulfilled from a day of swimming and snorkelling and sketching on the beach in the sunshine. It was the perfect tonic, and she was 100 per cent here for it.

6

'Oh, hello.' Gina was startled from her reverie to see the woman from the airport who'd reminded her of Charlotte waving enthusiastically and walking towards her table. Gina glanced around wondering if Deedee had returned and the two were friends, but she was still at the bar with her back to the table. The woman was now wearing an electric blue jumpsuit cinched in at the waist with a gold-buckled belt and matching metallic gold gladiator sandals, and she had an almost-finished cocktail in her free hand which looked like a raspbouzo too. 'And snap! Aren't these delicious?' She waggled the glass in the air before taking a sip and placing it on Gina's table. 'Are you staying here as well?'

'Yes, they are,' Gina smiled, glancing at the woman's glass, 'and yes I am, are you staying here too?'

'Sure am. And what a coincidence. If we'd known, then we could have shared a taxi from the airport. Mind if I sit here for a moment? These sandals are killing me. I should have worn them in before coming away, but it was a last-minute job so, well... anyway, sorry to bore you about my swollen, sweaty feet. Perils of peri-menopause I suppose.' She shrugged. 'Do your feet also swell up like giant elephants' hoofs, or whatever it is they have?' And she leaned forward with a conspiratorial look on her pretty face.

'Uh, err... yes... sweaty, a bit. My sandals were slippery earlier...' Gina let her voice tail off, wondering if it was OK to be quite so upfront about the state of her feet. But then figured it must be OK when a total stranger was talking about perimenopause and telling you about their swollen, sweaty elephant hoof feet. Gina was secretly surprised to be honest, as she never would have guessed the woman sitting in front of her was anything other than poised and serene and definitely sweat-free. She looked so 'together' and glowing and without a care in the world... It just went to show that first impressions could be very misleading.

'Oh, I hate it when that happens,' the woman said. 'It's the same after a pedi and when you leave the salon and have to squelch your way back to the car because your skin hasn't had time to absorb the moisturiser properly and you're in such a hurry that you can't just sit back and scroll your socials for any longer. And I find that I'm always in a hurry, don't you?'

'Err, yes... yes I do,' Gina agreed, but for her it was usually when she was running late to her next cleaning job and caught in rush-hour traffic, or her previous client had asked her at the last minute to, 'be a love and change all the bedding in the *three* guest rooms,' because they had forgotten friends were coming to stay or whatever. Gina never complained and just got on with it, figuring it wasn't worth losing work over. But then it struck her that she wouldn't need to work all day every day with so many cleaning jobs when she went home, not now that she had saved up enough money and achieved her dream of coming back to Kalosiros. But then she also realised that if her and Colin's trial separation did become a permanent thing, then she would have to find a way to support herself completely in any case. Colin and Pam would move out, she assumed, so she would have sole responsibility for all the household costs, and she knew that what she earned from cleaning wasn't anywhere near enough to cover it all. Her mum's life insurance had paid off the mortgage when she died, which had made things easier of course, but it was still a daunting prospect with the cost-of-living soaring. Maybe she could top up her income with some extra night shifts cleaning the big office blocks in the nearby town to make ends meet. Because, on the one hand, the prospect of having her house to herself again suddenly felt strangely exhilarating – was it wrong that her next thought went to being able to sit in the big cuddle armchair by the window whenever she flaming well pleased? And watch whatever she wanted on the telly?

Gina swallowed down a dart of panic and took a deep breath, hating how trapped the situation made her feel, but hating herself too for the fleeting thought of feeling that she might *have* to make her marriage work because she literally couldn't afford not to. But what she did know for sure was that she couldn't make any hasty decisions. Certainly not when she still felt so let down and angry with Colin. No, big life-changing decisions like this needed thought. Plus, this wasn't the first time her and Colin had fallen out, although it had never felt as final as this, and he often had a knack of smoothing things out until she felt compelled to give things another go, rather than 'throw twenty-seven years of marriage in the bin' as Colin would say. And a part of her hated the finality of that prospect, the feeling of failure, the sadness that it didn't work out how she had hoped and imagined it would on her wedding day.

Anyway, she didn't want to think about it any more right now and so she pushed the worries to the back of her mind and took another sip of her cocktail.

'It's so nice to be here though and not have to think about normal life or having to hurry anywhere, I feel as though I have all the time in the world,' Gina said to the other woman.

'Oh yes, although technically I'm here on business... looking for a suitable wedding venue for a client. I'm a wedding and events planner, but I'm tagging some extra days on to have a bit of a holiday too. And so sorry, I've gabbled on and not even introduced myself, I'm Rosie, and I'll leave you alone in a bit, I promise. I'm just going to loosen the straps on these sandals, if you don't mind? In fact, sod it, I'm going to take them off... comfort over style, I say, don't you?' And Rosie quickly bobbed her blonde curls down underneath the table to see to the sandals.

'No, I don't mind at all, and err... yes, comfort is best, I guess. I'm Gina. And are you... travelling solo too?' she asked tentatively, when Rosie had finished with the sandals, remembering when Deedee had asked her the same question and how cool and glamorous it had sounded. She hoped she sounded the same way too. Gina had never met a wedding and events planner before, but figured it explained the breezy, super chic and classic style that Rosie clearly did so well. Gina reckoned it must be important to look romantic and stylish if you were going to organise someone's wedding or special event for them. Unless it was a registry office without an actual event, an in-and-out quickie with a pub lunch afterwards, just like her own wedding to Colin. He hadn't wanted a fuss, and they didn't have loads of friends to invite in any case, so it had made sense, sort of. Although in a way, Gina wished it hadn't made sense at all, wondering what it would have been like to have a big family and lots of friends to invite for a fabulous party. To put on a big do that needed a specialist like Rosie to organise, something really lovely as a big thank you to everyone for joining in and sharing the happy couple's joy.

'Yes, I'm travelling solo too,' Rosie confirmed. 'And brilliant isn't it?' Gina nodded and took another sip of her cocktail as Rosie continued, 'It feels like such a treat only having to think about myself for a change and not to have to deal with my teenage son,

Tom, for a few days. I love him with all my heart, but he's very high maintenance. He came out about a year ago, not that we didn't already know of course, but now that it's 'official' if you like... well, let's just say he likes to talk through all his dating trials and tribulations with me. And he's perpetually outraged about something or another... or heartbroken over some boy. But then doesn't want to listen to any of my advice. He's only eighteen and just started university, so has all that to navigate his way through too, but still... it's a lot, very intense.' Rosie paused to draw breath and pull a face. 'And my husband, Ash... well, he "doesn't get it" apparently.' Rosie rolled her eyes. 'So he's no help whatsoever and disappears off playing golf at any given opportunity while I'm mostly rollercoasting on mum guilt much of the time. Tom was outraged that I was "leaving him" to come here at such a crucial time in his life... his first term at university, anyone would think he's the only one of us ever to go – we all went through it didn't we?' Rosie let out a long puff of air while Gina nodded vaguely, remembering how she dropped out of her art course. 'Anyway, cheers.' Rosie lifted her glass as she stopped to draw another breath before flopping back in the seat and shaking her head, making her curls bounce all around her face. She swallowed the last of her cocktail for fortification.

'Oh yes, cheers. That does sound like a lot,' Gina replied, politely.

'Yes, and sorry for oversharing, it just always seems so much easier somehow to talk to a stranger.' Gina nodded again and smiled. 'Right. I had better leave you in peace,' Rosie said, then leaned forward and went to stand up just as Deedee returned with two raspbouzo cocktails, one in each hand. She placed one in front of Gina and then smiled at Rosie. 'Hello.'

'Hi,' Rosie replied, and smiled at Deedee as she sat down next to Gina.

'Sorry, it took an eternity, Gina... I got chatting to that extremely handsome bartender,' Deedee said, her eyes sparkling. 'There's just something about a man who can move a shaker around like that.' And she placed another gorgeous-looking pink drink in a martini glass on the table in front of Gina before turning to Rosie and asking her, 'Would you like this other cocktail? You're very welcome to have it and it would be my absolute pleasure to pop back to the bar.' Her smile widened as she lifted one eyebrow hopefully.

'Oh, that's very kind of you, but no... thank you,' Rosie said politely. 'I can't take your drink. I was just leaving; I've bothered your lovely friend, Gina, here for far too long as it is.'

'Please stay if you like,' Gina suggested tentatively, glowing inwardly at Rosie having assumed she was Deedee's lovely friend. Both women glanced at Deedee.

'Yes, please do, it's fine by me,' Deedee said immediately. 'The more the merrier, and it doesn't look like there are going to be any other free tables for a while in any case, so only fair that we share.' The three women looked around the terrace and saw that it was even busier now.

'Are you absolutely sure it's OK for me to share?' Rosie checked. 'Honestly, no need to... just to be polite.'

'Yes,' Gina and Deedee quickly replied in unison and then laughed.

'In that case, cheers! Thank you very much. But I won't take your drink. I want to see this sexy bartender too.' And Rosie raced off barefoot towards the bar.

7

An hour or two later and having lost count of how many rounds of raspbouzos they had enjoyed, the three women were laughing and chatting like they were old friends on a reunion trip. Someone had ordered a sharing platter piled high with stuffed vine leaves and tangy tzatziki, black and green olives, houmous topped with chick-peas and pomegranate seeds and drizzled with olive oil and fresh lemon juice and warm pitta bread for dipping. Gina was having the time of her life laughing and letting her hair down with her new friends. She wondered if it was the alcohol or the company or the fact that Rosie and Deedee didn't know the boring details of her life as a cleaner, the invisible woman just going through the motions that she was back home in England. Because here she could be whoever she wanted to be, a little bolder, freer, and to be honest, she already felt much more like her old self, the person she was in the early years of her marriage, with a zest for life, before the disillusionment set in. She was on the cusp of an adventure, a turning point, and it felt exhilarating as she looked around and soaked up the buzzy, vibrant atmosphere. Deedee and Rosie made her laugh and feel alive, in stark contrast to the exhausted state she would usually be in at this time of the evening slumped in front of the TV at home.

'Gone to Greece!' Rosie exclaimed, nodding her head in awe. 'Love that!'

'So let me get this straight, darling… you just left a note on the fridge?' Deedee asked Gina, moving her lips into an O shape before popping the last olive into her mouth.

'Yes, that's right… but it wasn't completely out of the blue, Colin did know about the holiday, in fact he was supposed to be coming too, but well… he dropped out at the last moment and so here I am on my own. Travelling solo!' Gina lifted her eyebrows and shrugged mischievously, buoyed by the cocktails, and the relaxed, hedonistic atmosphere out on the terrace. Music was playing now, or 'deep house chill-out tracks' as Rosie had told them it was called, having spent several summers in Ibiza in her twenties frolicking about in foam parties.

It felt nice being part of a female friendship group again and although Gina had only met the two women just a few hours ago, they all seemed to have clicked, and she felt welcomed and at ease with them both. Deedee and Rosie were vibrant, warm and friendly, they listened and seemed genuinely interested in what she had to say, something Gina wasn't used to. At home, Colin and Pam were glued to their phones much of the time and rarely even bothered to glance up when she spoke, unless it was to ask her to, 'be a love and pop the kettle on' – Pam's favourite request, or Colin who was fond of tagging on, 'and some biscuits on a plate seeing as you're in the kitchen,' from his feet-up position on the La-Z-Boy section of the sofa.

As the three of them had been chatting and laughing, Gina realised just how much she had missed her friends from school and art college over the years, and an idea came to her; maybe she could look them up and try to reconnect when she got back home.

She didn't do social media, mostly because she didn't really go anywhere that interesting, or actually have any proper friends to go for a bottomless brunch with and tag in pictures next to an espresso martini cocktail tree. And because Colin had said social media was 'for fools with too much time on their hands' and they shared an email address which he had organised and she would need to use to sign herself up to social media accounts, she had found herself going along with his belief because she supposed she hadn't wanted him thinking she was actually... a fool with too much time on her hands.

But listening to Rosie talk about her Instagram account earlier and the lovely pictures she had shown them of her 'grid', Gina was beginning to question Colin's thinking and decided she might like to have her own Instagram account too, figuring it would be the perfect place to save all the holiday photos that she was planning on taking and she could also connect and keep in touch with her new friends. Rosie had already taken some group selfies of the three of them enjoying their cocktails, and of the impressive sharing platter and the view of the lemon and olive groves with the beach at the bottom of the hill, and Gina wanted to be part of it all. She wanted to have the memories to look at and knew it would help to put a spark back into her life when the holiday was over and she went back to her normal day-to-day routine.

'Well, you're not on your own now, Gina. You are with us, and I reckon the three of us are going to have an absolute ball,' Deedee stated with a firm nod. 'Starting with the art class that the hotel is running on the beach tomorrow. Just think... paint, pastels, easels, hot sun, scenic views, waves crashing on the shore.' She moved the palm of her hand through the air as if setting the scene to really sell the art class to them. 'And I've heard that the art teacher is very easy on the eye indeed. Shall I sign us all up for it?'

'I'm in,' Rosie said, chewing and swallowing a piece of pitta bread, before adding, 'as long as it doesn't clash with my meetings. I've got two potential wedding venues to view. You can come with me if you like. One of them has the most amazingly luxurious Thelasso spa "with an outside sea water infinity pool amidst its very own lush lemon and olive groves" it said in the brochure, and I can get us complimentary passes. We can swim, sunbathe, and have whatever beauty treatments we fancy too.'

'Ooh, yes please, I do love a spa day,' Deedee said, nodding. Gina, with a mouthful of cocktail nodded too, even though she didn't know what a Thelasso spa was, but a sea water pool set in lush lemon and olive groves sounded very exciting and so she was up for giving it a go, determined to broaden her horizons while she was here. Plus she might manage to get a lip and leg wax after all! 'And in that case, you'll be free, Rosie, as the art class is in the evening. I think it's so we can paint the glorious Greek sun as it sets over the sea,' Deedee confirmed.

'Oh, err, actually I'm not sure... it's been a long time since I painted anything,' Gina said on impulse as flashbacks of Colin with her canvas under his arm and the 'out with the rest of the rubbish' comment about her last creative attempt suddenly sprung to mind. 'No, I'll only embarrass myself...' She let her voice fade away, disappointed as her buoyant mood faded and she felt small, reduced again.

'Oh Gina, I'm sure you won't,' Deedee said, kindly, giving her arm a reassuring pat. 'And I haven't so much as lifted a paintbrush, not even at school... Mind you, I didn't do very much at all at school... No, there were far more exciting things to do *outside* of school.' She let her voice trail off as she winked at Rosie and Gina.

'Aaaaaand?' Rosie prompted, turning circles with her hand to encourage Deedee to elaborate. 'You can't stop there... we need details, don't we?' She nudged Gina with her elbow.

'Um, yes. Yes, we definitely do,' Gina agreed enthusiastically, pleased to be talking about something else other than the art class.

'Well, let me put it into context, I was actually a very well behaved and diligent pupil until the age of about fifteen or sixteen,' Deedee started, tucking a stray lock of silvery hair behind her ear. 'But then things changed dramatically when my hormones kicked in and I discovered boys. It was the sixties after all, and my boarding school was in Switzerland so let's just say that I became very proficient in skiing... and French kissing. And skinny-dipping in cold lakes after hot and very steamy saunas.'

'Deedee! You minx,' Rosie gasped, feigning shock.

'You know, that's exactly what my father said when I got expelled!' Deedee shrugged and gave her cocktail a quick, non-plussed stir with the straw. 'Though I could tell he wasn't really cross, as he swiftly followed it up by saying, "I hope it was worth it" with a twinkle in his eye, and I have to say that it most definitely was. I'd had the time of my life in Switzerland, and then got to return to London, to a little flat in Chelsea that my father set me up in, on the proviso that I at least got a job and paid for my own shenanigans if I wasn't cut out for academia. I was very spoiled. So then I had an even more exciting experience modelling for the new, trendy fashion houses at the time like Biba and Mary Quant, plus cabaret dancing in nightclubs.' Deedee paused as if remembering her past fondly, before laughing gently and adding, 'Yes, I spent many glorious evenings unfolding myself from a giant Fabergé-style egg!' A short silence followed as Gina and Rosie waited, wide-eyed, for Deedee to carry on. 'And there were sensible things too like hosting dinner parties – I did learn how to bake a brilliant soufflé and mix a marvellous martini at boarding school – although that was at the party of a friend's much older sister, so I suppose my expensive education wasn't completely wasted,' Deedee chuckled, as Gina listened in awe, thinking how otherworldly and glamorous it all sounded. 'Anyway, getting back to the art class – it's one of my bucket list goals. I've always fancied the idea of perching on a rock on a beautiful beach with an easel to hand, and wearing a kaftan and a silk scarf tied around my head like a proper artist. It could be very romantic in a whimsical way.' She laughed again and gave Gina a hearty nudge. 'We'll have fun together, Gina, and will promise not to take it too seriously. Please don't worry about being embarrassed,' she said gently. 'And from the sounds of it... and if you don't mind me saying so darling, you need hormones!'

'Hormones?'

'Yes, I reckon you could do with a shot of HRT,' she paused again and looked directly at Gina. 'Husband Replacement Therapy!' Deedee explained with a forthright look on her face as she drained the last of her raspberry ouzo.

Rosie and Deedee sat motionless waiting for Gina's answer. After clearing her throat and pressing her lips together in thought, Gina started nodding slowly, warming to the idea of the art class, and then suddenly thinking what a shame it was that she had let Colin's mean words get to her and spoil something that she had loved doing so much. Especially here on the island, all those years ago, sitting with Nico on a rock, sketching the magnificent view of the beautiful blue waves and the sandy shoreline skirted by grass-topped cliffs. Gulls soaring and swooping as the Greek sun set over the sea. It had been truly perfect, and she felt a surge of excitement at the prospect of having the chance to paint the scene again tomorrow evening, without Colin here to criticise her efforts.

'You know, I think you're right, Deedee! Bring on the HRT,' Gina announced, grinning from ear to ear. Yes, she had made her mind up and was going to get involved.

'Wahey! We are doing an art class together.' Rosie clapped her hands in celebration and Deedee stood up and scooted over to the giant, white wooden-framed easel in the corner where the hotel's activities were listed, and with a flourish she added all their names onto it underneath the 'Art at Sunset' class.

'So has your husband tried to contact you at all?' Rosie asked Gina, resting her elbows on the table, a look of concern etched on her face.

'No idea... I put my phone away,' Gina said, the sound of nonchalance in her own voice surprising her.

'Well good for you!' Rosie said firmly. 'And it's his loss... This island is such a magical place.'

'Have you been here before?' Gina asked.

'No, this is my first time but as soon as I started researching "wonderful Greek island wedding locations" as requested by my clients, I could see that this was the perfect place to look.'

'How about you, Deedee? Have you been here before?' Gina asked as the older woman arrived back at the table and sat down.

'Oh yes, many times. I run a travel agency back home in England. Travelling is what I do and Kalosiros is one of my favourite places to visit. And my oldest and dearest friend, Yiannis, a fashion photographer from my modelling days, keeps a boat here in the harbour, so I try to catch up with him whenever we are both visiting – he lives in New York now. I'll see if he can take us out for a sailing trip sometime... if you'd both like to?'

'Ooh, yes I'm definitely up for that,' Rosie said, closely followed by Gina.

'Yes, me too. Thank you, that would be wonderful,' she agreed, thrilled to have another exciting activity to add to her holiday itinerary.

'And have you been here before, Gina?' Rosie asked.

'Yes, lots of times actually. My mum and I used to have our holidays here every summer. But I haven't been back for many years now.'

'Ah, so this place holds special memories for you,' Rosie smiled, tenderly.

'Yes, very special, they were happy times and with memories of my mum; she's no longer with us now,' Gina confirmed, thinking of Shirley but then suddenly thinking of Nico too and the lovely carefree summers they had spent together.

'Extra shame then that your husband didn't want to join you,' Deedee said, swiftly followed by, 'Sorry, that came out the wrong way. What I meant to say was that it would have been nice for you to have had the chance to show him around, to take him to the places you visited with your mum all those years ago and share the memories with him.'

'And to have a romantic time together. A dreamy wedding vow renewal, perhaps?' Rosie jumped in keenly, lifting her eyebrows in hope. 'There are some absolutely stunning locations on the island, and I'd be very happy to help you find the perfect place.' Silence followed as Gina and Deedee stared at her. 'Sorry, it's the hopeless romantic in me. I am a wedding planner after all.' She lifted her shoulders and tilted her head sideways in apology.

'Hmm, not sure a vow renewal is on the cards any time soon.' Gina exhaled hard. 'But showing him around and having a nice time together had actually been my intention when I booked the holiday. But I should have known that Colin isn't really interested in my past. Or our future together, now it seems...'

'Why on earth not?' Deedee said, shaking her head.

'My husband is a bit like that too.' Rosie jumped in again after flashing a look at Gina, who sensed that Rosie knew she felt uncomfortable. 'Yes, Ash lives his life very in the moment, doesn't see the point of "picking over the past" as he calls it. And I can just imagine his face if I suggested a romantic Greek island getaway. His first stipulation would be "as long as the hotel has got Sky Sports!". All this would be wasted on him.' She rolled her eyes as she gestured with an open palm around the terrace and to the stunning views beyond.

'Actually, come to think of it one of my husbands was like that too, refused to talk about the past, or well, about anything at all very much, unless it was all about him. Now that was his favourite subject!' Deedee interjected.

'One of them?' Rosie asked.

'Yes, husband number one, a brute, and it's such a shame that I didn't discover what he was really like until *after* we married. But then he was on best behaviour beforehand, with an eye on my inheritance, and so behaved impeccably until we went away to Sardinia on our honeymoon. I was young and naïve,' Deedee sighed. 'I've been married three times, actually. But the first two were practice runs for Joe, my late husband of twenty years and the love of my life. He died three years ago.'

'So sorry, Deedee.' Gina smiled sympathetically.

'And I'm very sorry too, Deedee. Was he ill?' Rosie asked.

'Yes... cancer, although he had a good innings and didn't suffer for too long towards the end,' Deedee said solemnly, and the three women fell silent for a second or two. 'Anyway, please, let's not dull the buoyant mood. Joe would never have wanted that; he was so charismatic and a dazzling raconteur, and if he were here now then he'd be charming you both and entertaining us with his endlessly fascinating stories from Hollywood – he was a casting director and had all the stars on speed dial.'

'Wow, how exciting.' Rosie widened her eyes.

'Yes, we had the most marvellous life together and it was wonderful travelling to film premieres and going on location, which is where we first met – at the Cannes film festival. I had auditioned to be a Bond girl, back in the day, and he remembered me, and well... that was that! You could say that it was love at first sight.'

'Ah, it sounds so thrilling and romantic,' Gina beamed.

'It was, but it's all memories now,' Deedee said wistfully and dipped her head momentarily. 'Anyway, how about we go out for dinner?' She looked back up and pressed her palms together as if to bring the clearly sensitive conversation to a close. 'If you both fancy doing that? Then we can chat some more and get to know each other better. And I can recommend the most wonderful little taverna we can go to that does the best salt-baked fish you will ever taste. It's in the harbour, not far from here, and they literally pluck the fish fresh from the sea and bake it in their clay oven before chiselling the salt away at your table.'

'Ooh, yes, I'm up for that,' Gina replied right away, 'but shall we have an another raspbouzo before we go?'

'Good idea. Cheers to prinks,' Rosie said.

'Pri...?' Gina started tentatively, wondering if she had misheard, given the conversation they had just had about their respective husbands and their lack of emotional intelligence or sense of romance.

'Yes, you know... pre-dinner drinks. Prinks!' Rosie interrupted, laughing, and picking up her empty cocktail glass and chinking it at a jaunty angle up in the air against Deedee's and Gina's as they lifted theirs too.

'And it must be my turn to take a trip to see the bartender this time.' Deedee winked, waving an elegant hand in the air, and making her stack of solid gold Cartier love bangles jangle together. 'I may be old, or as I like to say, experienced... but I still know how to have fun.'

'So you're a queenager too in that case!' Rosie said. 'It's what my son, Tom, says to me after I've had a good night out with friends,' she explained. 'Mind you, he thinks anyone over the age of thirty is *really old*.' She rolled her eyes dramatically.

'Gosh, thirty isn't old, or forty, or fifty come to think of it,' Deedee said.

'Or sixty – how old are you Deedee, if you don't mind me asking?' Rosie said.

'Sixty-nine.'

'*Really?*' Rosie and Gina said at the same time, both clearly absolutely flabbergasted.

'Yes, although inside my head I'm still about twenty-five,' Deedee laughed.

'Well, you look incredible,' Gina said, wondering what her secret was.

'Thank you. It's the sex!' Deedee stated, as if reading Gina's mind. 'And yoga and Botox and a healthy diet of course. But mostly the sex,' she paused, and all three women giggled and shushed themselves like teenagers as they gave furtive glances around the terrace full of families, some with very elderly grandparents dressed all in black and looking very staid, and young children playing around their tables.

'So, do you have a lover?' Rosie asked, dropping her voice, and leaning in close. Gina dipped her head and huddled in further so she could hear all the details too.

'Of course, Luca, younger than me and lives in Italy so it suits us both to hook up when he's in England on business,' Deedee told them in a low, matter-of-fact voice, her eyes twinkling like a Christmas tree. 'I'm a firm believer in sex not being taken off the table for women of our age. Well, *my* age... you two are much younger than me.'

'Good point about the sex, I'd hate to go without, but then I am fifty and have been married for twenty years and so it is a bit samey to be perfectly honest,' Rosie shrugged. 'Ash and I could do with spicing things up a bit. I did buy one of those faux-fur paddles and a crop for us to try out, but then I couldn't really be bothered with it all. How about you, Gina? How's your sex life?' Rosie turned to look at Gina as she took a big slurp of her cocktail.

A beat of silence followed.

'Oh, um... err,' Gina spluttered, totally unprepared for this line of questioning, but managed to gather herself swiftly enough to say, 'I'm forty-nine, so a similar age, and well... yes, a bit samey too,' and then shrugged just like Rosie had in the hope of covering up just how uncomfortable she was feeling, not wanting to tell her new friends that she couldn't actually recall the last time she had sex or remembered enjoying it. And she could just imagine Colin's face if she produced a faux-fur paddle and proceeded to spank him with it. He would think she had lost her mind. Or been watching too much *Love Island* upstairs in the bedroom by herself, as he wouldn't have it on in the lounge. He blamed *Love Island* for just about everything and anything to do with immorality or wayward behaviour. It was akin to social media and the ultimate example of 'fools with too much time on their hands' according to him. But Gina enjoyed watching it, and an hour or so to herself to switch off and watch beautiful young people seemingly having the time of their lives without a care in the world.

'Well, I think we have just about covered all the important details for now.' Rosie pulled a faux solemn face, prompting them all to snigger some more.

'Yep, I think so too,' Deedee nodded in agreement, 'that's settled then... so cheers to us three queenagers and the fabulous time we are all going to have together on this beautiful island!'

'Cheers to being a queenager,' Gina laughed, lifting her glass, a giddy optimism bubbling back up inside her again. She was looking forward to the rest of the evening and had a feeling it was going to be a lot of fun. As long as the conversation stayed away from her sex life, or to be more precise, the complete lack of it.

Because it had been that long for her, she feared it was like a pile of autumn leaves down there...

8

By mid-afternoon the next day, Gina was sprawled on a sun lounger in the shade of a large lemon tree with Rosie's wide-brimmed floppy sun hat covering her head – which felt as if a herd of pygmy goats were pummelling their hard little hoofs all around the inside of her skull. She had mainlined at least a litre of water so far and devoured a plate full of pastries for breakfast at the hotel. Then, on arriving here at the Thelasso spa, had also forced down a Bloody Mary on Deedee's insistence, drawing the line at her suggesting they ask the spa manager to plop a raw egg into the vivid, vermillion coloured concoction and stir it all up with a giant celery stick or two. Gina hated celery at the best of times so definitely wasn't going to entertain it today, feeling the way she did, which had to be the very worst way ever. Hideously hungover.

'How are you feeling now, Gina?' Rosie whispered from the sun lounger to the left of Gina's.

'Delicate.' Gina tentatively lifted the rim of the sun hat to see if her eyes could cope yet with dazzling daytime Greek sunshine. She was sure it seemed shinier and brighter and, well, just... way more extra than it had yesterday!

'But worth it, yes? We had such a fabulous evening,' Deedee chipped in softly from her sun lounger on Gina's other side.

'Yes, it was, but I don't think I should have tried that brown coloured shot after dinner,' Gina croaked and then shuddered as the sweet brandy taste bounced back into her mind.

'*Shots*, plural, darling. You couldn't get enough of the Metaxa.' Deedee sat up and after swinging her long, toned legs over the side of the sun lounger, she reached out a hand and patted Gina's arm.

'What do you mean?' Gina asked.

'Can you not remember?' Rosie asked, also sitting up and turning to face Gina.

'Oh yes, I remember the delicious dinner. The salt-baked fish was so good. And those raspbouzos.'

'Ah yes, we did get a bit carried away on those,' Deedee laughed.

'So how many of the Metaxa shots did we have?' Gina sighed, sitting up carefully in case the honey-coloured paving stones surrounding the saltwater infinity pool started blurring and undulating again.

'Weeeeell...' Rosie glanced at Deedee before carrying on, 'you did have quite a few. Four or five, six tops... perhaps!' She winced.

'Oh God. What was I thinking? And why didn't you stop me?'

'Um, we did try to, darling, but you were very insistent. And at one point you wanted to run along the harbour wall and leap onto the beach to go dancing on the sand and sing that Abba song...' Deedee paused to ponder, her eyebrows dipping. 'Which one was it, Rosie? Can you remember the title?'

'Fernando!' Gina answered feebly, knowing right away which song it would be, then shook her head and instantly wished she hadn't when the horrible swimmy sensation made a rapid return and she had to grip the sides of the sun lounger just to garner a modicum of fortitude.

'That's the one. And you're a very good singer, Gina… have you ever considered a career as a wedding entertainer?' Rosie suggested, earnestly. 'I reckon you would be very popular; I could certainly get you some bookings. An Abba tribute turn even. You sure know all the lyrics to all their songs, and you really got stuck in doing all the dance moves too.'

Gina looked at Deedee and then to Rosie again, feeling utterly aghast at the show she must have made of herself. What on earth was she thinking? Colin always said that she could be a 'bit unpredictable' when she had cocktails. On the rare occasion they went to a social event, he always brought up the time they were invited to his boss's wedding all those years ago when she'd had several Sex on the Beach cocktails and had joined the conga line led by the best man and had made 'a right show of herself' as Colin had told her when she tripped over and flashed her knickers for everyone to see. So she had tended to stick to fizzy water from that night on, not wanting to embarrass herself like that ever again. But then it dawned on her that she supposed it was a good thing Colin wasn't here last night, or she'd never have heard the end of it! Plus she *had* actually enjoyed herself; she remembered laughing and feeling free for the first time in a very long time, even if she still wished she hadn't shown herself up.

'Oh God, all over again.' Gina pressed her palms over her face. 'I'm so sorry, was I actually singing? Out loud, in the taverna? In front of everyone?'

Both women exchanged looks before Deedee broke the news. 'It was only for a little while,' Deedee soothed, patting Gina's arm again, 'in the taverna and then—'

'It's all coming back to me,' Gina said vaguely, 'but weren't we *all* singing and dancing?'

'Oh yes, it was very lively, and to be fair there was a band, a traditional Greek one with three guys playing syrtaki music on their bouzouki guitars which was very rousing in a *My Big Fat Greek Wedding* way. And everyone in the taverna was up on their feet clapping along at one point,' Deedee said.

'And the belly dancer was amazing too,' Rosie chipped in, brightly. 'It was when she appeared that you were inspired to give it a go.' Her voice faded on seeing Gina's horrified face.

'Oh please, stop it. It's definitely all coming back to me now. I was swaying my hips around thinking I was Shakira on the stage at Wembley or whatever, wasn't I?' Gina sighed. 'No wonder I've put my back out too, I could barely walk this morning and had to hobble into the shower.'

'Yes, just a bit... but you were good. *Really good.* Your hips definitely don't lie,' Rosie smiled, quoting the Shakira song, and placing a supporting hand on Gina's arm. Gina managed a small smile back, thankful for her new friend's vote of confidence in her.

'But how come you both seem so perky and bright eyed? Didn't we all do the shots?' Gina asked.

'Sure, but I was sort of working too, and taking calls from my clients, so I alternated my drinks with fizzy water,' Rosie started. 'And I'm guessing perhaps you aren't as used to... um, that sort of thing—'

'I think what Rosie is trying to say is that you aren't like us,' Deedee took over. 'That perhaps you're not used to drinking quite so much alcohol and partying quite so hard.'

'That's true,' Gina agreed quietly. 'I think I might have got a bit carried away, with it being my first evening here and I was so determined to have a good time, and well... I've waited a long time to come on holiday.'

'Well, there's no rush to get back in the saddle and ride the party horse, as it were,' Deedee paused, and then swiftly added, 'and it was wonderful to see you having such a fun time, it's a good thing. But darling, we've all been there, overindulged and paid the

price the next day. God, I wish I hadn't partied quite so hard sometimes, the recovery is far more intense when we are not in our
twenties or thirties any more.'

'Hmm, well I sure as hell don't want to feel like this again,' Gina
groaned. 'So what happened after the taverna? You said, "in the
taverna and then", but I interrupted. Was it really bad? Do I even
want to know?' She wasn't sure, as flashbacks of dancing on the
sand and then running around with her arms flung out wide
saying something about a warm wind in her hair came to mind.
And possibly hugging a large rock!

'Oh, you were fine!' Deedee said, flashing a look at Rosie. 'We
all had a fantastic time, singing and dancing on the sand and then
we hopped in a taxi and came back to the hotel for a good night's
sleep.'

'You might have needed a little help to pull your sundress off
over your head and be persuaded to go to bed and not try to order
a McDonalds Big Mac from room service. They don't do McDonalds burgers here in any case,' Rosie chipped in, 'but all pretty standard stuff after a good night out.'

'Hmm, I do have a vague memory of craving a big burger,' Gina
sighed. 'And thanks for helping me get to my room by the way, and
making sure I took my contact lenses out too. I can't tell you how
much of a relief it is being able to open my eyes, just about, today.'

'Ah yes, a basic,' Deedee agreed, 'I forgot about my lenses one
time and ended up having to see an optician to peel them from my
eyeballs the following day. Mind you, this happened when I was a
teenager on holiday with my father in Portofino and the optician
was the most handsome man I had ever seen – once he had done
the deed and taken the lenses from my eyes and I could actually
see him properly, of course.' She laughed lightly. 'We ended up
dating for a while and I thoroughly enjoyed riding behind him and
holding my hands around his very muscular abdomen as he took

me sightseeing on the back of his scooter. So there was an upside to that little misdemeanour, I suppose, as I would have spent the entire holiday on my own otherwise, bored out of my mind because my father was always busy with his business meetings.' She smiled wryly and lifted one shoulder nonchalantly as Gina listened in awe again to the seemingly glamorous and eclectic life her new friend had led. Although Gina couldn't help wondering if there might be a tinge of sadness there too, as she thought of a young Deedee having to find her own amusement while on holiday with a dad who was too busy working to spend time with her. 'So do you remember anything else about last night?'

'Um, yes, I remember trying to mountaineer up the side of my super king big bed before giving up and flopping on the chaise longue instead, which is probably why my neck hurts from sleeping scrunched up into a tight ball.' Gina groaned all over again as she tilted her head to one side in an attempt to release the painful crook in her neck. 'And I'm so very sorry for making a show of myself. I don't normally behave that way.'

'Don't be daft. You didn't make a show of yourself, you had a good time, and you had every right to... especially when you are on holiday,' Rosie said firmly. 'But there is something we want to ask you about?' Rosie looked at Deedee as if for affirmation that she should say something.

Deedee nodded in agreement.

'Go on...' Gina prompted slowly, wondering if she really wanted to hear what her new friends were going to say.

'Who is Nico?'

9

'Nico?' Gina repeated faintly, a warmth flooding her cheeks. Oh God, what had she told them? A beat of silence followed as Rosie and Deedee waited for her answer. 'He's um, just... an old friend.'

'Oh, so not a secret lover?' Rosie looked deflated.

'No, definitely not, I'm still a married woman, just about,' Gina protested, horrified that they were clearly thinking she was having an affair. 'I haven't seen him since I was a teenager.'

'So he was a holiday romance then?' Rosie's eyes lit up again in hope, the wedding planner in her seemingly keen to hear of a romantic fairy tale, Gina could see.

'Ah, yes that would explain it.' Deedee looked sideways at Rosie who nodded as if this confirmed something Gina had said last night. Both women leaned in closer to her as though for a cosy chat, clearly keen to find out all the dreamy details.

'Explains what?' Gina asked tentatively.

'Well... you were saying that you loved him, this Nico. That he was the "love of your life" and that you "never ever should have let him down all those years ago". You seemed convinced that karma had got you in the end. What goes around comes around, you said, and that this was the reason why Colin kept letting you down, it was payback for you forgetting about Nico,' Deedee recalled. 'Or words to that effect. You *were* a little discombobulated at times, and being very hard on yourself, Gina.'

'And you told us what a wonderful kisser Nico is, and how hot he is and when you were running on the sand you were calling out his name and asking him to forgive you and singing something about bring me sunshine—' Rosie added.

'Oh, stop, please.' Gina closed her eyes for a moment and inhaled hard through her nose before opening her eyes again. 'Can we just drop it?'

'Err, nope,' both Rosie and Deedee said firmly in unison.

'Come on, please, we need details. Nico obviously makes you very happy as your eyes lit up when you talked about him last night and it was like a big weight had lifted off your shoulders, you seemed lighter and younger and well, if you don't mind me saying so, a hell of a lot happier than when you talked to us about Colin and the way he carries on,' Rosie added. 'And I have to say that I'm actually pleased your husband let you down at the last minute. If you ask me, it's about time you were able to relax and have a good time,' she finished, letting her voice fade as if she was worried that she had said too much.

'*Estranged* husband!' Deedee clarified before quickly adding, 'Gina, is this why you are really on a trial separation, so you can explore your relationship with Nico?'

'No!' Gina sat properly upright now, her hangover shifting as she tried to gain a semblance of control over the conversation. 'Absolutely not. There is no "relationship with Nico",' she said, doing silly quote signs and pulling a face. Suddenly there were tears sparkling in her eyes and she had no idea why, but she was very grateful for the big sunglasses she was wearing.

'OK darling, we really don't mean to upset you,' Deedee said soothingly as she took hold of Gina's left hand. 'But you also told us about the problems in your marriage, and from what I can gather, it sounds like you might want to consider making the separation a permanent thing! Sorry to be blunt—' She stopped talking abruptly.

'Go on,' Gina coaxed, using the side of an index finger to surreptitiously dab at a tear that had escaped from the corner of her eye as she tried to work out what was wrong with her. Why was she getting so emotional at the mere mention of Nico's name? Or was it Rosie's assumption that she was having a love affair? A wild, passionate secret romance, and something that she had never experienced... Or could it be that somewhere deep within her, there was a part of her that wished it were true? Imagine that! The giddy feeling of being in love, truly, deeply, and desired again, carefree and flying high as she had once felt many years ago. Where did that go? Smarting, she caught her breath and then swallowed hard, focusing on slowing her heartbeat that was hammering almost right out of her chest.

'Well, to be perfectly honest, Colin really doesn't sound like he's on your side, Gina.' Deedee smiled kindly, if a little apprehensively as Gina chewed the inside of her cheek. She knew that what Deedee was saying was true, but it didn't make it any easier to face. No, it was painful and embarrassing, and to be honest, she felt ashamed, foolish, nobody wanted to hear that their husband wasn't good and kind or at least on their flaming side. Wasn't that a bare minimum requirement of a marriage – it was meant to be a mutually loving relationship where you had each other's backs? And the wild thing was that she did love Colin and had always been on his side, but... well, things had changed. And she didn't know when exactly, only that they had.

'The two things aren't connected,' Gina said, trying to separate it all in her head: how she felt her about Colin compared to her memories of Nico. Two romantic relationships, but each so very different.

'Oh, well that's a shame,' Rosie said, pushing her bottom lip out in disappointment.

'So who *is* Nico? You still haven't told us,' Deedee asked, taking her hand away and adjusting her sunglasses so she could peer over the top of them to scrutinise Gina.

'If I tell you, then does it mean you'll leave me alone and let me lie back down? Because this hangover is in desperate need of some rest and more carbs, so possibly a big bowl of houmous and hot pitta bread would help. And a can of Fanta Orange too?' she asked, remembering the comfort she always felt when she had shared this treat with Nico sitting on the steps outside his grandparents' taverna on the beach.

'We can do that, snacks coming right up.' Both women nodded in agreement. 'As soon as you've told us about Nico!'

'OK, so Nico is a boy that I used to know. We spent lots of summers here together.'

'Go on,' Deedee prompted. 'How old were you when you last saw him?'

'Oh gosh, I can't remember—' Gina said.

'Please try,' Rosie smiled, scooting over to Deedee's lounger to sit beside her. 'Did you make love on the sand underneath a velvety moonlit sky?'

'*Rosie!*' Deedee nudged her with her elbow.

'What?' Rosie exclaimed. 'I'm only saying what we are both thinking, no point beating around the bush. We need all the deets, as my Tom would say.' Then she placed her elbows on her knees and propped her hands underneath her chin as if to listen more intently.

'Yes, we do,' Deedee agreed. 'But Gina said she was a teenager when she last came here so the holiday romance could just have been an innocent crush, we can't assume that sex was involved—'

'I was nineteen when I last saw him,' Gina interrupted, quietly. 'And yes, we did make love on the sand, underneath a velvety moonlit sky. I was seventeen then, and it was my first time and still probably the most romantic moment of my life. It was incredible.' She looked away, grateful again for the shades so they couldn't see the pool of tears that had collected at the corners of both eyes now, and that she still couldn't really explain why. She thought it might be something to do with a sudden sense of regret, a sadness for that young woman inside her who had been so full of life and all that it had to offer back then. Karma could possibly have played a hand, but Gina also knew that she had let her teenage self down.

'I knew it!' Rosie reached a hand out to pat Gina's knee. 'So did you spend every summer together?'

'Yes, from the age of about seven or eight. I think his parents, or was it his grandparents...?' She paused to consider but couldn't remember. 'Well, his family were friends with the woman who ran the little holiday apartment complex where we always stayed,' Gina said, trying again to remember, 'and I suppose we sort of grew up together. Nico's grandparents owned a beach taverna and so he was always here in the summer and then when it turned romantic – I was about fifteen when we had our first kiss – we wrote to each other through the winter months and would get excited, counting down the days until we could be together again.'

'Oh my God, that is so romantic,' Rosie swooned, crossing her hands over her heart. 'It's like a Hallmark film.'

'It was wonderful, that's true. But there was no happy ending. We were both young,' Gina said softly, in contemplation. 'And when I got home at the end of every holiday Nico used to send me photos of our summers together, the good times with our families having fun in the taverna and I'd send him photos of my life in

England, silly pictures of me on the village green where I live in Tindledale, in front of Big Ben on a day trip to London, or the English seaside, that kind of thing. He used to talk about coming to England to do his medical training... He wanted to be a doctor, you see, or an artist – he had a passion for painting landscapes too, and so loved seeing the pictures of all the tourist sights.'

'And what happened next?' Deedee asked.

'My mum became ill with breast cancer, and we didn't come here again,' Gina told them. 'Nico and I kept in touch for a few years, and we fell in love through our letters. But it was a long time ago, so no social media or mobile phones then of course. The closest we came to keeping a connection back then was exchanging friendship bracelets,' she smiled on remembering the bracelet she had given Nico on the beach. 'He invited me to go island hopping with him one summer and I would have loved to, but then my mum died, and I met Colin soon after and, well, my life changed. I stopped writing to Nico for a while and didn't hear anything more from him. Until a postcard from him arrived out of the blue one day – I remember it clearly as it was my birthday and I had taken the day off, so it was a nice surprise when the postman popped the postcard through the letterbox, and I saw the gorgeous Greek beach scene with a little sailboat bobbing on the blue sea sitting there on the doormat with a "happy birthday, love Nico" message on the back. It cheered me up as it was a rainy, grey day outside and I was home alone. Pam was out shopping, and Colin was at work, and I think they had both forgotten it was my birthday,' she shrugged resignedly, putting on a brave face. 'But when I went to find Nico's address in the memory box where I kept all the letters and cards from him, the friendship bracelet he had given me, and the photos and souvenirs too of all the holidays, it had disappeared. Colin said he thought the box might have been moved into the loft when we cleared out my mum's old bedroom to decorate it, but I looked in the loft too and never did find the memory box and so... I guess that was that.' Gina let out a long breath as she looked away.

'Oh love, that must have been really hard for you,' Rosie said, solemnly.

'Yes, it was. I felt as if a part of my mum had gone all over again. There were loads of photos of all the good times we had here together. It wasn't just the letters and postcards from Nico, it was my whole childhood, the happy bits, you know. It was as if my past had been erased. This was long before storing photos on phones was a thing, so I have very few pictures from my childhood now and none at all of my mum. I did have lots of photo albums in a cupboard, but they were ruined when a pipe sprung a leak and drenched them all in water. Nothing was salvageable apart from one picture of me and Mum; I'm smiling and cuddling into her, but she's side on so I can only see the profile of her face. People used to say that I looked just like her, but I can't remember. I can't see her face in my mind any more, if you know what I mean?'

'Yes, we know,' Deedee and Rosie said softly in unison.

'Then we need to find Nico!' Rosie announced, standing up with a determined look on her face, her eyebrows knitted, as she tightened her sarong over her bikini and started pacing around as if she was deep in thought trying to come up with a plan.

'No, please, it was such a long time ago... He probably won't even remember me now,' Gina said, waving a hand in the air.

'Maybe, but he might do. You remember him, so why wouldn't Nico remember you? And I was thinking that he might have some holiday pictures. You know, some of you and him and everyone in his grandparents' taverna having a lovely, happy holiday together. Photos that might have your mum in them so you can see your resemblance to her again,' Rosie emphasised. 'It's certainly worth trying, isn't it?'

'Yes, it would be really wonderful to have that sense of closeness back and to have some happy, holiday pictures of Mum again,' Gina said slowly, trying to think it all through, 'but what if—'

'No buts or what ifs! Life is too short, trust me!' Deedee joined in. 'When Joe died, and you'll know this too, Gina, from when your mum died, you realise that memories are all you have, they're precious, but the ones inside your head can fade. I have albums full of photos of me and Joe, and films too that I can watch and see his face again. They're just as precious too and can make all the difference. So I can't bear to think of you not even having a handful of photos to look back on, to help keep alive the memories of the good times with your mum. To not even be able to see her whole face...' Deedee shook her head and then fell silent. Rosie and Gina glanced at each other before looking at Deedee who seemed very worked up now.

'Are you OK?' Rosie asked Deedee.

'Yes.' Deedee straightened the strap of her bikini top and sat up on the lounger. 'Actually, no, I'm not OK, I am cross. And I might be way off the mark but I'm going to say it anyway. Gina, do you think it possible that Colin could have got rid of the memory box?' Silence followed. Rosie took a sharp intake of breath. Gina's mouth dropped open. 'I'm sorry, Gina, because I don't want to cause you any additional pain on purpose, and I know we've just met but after last night it's as though we covered a lot of ground in getting to know each other. So I feel like we've been friends for a long time already and I know that I've never met Colin, but after everything you told us about him last night... Well, it just sounds strange to me that such a precious thing as your memory box – with photos and memories of your deceased mum and from your childhood and all those happy holidays with Nico – would just vanish from inside your own house!'

Gina gripped the edge of the sun lounger again and found

herself nodding slowly as a horrible sinking feeling took over and a realisation dawned on her.

'It's possible, I suppose,' she said, her voice shaky as she remembered a hurtful comment Colin made when Nico had written to tell her he was coming to England and would love to meet up, saying, 'That Nico only wants you for sex and he's got another thing coming if he thinks he's going to rock up here and expect to meet up with my wife and carry on where he left off the last time he had his way with you!' And so she hadn't met up with Nico, even though their relationship by this time had changed from being romantic and had deepened into one of true and ever-lasting friendship, or so she had thought.

'Oh, Gina,' Rosie said, 'if Colin did get rid of the memory box in a fit of jealousy or just plain, cold meanness, then that is inexcus-able, but if he didn't then you still lost touch with Nico, and you have a shared past. A history together. He's an important reminder wrapped up with the memories of your mum. And if there is a slim chance that we could find him and see if he has some photos from those times of your mum here on holiday with you, then I agree with Deedee, it has to be worth giving it a go.'

'And we could start with his grandparents' taverna! Can you remember anything about it?'

'Yes, it was called Toula's, and it was on the beach, not far from the harbour,' Gina told them.

'Then that's a good start. And there's the holiday apartment complex where you used to stay. We could try there and see if the woman who runs it is still in contact with Nico's family, or whoever the connection is with.'

'And if we have no joy with those two leads then we can get on social media and look for him—'

'But I can't remember his surname,' Gina jumped in. 'It's so frustrating as it used to be emblazoned on my mind, but not these days, I get terrible brain fog and can't remember my own name some days.' She rolled her eyes. 'And there are bound to be hundreds, if not thousands or even millions of men called Nico in the world.'

'Good point,' Rosie interjected. 'Then in that case, we will just go on a "treasure hunt" around the island and look for all the Nicos until we find your one. Or someone who knows him at least. Any leads we can find will help track him down for sure.' She nodded, resolute, her eyes seemingly dancing in delight at the prospect of reuniting Gina with her first true love.

'Can I have the houmous and hot pitta bread now? And the can of Fanta please?' Gina asked, hoping that would be the end of it, but it wasn't to be. Deedee and Rosie were determined.

'Yes. Have a little nap and I will bring you the biggest bowl of houmous and carb mountain of hot pitta bread to have when you wake up and then we can come up with a plan, starting tomorrow morning,' Deedee told her, leaving no room for Gina to quibble.

'Good idea! I'm thinking the taverna first and then the holiday apartment complex – can you remember the name of it, Gina?' Rosie asked, pulling a big notepad and a fluffy pink pom-pom-topped pen out from her tote bag that was propped against the side of her sun lounger.

'No, sorry I can't.'

'Or where it was on the island?' Rosie found a fresh page in her pad and was already writing 'Gina and Nico's Reunion' at the top and underlining it, not once, or twice, but three times. Gina swallowed down a dart of panic.

'Sorry, again, no I can't. But it wasn't far from the beach taverna as I remember walking from there back to the holiday apartment,' Gina told them, wishing all over again that she hadn't had quite so many raspbouzos and shots last night and bared her soul, or so it seemed, about the state of her marriage and a holiday romance that ended thirty years ago. Nico was probably happily married by now to a wonderful woman and wouldn't welcome an overexcited wedding planner with her friends in tow tracking him down, even if they did manage to, which was highly unlikely in any case, she supposed. Secretly hoped. Because what if they did find him, and he was nothing like the memory she had built up inside her head? She had read somewhere that you should never meet your heroes, and this felt like a similar kind of thing. Could it ever be a good idea to revisit something that was so incredibly magical many years ago and risk it just not being the same a second time around because the original memory would then be spoiled forever? She wasn't sure she could handle the anticlimax of it on top of everything else she had going on with Colin and her disastrous marriage. Plus, what would Nico think of her? She was hardly the young, lithe, lively girl he once knew – in fact, she was barely recognisable now with her fluctuating moods, the extra weight around the middle, the dark circles under her eyes and the stubborn wiry grey whisker on her chin that she had to keep plucking out with a pair of tweezers. And then there was Pam's 'frumpy' comment to contend with, worming its way back into her consciousness and filling her with a horrible thread of self-doubt. No, the look of dismay on Nico's face, if they were to find him, would be utterly unbearable.

'Yes, if there is one thing that I know all about… it is romance!' Rosie carried on, waggling the pom-pom pen in the air as if to punctuate this point. 'True love always finds a way when Rosie is on the case. Did I tell you I used to run a matchmaking service too before I went all in on the wedding and events planning business?' She paused, but then carried on before Gina or Deedee could get a word in edgeways. 'Oh yes, and very successful it was too. So leave this to me! I've got you Gina and will not let you down. This is my promise to you.'

Gina sighed inwardly as she carefully lowered herself down on the lounger and pulled Rosie's floppy sun hat back over her head. All she could think of right now was having a nap and then working her way through the promised snacks, in the hope of feeling well enough to paint something half decent in the art class at sunset tonight. She could worry about Rosie's reunion mission in the morning, by which time – with a bit of luck – Gina hoped she might have forgotten all about it.

10

Rosie and Deedee came through on their promise and so after polishing off the deliciously smooth homemade houmous and last piece of hot pitta bread, Gina had swallowed down the sugar hit from the Fanta and lowered herself into the sea water infinity pool at the spa. She had managed to swim a few lazy lengths to help shift the hangover from hell and then treated herself to a hot stone full body massage and the long overdue lip and leg waxing session, so she now felt brand new as she walked across the sandy, grass-capped, cliff-lined beach to join the others for the art class.

The gloriously golden Greek sun was already starting to sink and cast a magical hue over the sea water as it gently swayed back and forth. Cicadas buzzing in the lush, green tamarisk trees in the sand dunes sounded evocative. Fire lanterns hanging from wooden posts in the sand lined a towpath to where the class was being held so Gina slipped off her sandals and let them swing from the fingers of her right hand so she could savour the sensation of the sun-baked sand under the soles of her feet. She surreptitiously adjusted a strap of the fresh maxi dress she had put on after her shower. She'd also smoothed some self-tanning cream over her arms and legs in an attempt to jumpstart a natural tan and help banish the thoughts of frumpy self-doubt from her head. She always felt better with a sun-kissed glow, as they called it in the adverts. She'd even painted her toe nails a lovely coral colour to make her tan pop, and then spritzed herself in the body spray from Anne's hamper and so was now enveloped in a pina colada scented bubble of anticipation, mingled with apprehension, on seeing all the people milling around on the beach ahead. Gina hesitated. Stopped walking. And for a hot minute Colin's 'rest of the rubbish' comment was inside her head again. Only briefly, but enough to make her balk momentarily on wondering what her painting might turn out like. It was years since she had last picked up a paint brush, so what if she had forgotten all that she had learned in those lessons at art college and ended up producing something silly and they all rubbished it like Colin had? She contemplated going back to the Hotel Mirabelle, ordering room service and having a quiet night on the balcony with her book. She wasn't used to groups, spending most of her time alone at her cleaning jobs, and it was comfortable, she felt safe and knew where she was at when it was just her with Mr Muscle and a Minky sponge for company.

Tucking a stray curl into place, she pressed the tips of her nails into the palms of her hands and tried to shift her thoughts because another part of her wanted so much to step out of the comfort zone she had been in for far too long. It had felt like a prison at times. The monotony of doing the same thing every day, going to work and then being at home every night with Colin and Pam. Never trying new things, not a club, a choir, a gym class nor even dinner in a nice restaurant. She was so ready for this, an adventure, to try new things but then look where it had got her last night. Deedee and Rosie had been lovely and kind about her trolleyed state, singing and dancing about the place, but it didn't change the fact that she had made a fool of herself.

The top and bottom of it was that she just hadn't lived, not properly, not like other women her age who had done all the fun things and had reckless shenanigans in their younger years. But then it also dawned on Gina that Rosie was the same age as her and Deedee was older and they were both still having fun, adventurous lives, travelling solo and trying new things so there really was time for her too. Yes, she needed to find a way to stop worrying about the 'what if's' and harking back to the past. Even though she had already made a promise to herself not to do this, it felt hard... three weeks to form a new habit, is what she had heard, and she was really only a few days in.

Lifting her head from its force-of-habit downward position, she resolved, yet again, to persevere, reciting to herself, 'good evening, nice to meet you' as she carried on walking across the sand towards where the art class was being held, so she was properly prepared to meet new people without stumbling over her words if the fuggy head made a sudden appearance.

'Gina. Over here, darling. I've saved you an easel.' It was Deedee with a wide smile and waving enthusiastically from an elevated area of the beach, and true to her word, she was wearing a brightly patterned silk headscarf wrapped around her head with a matching floaty kaftan swathing her long-limbed yoga body and looking every inch like an authentic artist in residence. Gina smiled on seeing her new friend looking so happy, achieving her bucket list dream of being an artist on a Greek island beach. 'There's an easel here for Rosie too,' Deedee said. 'Did you see her on your way here? She's not arrived yet.'

'Oh no, I haven't, hopefully she'll turn up soon,' Gina called out, lifting the hem of her long dress so she could climb up onto the dense, grassy, flat surface of the sand dune that was shaded from the still warm evening sun by a very lush tamarisk tree. 'Thanks for this... You got us the best spot I see. And you look fabulous in your "artist-in-residence" outfit.' Gina settled herself on a stool next to Deedee and looked across the sunlit beach, admiring the electric blue sea water swirling and swaying over the silver sand, the shrub-covered cliffs skirting to form a secluded cove. Deedee had managed to bag three easels that had been set up on top of the highest sand dune with a lovely, elevated view of the Greek beach and beyond.

'Thanks Gina. You also look gorgeous too in your "breezy beach babe living her best life" outfit.' Deedee smiled warmly, giving Gina an enveloping hug. 'How are you feeling now?' She let Gina go. 'I hope I didn't upset you with my theory about Colin and the missing memory box?'

'No, you didn't. I'm OK, good in fact. I feel much better now the hangover has lifted, and to be honest, Deedee, I just feel a bit foolish for not considering that Colin could have hidden, or worse still, got rid of my precious memory box. He threw a painting I did on the bonfire one time, so it is entirely possible.'

'Oh Gina, that's no reflection on you. How horrible of him. You mustn't feel foolish... but I do totally understand how easy it is for those feelings to slide up on you when the balance is off kilter in a relationship. My first husband did similar things – ripped up a Mary Quant miniskirt because he claimed that I looked like a cheap sex worker in it – I then didn't wear a short skirt again while I was with him, which was a shame really as I had been rather fond of my legs prior to that point. But for years after, his criticism riddled me with insecurity.' She flipped her lovely legs out from beneath the stool she was sitting on, crossed them at the ankles and pointed them in the air like a ballerina.

'Well, your first husband was wrong to criticise and cause you to feel insecure, you have amazing legs and always look fantastic,' Gina smiled and nodded in admiration.

'Thank you, darling. My first husband had a very fragile ego, and you know coercive control is a recognised crime nowadays.' Deedee squeezed the top of Gina's hand.

Silence followed as the two women sat together each contemplating their shared thoughts. From their vantage point, Gina and Deedee watched the other guests arriving for the class, but still no sight of Rosie. Or the art teacher. A waiter from the Hotel Mirabelle wandered over to them.

'Good evening, ladies, can I bring you some cocktails, or wine if you prefer?'

'No, thank you,' Gina answered right away, welcoming the distraction from her thoughts. She had been thinking about the memory box and Colin taking it and how naïve she had been not to even contemplate this at the time. She had trusted him implicitly and if he had taken the box, which let's face it was the most likely explanation, then the realisation of this felt so incredibly hurtful. Turning to Deedee, she put a smile on her face and quickly whispered, 'I'm doing a detox tonight. I don't want to tempt fate and stoke the hangover from hell. It only shifted completely in the last hour or so, after I polished off the rest of the complimentary baclava back in my room!'

'In that case, I'll join you and detox too, Gina.' Deedee turned to the waiter. 'Can we have two mocktails please? Virgin Apollos? Actually three would be better, one for our friend as well who should be joining us soon,' she explained. Then over her shoulder to Gina, she added, 'I tried an Apollo the last time I was here on the island and they are very good, fruity, and sweet and just like the real thing, but with none of the headache the next morning.'

'Sounds like just the thing!' Gina grinned, relieved that Deedee wasn't pushing the Bloody Mary option onto her again.

'And some snacks would be marvellous too, please,' Deedee added.

'Of course,' the waiter smiled easily. 'I will bring you the mezze board with lots of *saganaki*, stuffed vine leaves, prawns, calamari, feta, pitta, olives, spanakopita... you like all this?' Gina nodded, grateful that the hangover had gone, and her appetite had returned, immediately thinking of the delicious *saganaki*, or little pan-fried dishes as they were, if she remembered the translation correctly. Memories of sharing the warm melting cheese and garlicky prawn dish with her mum for the first time when she was about ten years old at Toula's taverna on the beach and thinking how grown up and sophisticated she had felt. The spanakopita was another favourite, a tasty filo pastry pie stuffed with spinach and feta and sprinkled with pine nuts – simply irresistible. She could feel her stomach rumbling in anticipation of tasting all these foods that were bound to evoke her happy holiday memories once again. Colin might have thrown away the photos from the past but there was nothing stopping her now from revisiting those memories and enjoying them all over again. Although the joy was bittersweet without her mum here too.

'Oh yes, please. *Parakalo*,' Deedee added politely in a perfect Greek accent to show her thanks before the waiter turned and wandered back across the sand towards the wooden beach bar that the staff from the Hotel Mirabelle had set up underneath the shade of more tamarisk trees.

Moments later, Rosie appeared padding across the sand closely followed by the art teacher, Gina assumed, going by the big pile of canvases the man was carrying, stacked so high his head was hidden from view. She waved to get Rosie's attention as Deedee had her phone held up in the air and was busy taking selfies of her easel set-up, with the picturesque Greek beach for a backdrop.

'Rosie, we are over here,' Gina yelled a little louder than she intended as everyone on the beach turned their heads towards her, including the art teacher who had started sharing the canvases out so the pile had reduced, and she could see his face clearly now. Oh no. A rivulet of sweat immediately snaked a path down between her boobs as her cheeks tingled with heat. Cristos! *But he's the receptionist. Not the art teacher, surely.* She inhaled through her nostrils and directed a long, maelstrom of cooling breath out and down over her body, inwardly praying that the sweaty map of Australia wouldn't make a sudden appearance. Gina flapped a hand across her face before attempting to hide behind her easel, but it was no use, as Cristos was up on the sand dune and underneath the tamarisk tree in one athletically swift movement. He was standing right in front of her now with a wide smile spread across his ridiculously beautiful face.

'Gina. I'm very happy to see you here. Are you ready to paint?' he asked enthusiastically as he placed a canvas on her easel, seemingly oblivious to the sudden effect he was having on her. A burst of his now familiar scent mingled in the air around her, sparking a tingling sensation down the length of her back. She instinctively cleared her throat and sat up straighter, wondering what on earth was happening to her. She had butterflies. Actual butterflies. Fluttering in the pit of her stomach and radiating down her thighs and turning her on. And it was ridiculous. She was forty-nine years old for crying out loud! So why was her body behaving like she was a teenage girl with raging hormones having her first crush? Especially with a man who she had already made an absolute fool of herself in front of. Bloody typical that her libido, which had ghosted her for the last however many years, let's not forget, would make such a monumental return right now. The magnetism, sexual chemistry, or whatever it was that she was experiencing, was so intoxicating, it was all she could do not to reach out a hand, slide it underneath his T-shirt and run her fingertips over his exceptionally muscular abdomen and up to his chest. And now images of him flinging her onto the giant 'princess and the pea' style bed in her hotel room flashed into her head, of getting naked together, her straddling his hips and having hot, wild, passionate sex. All night long.

'Gina. Gina. *GINA*?' Rosie prompted in an urgent whisper voice, giving Gina a gentle nudge as she walked past to find her easel on the other side of Deedee.

'Oh, um.' Gina swallowed as she came to and realised that she had momentarily been sat in some kind of stupor, with her mouth hanging properly agape. She immediately reunited her jaw with the rest of her face and tried to hide her head by busying herself in adjusting the canvas and sorting through the box of paints at her feet. What was the question? Her mind had done that weird thing again. She couldn't remember. Her head felt as if it was stuffed full of cotton wool. And her face felt like it was on fire and in danger of spontaneously combusting. Not to mention her legs which were currently trembling... but not in a bad way.

'Yes!' Deedee stepped in. 'Yes, we are all very excited to paint the sunset, aren't we Gina, Rosie?'

'Yes, oh yes we are,' they chorused, nudging each other, with Gina flashing Deedee a very grateful smile.

'Good, so we make a start,' Cristos prompted, inclining his head slightly and glancing at Gina with a cute smile before he turned and nearly leapt off the sand dune in another very athletic move. She bit down on her bottom lip and focused on steadying her breathing.

'What was that all about?' Deedee asked as soon as Cristos was out of earshot.

'What do you mean?' Gina squeaked, keeping her eyes fixed on the blank canvas on the easel in front of her as she tried to will the furnace on her face and neck to leave her alone. And the swirling sensation still going on in her thighs to subside.

'*That!*' Deedee subtly circled an index finger in Cristos's direction. 'The moment. Or whatever just happened there. Are you OK, darling? Is it still the hangover?'

'No, no, the hangover has gone now. I don't know what happened. I just felt hot, and then my mind suddenly went sort of...' she paused before settling on, 'wild,' which wasn't entirely untrue. Gina looked away, feeling self-conscious.

'Oh, it happens to me all the time,' Rosie said breezily as if to rescue Gina, before standing up and moving her easel and stool so the three of them were sitting closer to each other in a little semi-circle underneath the tree. 'Goes with the elephant hoof feet... It's the blooming perimenopause. A rollercoaster of emotions and sometimes my brain seems to cut out too... Just like that.' She did a dramatic click with her thumb and finger up in the air between them. 'It drives me mad.' Rosie tutted and let out a long breath.

'Well, that will be your hormones, darling. I take it neither of you are on HRT?' Deedee gave them a look with one eyebrow cocked curiously. Rosie and Gina both shook their heads. 'In that case, I will give you the number of my doctor, a fantastic woman, an expert in women's health and the menopause, and you can Zoom her when you get home. She will talk you through it all. Honestly, there's no reason why either of you should have to put up with sudden memory loss or elephant hoof feet or whatever you call them Rosie, or indeed all the other horrible symptoms,' Deedee said, pragmatically. 'Not that I'm pushing drugs onto you, absolutely not, but I think it's always good to have options, to find out the facts so you can make an informed decision about your own body and if you need to top up your dwindling hormones.'

'OK, I can get on board with that, I like options,' Rosie shrugged and then nodded slowly in agreement. 'But I think I've just been in denial for far too long... Not wanting to admit to myself that I really am getting older.'

'Hmm, well what would you sooner do... Plod along on your elephant hoofs being in denial and letting things just happen to you, or take action and get your zest for life back and feel marvellous like I do? Honestly, I think you will thank me when your libido is properly switched back on and sex is fully on the agenda again.'

'That's definitely true.' Rosie widened her eyes.

'Good. Because soon you'll be riding your husband in a reverse cowgirl and getting your bare backside spanked with that faux-fur paddle, thinking all your Christmases have come at once! Pardon the pun.'

A short silence followed as both Gina and Rosie stopped moving to stare open mouthed at Deedee before subsiding into fits of laughter.

'Oh God, Deedee, you are naughty, but bloody hilarious too,' Rosie said, the first to recover. 'And thanks for the lecture.'

'You are very welcome, darling.' Deedee did one of her forthright nods and the three of them sniggered some more and for some insane reason Gina's thoughts went to Nico and the sex they had enjoyed together... It had been tender and sensual and intense. She had loved it a lot and had never forgotten. She'd even secretly thought about it on occasion over the years, fantasising when things had first started feeling off with Colin. Touch was something she had missed immensely in her marriage these last few years, devoid of even a cuddle. She'd lost count of the nights where Colin had positioned himself on the far side of the bed with his back to her, seemingly oblivious and snoring in answer when she attempted to talk to him. It was a lonely place lying awake in the dark next to someone who barely noticed you.

'Ladies, please... Are you ready to create your sunset scenes now?' Cristos called out from across the beach as a polite but firm way of telling them to stop talking and pay attention.

'Yes, sorry,' the three friends chimed, smiling, and exchanging looks. Cristos then gave them all some tips on planning their painting, how to think about creating perspective and blending colours and to start with capturing the beach view and the different shades of the sea, leaving the actual sunset element to last by which time the sun would have actually set. That is if they wanted to have the sunset as the focus of their painting, which everyone did, given that they all smiled and nodded in agreement. Every now and then Cristos turned his own canvas towards the group so they could all see how he was building up the layers of his painting. Gina was fascinated and felt a pang of nostalgia for those lectures she had loved at art college.

'Now you must start and don't think too much about it. The painting must come from the heart, with your passion. Just blend and paint and trust that you will create something beautiful,' Cristos said, lifting his arms out wide as if to embrace, and then frame, the stunning scene set out before them all. 'And I will mingle around to see what you are doing,' he added, his Greek accent sounding even stronger and sexier, Gina thought, transfixed by his charisma and obvious love for the art. It was incredibly appealing and in stark contrast to Colin, who hated anything to do with spontaneity or creativity, she couldn't help thinking too.

'Gina.' Rosie leaned sideways to whisper to her. 'The art teacher can come and mingle up here anytime he likes,' she swooned, popping a plump stuffed vine leaf into her mouth from the platter that had been set up on a small wooden table beside them. 'Talk about red hot, he's an actual Greek god walking among us.' She fanned herself dramatically as she chewed and swallowed and then picked up a brush to daub over the red paint on her palette before swirling a big fiery ball in the middle of her canvas with an exhilarating flourish. Smiling to herself, Gina tasted a forkful of the delicious spanakopita, savouring the spinach and tangy feta taste and then made a start too, mixing and blending and relishing the nostalgic scent of the paint mingled with an anticipation to be doing something she loved again.

Soon her initial reservation had vanished, and she felt fully immersed in the creative process only pausing from dotting flecks of white paint on the crests of the waves rolling over the sand when Rosie gently nudged the side of her thigh with her hand. 'Gina,' Rosie whispered again, 'that frisson, chemistry or whatever happened earlier between you and the art teacher was electric. Mind you, like I said, he is extremely hot. And talented too... did you see his painting?'

'Cristos?'

'Ooh, you know his name?' Rosie breathed, her eyes widening. 'Have you met him before this evening?'

'We first met when I checked in...'

'*First?* And so there's been other times too?' Rosie prompted, clearly keen to hear more of what she seemingly imagined was a string of steamy encounters between Gina and Cristos.

'One other time, but it was nothing... Just him showing me the way—'

'Oh my God, I bet he did!' Rosie fanned herself some more. 'Details please? Was he hot as fu—?'

'NO,' Gina jumped in. 'Absolutely not, nothing like that, he showed me where the bar was, that's all.' She let her voice tail off, not wanting to elaborate further and be reminded all over again of the massive show she had made of herself, with her crusty top lip and comedy stagger.

'So no intimacy at all?' Rosie's face dropped in disappointment. 'Well, in that case, if we can't find your Nico, then I will matchmake you with Cristos instead, he's clearly into you. I saw the way he locked eye contact with you and remember, I am an expert in this stuff. Oh yes, I can spot it all a mile off. Leave it with me.'

'Whaaat? Noooo, there was no intimacy!' Gina spluttered, simultaneously marshalling her thoughts around everything Rosie was suggesting, especially the 'your Nico' comment which admittedly, and to her surprise, did give her a warm fuzzy feeling, as she momentarily tried it on for size, but then just as swiftly discarded it as preposterous; she already knew that this was a fantasy so what was the point of teasing herself with something that was never going to happen. And as for Cristos, that was a preposterous idea too and Rosie was deluded if she thought she could pair her up with him. 'Cristos isn't interested in me. He probably just feels sorry for me. Plus, I am still a married woman, technically, even if we are having a trial separation.'

'Of course, I get that,' Rosie said, quickly backtracking. 'But also, why on earth not? Why wouldn't Cristos fancy you? You're a very attractive woman. Don't let your husband not valuing you as he should live rent-free inside your head and make you doubt your own self-worth.' And just like that, Rosie had got to the heart of Gina's insecurities. Both women took a deep breath. 'Sorry, I shouldn't have said that,' Rosie added in a calmer voice now, as she glanced downwards and shook her head before fiddling with her gold layer necklace.

'Please don't be,' Gina said quietly. 'It's true. I have let "things" get to me and change how I feel about myself. But I am working on sorting it out if I can...'

'Of course you can! And good for you. Take it one day at a time, yes? You'll get there,' Rosie said gently and gave Gina's thigh another pat. They carried on painting.

A couple of hours later, the class came to a close and Gina started packing away the paints she had used. Cristos appeared at her side just as she popped her brush inside the jug of water that one of the waiters was passing among them.

'Thank you,' she said, as the waiter walked on to the next group of holidaymakers over by the wooden beach bar.

'Gina, please wait a moment?' Cristos asked, as she went to take her canvas off the easel so she could take it back to the hotel. She thought she might prop it against the railings on her balcony to properly dry and then see if it would fit inside her wheelie suitcase to take home. It would be a nice souvenir of her holiday and a reminder of the sense of déjà vu she had experienced while painting it here on the beach which was very similar to where she and Nico had sat on the rock and painted together as teenagers. 'You mind?' he added, touching her arm, and sending another spark of electricity to surge right through her. He took the canvas from her and held it at arm's length, his head tilted to one side. Silence followed as he studied the painting. Gina held her breath and glanced first at Rosie and then at Deedee who were both stood behind Cristos, each with their own canvasses in their hands. Some of the others from the class had wandered over and were now gathered around all looking at Gina's painting. She could feel her heartbeat quickening as she waited for Cristos's verdict, inwardly hoping he would be kinder than Colin had been about his portrait. The sunset painting had turned out a lot better than Gina thought it might, and more importantly she had absolutely loved the experience. It had felt cathartic, meditative almost. 'Why do you not tell me you are an experienced artist?' Cristos asked, his conker brown eyes dancing in delight as he smiled and turned his head from side to side to scrutinise Gina's canvas from all angles.

'Oh, well, I suppose I'm not really that experienced,' Gina started, feeling her cheeks flare up on being in the spotlight all of a sudden. People were nodding and muttering words of admiration as they took it in turns to get a close-up look of her painting.

'It's captivating,' someone said.

'I wish I could paint like that,' another person commented.

'Gina, this painting is outstanding. You have a real talent,' Cristos told her. 'The way you have caught the light on the sea and the different colours in the sunset is surreal. The contrast, the fine brush strokes, the emotion, the *passion*! You have it all here.' Cristos tilted his head some more and then turned to look at Gina straight on, doing that 'only woman in the world' thing again and making her melt just a little bit more. The fluttery butterfly feeling from earlier returned even more intensely. Rosie and Deedee were both seemingly beaming with pride and nodding too as if to punctuate Cristos's appraisal of her artwork. 'Please – would you like to display your painting in my friend's art gallery, so everyone on the island can come to see it and enjoy it?'

'Um, oh, well—' Gina started, taken aback. She could feel her heart pumping like a piston now with the sheer intensity of the moment. The close proximity of him. The praise of her painting. Mixed all together it was a heady cocktail, intoxicating and over-whelming.

'Yes!' Deedee immediately said, pressing her own canvas into Rosie's free hand and practically sprinting over the sand to stand next to Gina. 'My friend would love to display her exquisite paint-ing,' she told Cristos firmly, and then turned to Gina. 'What do you say, darling? It's about time your art was recognised for the talent that it is, don't you think?' Deedee flung an arm around Gina's shoulders and gave her an encouraging hug. Rosie winked at her and swivelled her eyes in Cristos's direction with a subtle nod of her head as if to say, 'A-ha, I told you so'.

'Oh, um, OK. I guess so,' Gina grinned, a surge of relief and a simmer of pride swelling up within her... A feeling she hadn't felt in a very long time. 'Yes, yes thank you, that would be lovely.'

'Good, I will send a message with a photo of your painting to my friend and will take it to his gallery. You can come and see how it looks there tomorrow, yes?' Cristos explained.

'Thank you,' Gina repeated, beaming now from ear to ear as she took another look at her canvas with the beautiful beachy sunset painting on.

'Let's get a picture first,' Rosie suggested, dumping her own canvas on the sand, before handing Deedee's canvas back to her and whipping out her phone. 'How about you hold your painting up in front of you, Gina?' she added, getting into position like a pro on a photoshoot.

'Um, sure,' Gina said, still dazed as Cristos handed her the canvas and then standing slightly behind her, he leaned in and proudly placed a hand gently on each of her shoulders as if show-casing his star pupil with her gorgeous Greek sunset painting. Gina kept her smile in place and fixed her eyes on Rosie's phone, willing every iota of willpower she possessed to show up, so she didn't succumb to the close proximity of Cristos's firm body practically pressed up against her back that felt as if it was on fire, the fluttery butterfly feeling fuelling up into a full-on furnace of desire now. Oh God. The temptation to move her body backwards just a teeny tiny bit to rest against his solid chest was almost too much to bear. She found herself craving physical touch, something that had been missing from her life for a long time. She curled her fingertips tighter around the sides of the canvas and inhaled hard through her nose, inwardly galvanising herself to 'get a flaming grip girl!'.

Seemingly oblivious, Rosie carried on taking pictures, lifting, and lowering her phone and shifting position until she was satis-fied that she had the money shot.

'OK, fab, that should be enough pics, I have at least twenty so there's bound to be one that's good enough for the grid,' Rosie laughed, and Cristos stepped away from Gina. She gave him the canvas to take to the gallery while discreetly slowing her breathing which felt as if she had just run a record-breaking sprint. He smiled at her and held eye contact looking like he was going to say something else but then changed his mind.

'So Cristos, where is your friend's gallery?' Rosie asked, not missing a beat in making sure they had all the details.

'In the old piazza on the top of the hill, I can write the address for you. Ask for my friend. His name is Nico!' he said, before pulling a pen from the back pocket of his jeans and heading back to the bar, in search of a piece of paper, Gina presumed.

A beat of silence followed as Gina, Rosie and Deedee stopped moving.

Could it be?

The three women stared at each other, open mouthed and eyebrows raised as they collectively wondered if this was some kind of serendipity at play?

'Wouldn't it be amazing?' Rosie gushed. 'And Gina, you did say that your Nico dreamed of being a doctor... or an artist. I wonder is it possible that he pursued this passion and opened his own art gallery right here on the island? It could happen, it really could. It could be fate bringing you both back together again.'

11

The following morning Gina, flanked by Rosie and Deedee, stood outside the art gallery waiting for it to open. The three new friends had met for an early coffee in the hotel with Rosie insistent that they come here right away to, 'reunite you with your first love, Gina', she had rhapsodised with a very determined look on her flushed face, adding stuff about Hallmark films and destiny, and it was giving Gina giant waves of panic.

'Maybe we should come back later,' Gina suggested, funnelling her thoughts instead on admiring the beautiful whitewashed two-storey building with an arched wooden door painted a pretty pastel blue and a balcony above bursting with an array of vibrant pink, purple and white geraniums cascading over the sides. The gallery was in the corner of a small, cobbled piazza at the top of a narrow, winding street with several boutiques and a cafe that had a striped awning and seats outside. A slinky tortoiseshell cat, lying on a step near the cafe, stretched out and yawned lazily, basking in the already warm, hazy morning sun.

The sound of the sea soothed as the old town of Kalosiros stirred for the start of a new day in paradise, or so it seemed to

Gina as she soaked up the atmosphere and reflected all over again that it truly was a wonderful place here. Even though she had only been back on the island for a few days, she was already beginning to wish she could just stay here forever and never have to return to her old dull life where the highlight was trying out a new cleaning product with a seasonal scent. But she also knew staying here forever, and just not going home, was a fantasy and so she was doing her best to block the teasing thoughts from her mind because in just under two weeks she would have to go home and face the music. Plus, she'd have to face Colin and confront him over the memory box, and it would turn into a scene. Or, and this might be even harder to deal with... Would Colin be nice and loving enough that she retreated back into her old ways and never made the changes that she knew needed to happen? She had taken her mobile out of the safe last night to see if she could work out how to set up her own Instagram account. But after the usual million messages a day from Colin had pinged through one after the other onto the screen, the last one sent the day before, asking, no demanding, to know why she was ignoring him, it had then gone silent. It was then, when she was taking some pictures of the hotel room and the breathtakingly beautiful view of the lemon orchards and the beach, that a new message had flashed up on the screen. And it was different to all the others.

COLIN

> You've made your point love. I should have come on holiday with you. I love you and wish you would come home so we can sort this out xxx

And she had wobbled. Colin rarely said he loved her, and he never put kisses, not even in a birthday card. It had confused her and so she had put the phone back in the safe to give herself some space to think about the message.

'Oh no, I think we should wait,' Rosie said, punctuating Gina's thoughts. 'What if we miss him? Nico might come along to open up the gallery and then disappear somewhere.' Rosie pressed her nose up to the window. 'He could have an assistant or someone else who manages the gallery. We need to find out right away if he's *your Nico* which will be truly wonderful. It's so exciting... We really are fully involved in a Hallmark film here.'

'Rosie, please, stop saying that,' Gina said in a hushed voice, furtively glancing around. 'It's very unlikely to be the same Nico. Plus, he's not *my Nico*. I never heard from him again after that post-card on my birthday, so he probably met someone else and forgot about me. He might be married. He might be—'

'And he might not be!' Deedee joined in, elbowing her way in next to Rosie at the window so she could take a look inside the gallery too. 'Hmm, but I can't see your painting on the wall.'

'Exactly!' Gina said. 'Cristos most likely hasn't even brought the painting here yet. How's it going to look if he arrives, and we are all here waiting like three extra eager beavers?'

'Ah, good point.' Deedee stepped back from the window. 'Not cool. Darling, you don't want to look like an over-grateful amateur, absolutely not. You are an accomplished and very talented artist, Gina. Say it with me,' she laughed, and Gina thought she sounded just like Anne had on that day with her 'woman of substance' power pose. 'Yes, a special talent and as such, you will breeze in at some point today to see your latest masterpiece,' Deedee kept on.

'Well, I wouldn't go that far.' Gina shook her head.

'But what if the gallery owner really *is* your Nico? It could be possible, and they do say that love works in mysterious ways,' Rosie said breathlessly. 'Maybe this is the reason why Colin dropped out at the last minute. So fate, or whatever, could help you find your way back to your first love. It's going to be so romantic when you two love birds are reunited after all these years, and I don't want to miss the moment. And I can't come back later today; I have two more potential wedding locations to look at this afternoon.' She turned back to the window. Deedee looked at Gina before taking charge.

'Right, come on Rosie, let's go and get a coffee—'

'But—'

'No buts, we can sit outside the cafe over there on the other side of the piazza and then we will see when the art gallery opens. I'm sure it won't be too much later.' She glanced around the piazza where doors were being unlocked and wooden shutters flung open. 'See, some of the other shops are opening up now. Come on.' And Deedee walked over to the cafe on the other side of the piazza with a perfect view of the gallery. Gina followed her inwardly breathing a sigh of relief on realising that they would probably see the gallery owner walk along the street when he arrived which meant that she would be able to see if it was 'her Nico' as Rosie said, or not (most likely) without having to go inside and actually stand right in front of him and deal with his disappointed face when he probably wouldn't even recognise her. All with Rosie right up close and ready to burst in a fit over exuberant romantic wanderlust or whatever. No, it would just be too awkward and incredibly crushing when it wasn't like a scene from the Hallmark film that Rosie was imagining. It would be far better to see the gallery owner from a distance, point out that he wasn't actually 'her Nico' and then they could discreetly leave and that would be the end of it. They could go back to being on holiday and having a fantastic time together.

Nearly an hour later, and having drunk two exceedingly strong Greek coffees, and with no sign of the gallery owner arriving, Gina was feeling very jittery and had stood up with the intention of going back to the hotel to sunbathe by the pool when the blue door to the gallery opened.

'At last!' Rosie leapt out of her seat, popped her shades up on top of her head, presumably so she could get a better look at the person inside, Gina assumed, and dashed over to the gallery. Deedee followed with Gina close behind, the panic swelling inside her all over again on spotting Rosie's phone gripped between her fingers, primed to take pictures of the reunion, or worse still, make a film!

Inside, and Gina stopped abruptly. Her canvas was there on the wall after all, tucked behind a pillar away from the window and glowing underneath a spotlight, the sunset scene almost golden in this light. An elderly woman behind the counter came around to stand next to Gina.

'My friend here is the artist!' Rosie said right away, her excitement on potentially finding Nico clearly making it hard for her to contain herself. The elderly woman nodded at Gina in admiration.

'Congratulations, you have a special talent, this piece is exquisite,' the woman said in perfect English to Gina before offering her hand to shake.

Gina took it and replied, 'Thank you. And for displaying my painting.'

'It's a pleasure. Do you want to sell the piece or just to show it? I will have many interested buyers if you'd like to sell it,' the woman said, her eyes widening in anticipation.

'Oh, I think just to show it for now, please, if that's OK?' Gina said, not having even contemplated that people might actually want to buy her painting.

'Sure, it's OK. I will move it over here by the door to attract people to admire it and then come inside and see the other paintings to buy,' the woman smiled knowingly as she unhooked Gina's canvas and carried it to a better spot by the gallery's entrance. Gina followed her.

'Thank you. I couldn't believe it when our art teacher, Cristos, told me. It's such an honour, a long-held dream come true, to see my work hanging in a real art gallery,' Gina said.

'Ah, yes, Cristos, he is a wonderful artist too. He has a keen eye for a beautiful painting...' And then lowering her voice, the elderly woman leaned in a little closer to Gina and added, '...and an eye for the beautiful tourist ladies too.' She chuckled and shrugged as Gina felt her cheeks flush.

'Oh, um...' Gina hesitated unsure of how to respond to this information, so swiftly moved on and added, 'Yes, Cristos said that his friend, Nico, owns the gallery. Is he here by any chance?' Gina took a deep breath just in case by some wild fluke it did turn out to be the same Nico that she once knew, figuring that now they were all inside the gallery, it was better to take control of what would be an absolutely awkward scenario if Nico was here, and Rosie made a massive drama of it all. She willed the elderly woman to say no, he wasn't here, in fact he lived millions of miles away and never actually came to the gallery any more, not ever. But it wasn't to be.

'Yes, he's here,' the woman said, and Gina took a sharp intake of breath. 'But he's sleeping.'

'When will he wake up?' Rosie piped up, glancing at her watch. Deedee nudged Rosie and she pulled a face.

'Sometimes he sleeps all day... My father is very old. He gets tired,' the woman explained.

'Your father is Nico?' Gina checked, almost sagging in relief. *No awkward reunion today! Yeayyy.*

'Yes, my father is Nico. And soon he will be one hundred years old.' The woman nodded proudly.

'How wonderful. It must be the glorious Greek air,' Deedee said politely. 'Thank you so much for displaying our friend's wonderful painting and it's a pleasure to meet you. We need to go now, but we will visit again.' And she stepped backwards, motioning for Gina and Rosie to come along too. But just as they reached the door, Rosie turned around to talk to the woman again.

'Err, I don't suppose you know any other men called Nico by any chance? Young, handsome ones I'm, um, guessing the one that we are looking for would be... Yes, very good looking. About fifty-ish, something like that. Gina, what does your Nico look like, can you remember?' Rosie paused to draw breath, giving Gina a scrutinising look as she nudged her with her elbow. 'What colour hair did he have? Mind you, it could be grey by now, or... Ooh, salt and pepper, that would be nice—'

'*Rosie!*' Deedee whisper-hissed as she swiftly looped her arm through the crook of her very persistent friend's elbow and hoicked her through the gallery's open door and into the street.

Outside, and the three women stood in a triangle staring at each other. Deedee was the first to talk.

'What were you thinking? Rosie, you can't be interrogating an old lady like that!' Deedee batted Rosie's arm, pretending to be cross as she rolled her eyes and shook her head. 'Honestly, you'll get us all locked up, for, I don't know, procurement or inappropriate behaviour or whatever. Word will whizz around this tiny island, warning all the lovely local Greek people to watch out for the crazy English woman hunting for a handsome Nico!'

'I know, I know!' Rosie looked aghast. 'I'm so sorry, I don't know what came over me. And sorry Gina, I didn't mean to embarrass you. I've always got a bit passionate when it comes to my friends and making sure they're happy. It's the hopeless romantic in me and after hearing about Colin letting you down over your dream holiday... well, I just want you to be happy.' She hung her head like a scolded puppy before glancing back up with sad eyes and giving Gina a big hug.

'No real harm done,' Gina soothed, hugging Rosie, and patting her back before letting out a long breath as they broke away from each other. 'And I am happy... happy that I've met you two; it's lovely to have friends after a long time of feeling isolated and I have to say, that it was a truly wonderful moment seeing my painting hanging there on the wall in a proper gallery,' she added, her pulse still quickening by the experience. It had sparked her enthusiasm further to take up her beloved art again. Maybe she could enrol in a course when she got home. Yes, the thought of it buoyed her and went some way in covering up the panic she had felt over potentially finding 'her Nico' just now, but there was something else going on inside her too, a deflated feeling, a dart of disappointment perhaps, and she wondered if she might like to see Nico again after all? If only to see if he did in fact have some photos from the past, or was it more than that? The thought lingered.

'I'm sorry,' Rosie repeated, turning to Deedee. 'Forgive me?'

'Of course I do, darling.' Deedee batted her arm again. 'Come on, let's find somewhere nice to go for brunch – a bottomless one preferably – we need to celebrate Gina's brilliant painting. But don't worry, Gina, we won't let you drink a trillion shots again.' She looked at Rosie for confirmation.

'Absolutely not! No, you need a clear head for when we do actually find your Nico,' Rosie instructed, like she was coaching a nervous client going on a blind date as she fished around inside her tote bag before pulling out her big pad and the fluffy pink pom-pom-topped pen. 'I need to cross the art gallery off my list of potential whereabouts for Nico,' she explained, taking the plastic lid of the pen off with her teeth. 'I reckon we should go back to plan A and try the taverna his grandparents owned and then the holiday apartment place. What do you reckon, Gina? If we get a move on, I'll still have time to come with you today.' She tapped the page with her pen and simultaneously glanced at her watch.

'Um, sure, maybe. But let's have the brunch and talk about it first, there's plenty of time before your meetings start,' Gina said, to buy herself an hour or so to work out what was going on inside her head and her heart right now, the dart of disappointment on not seeing Nico having taken her by surprise.

'Ah yes, good idea. We'll have a proper project meeting, and I can draw us a map of the island with a route planner! Come on.' Rosie pushed the notepad back inside her tote bag and then looped her arms through Gina's and Deedee's elbows and the three women were just about to walk away when the elderly woman appeared at the gallery's open door and called out to them.

'One moment please, I know the Nico you ask about. Very handsome, yes?' she said with a conspiratorial twinkle in her rheumy eyes. 'He is the doctor!' The woman clapped her hands together in joy at being able to help. 'You can find him in the clinic; it's near the old church by the water.' Gina, Deedee and Rosie stopped walking and once again they stared, open-mouthed at each other, all wondering if this time it really could be 'Gina's Nico'. The teenage boy she had known with a passion for painting but also with a dream of being a doctor!

'Oh, this is a great help!' Rosie said, un-looping her arms from Gina and Deedee so she could move closer to the woman. 'Thank you so much. And I'm very sorry about earlier. I got a bit carried away.'

'It's OK. We all like to find a handsome man, yes?' The woman raised a knowing eyebrow and they all laughed. Rosie, turning back to her friends added, 'Come on, brunch can wait! Let's go straight to the old church by the water – I know where it is as it's on my list of possible places for my clients' wedding ceremony – and see if we can find Nico's clinic.' And, after slipping her shades over her eyes and slinging her tote bag back over one shoulder with a renewed determination, Rosie lifted her elbows primed to pump and speed-walked off down the cobbled hill yelling to Gina and Deedee, 'Hurry up! This is going to be so romantic.'

12

'Oh no!' Rosie called out, having reached the doctor's clinic a few steps ahead of Gina and Deedee.

'What's up?' Gina asked, walking past the old church and towards the small, whitewashed building with a flat roof and a red and white cross symbol on the wooden door.

'I think it's closed. The door won't open and there's a hand-written note pinned here underneath the ring bell.' Rosie pointed to a piece of paper with Greek words written on it.

'What does it say, Deedee?' Rosie tapped the paper as the three women gathered together in the small doorway while Deedee tried to read the note.

'No idea, but my money is on it saying, "Closed for bottomless brunch" if this Nico has any sense, especially if he skipped break-fast too, like we had to!' Deedee gave Rosie a pointed look.

'Ah, I'm sure it doesn't say that. Doctors don't go for bottomless brunches. *Do they*?' Rosie swivelled her head towards Gina and Deedee with a baffled look on her face. 'Let's just wait a little bit,' she added, 'the note might say, "back in five mins" for all we know.'

'Look, the doctor isn't going to disappear, not if his clinic is right here. He's bound to turn up at some point, and I'm getting peckish. Come on, let's do brunch and come back later,' Deedee suggested.

'Yes, good idea!' Gina agreed immediately and fell into step beside Deedee who was already walking away towards a row of tavernas with tables and chairs outside, lined along the sea wall. A few minutes later, Rosie caught up and gave them a breathless update, 'The note says the clinic will be open again at four o'clock! I asked one of the fishermen.'

'Well, there you go!' Deedee smiled. 'Plenty of time for another one of those grazing platters we love to share with a nice bottle of crisp, chilled Savatiano Greek wine. It is after eleven o'clock now, after all.'

'But what about my meetings?' Rosie groaned. 'I only have an hour or so before I will need to leave you two to it. I'll miss the romantic reunion.'

'We could come back tomorrow,' Gina suggested, a plan swiftly hatching to pop back to the clinic later on by herself and see if she could catch a look at the doctor without an audience watching.

A short silence followed.

'Hmm, OK, well I suppose that will have to do,' Rosie eventually conceded. 'But let's keep an eye out in case your Nico comes back early. Look, there's a lovely looking taverna right there on the end with a bird's eye view of the clinic.' And she dashed off ahead towards the parasol-covered seating area outside to bag them the nearest table with the best uninterrupted view of the clinic. Gina and Deedee held back.

'I know she means well,' Deedee said to Gina as they strolled along the sea wall together, weaving in and out of a pair of pelicans that were pottering about, 'but she's in danger of spontaneously combusting into a big, romantic puff of love heart confetti at this rate.'

'Yes, and she's going to be crushed when the doctor most likely turns out not to be "my Nico",' Gina said, shrugging and lifting her palms.

'And what about you, Gina? How do you feel about it all?'

'You know, to be honest, I was horrified at first, panicked at the prospect of seeing Nico again and it spoiling the memories I've cherished for all these years of the wonderful times we had together, if that makes sense...'

'Absolutely, sometimes things are best left in the past, because in my experience, they are never as good a second time around. And you were both very young back then.'

'Exactly!' Gina agreed. 'He might not even recognise me... I hardly recognise myself some days,' she shrugged, 'especially when I remember the young woman I was back then. It's strange, as it's almost like those summers here with him happened to someone else – a carefree, confident person, full of optimism and a zest for life.' She smiled wryly. 'But then I found myself feeling disappointed when Nico wasn't at the art gallery earlier. It felt like a missed opportunity to ask if he does have some pictures of the happy holiday times we all shared together here with my mum.'

'And is that the only reason you felt disappointed?' Deedee scrutinised. 'What about Nico? Could you imagine yourself rekindling a romance with him? You do have a shared history together after all, and that can be a very powerful link binding two people together.' She stopped walking and turned to face Gina square on. 'If he's single, of course. And we do actually find him.' Deedee raised one eyebrow and tilted her head to one side. 'And you know, if he's still extremely handsome,' she paused to ponder, 'maybe it might not be a mistake to revisit the past after all.'

Gina waved a hand in the air and stopped walking as well but kept her gaze focused straight ahead on the blue and white gingham covered tables outside the taverna. 'Oh, he wouldn't be interested in me now, not romantically, it was such a long time ago... we were just kids. Like I said, I'd be surprised if he even recognised me, I don't look anything like I did when I was a teenager. Plus, he stopped writing and probably forgot about me.'

'Why do you do that?' Deedee asked, tenting her eyes from the dazzling Greek sun.

'Do what?' Gina turned to look at Deedee now.

'Put yourself down. Not value yourself. I heard you last night in the art class when Rosie was chatting about Cristos, who I have to say is utterly beautiful, seems like a really nice guy and clearly fancies you.'

'Um,' Gina started, unused to being confronted quite so directly and didn't know what to say. 'Well, I agree that Cristos is very handsome...'

'Yes, he is. But don't change the subject. Why do you not value yourself? Why do you put yourself down?'

Silence settled between them. But Deedee stood firm and even put a hand on her hip as she scrutinised Gina, who could feel the old familiar trickle of perspiration beading beneath her boobs.

'I'm working on it,' she managed, repeating what she had said to Rosie last night. 'It's a habit... and I guess I'm just not used to compliments. I've been trying to work out why I do it and I think it's a protection thing, you know... before someone else beats me to it.' She inhaled and swallowed hard before letting out a long puff of air.

'And darling, who might "beat you to it" as you say?'

'My husband,' Gina answered quietly, then added, 'um, my *estranged* husband.' A flush of shame heated her face, but she managed to look in Deedee's direction. To her surprise, Deedee didn't say anything else. Instead, she stepped forward, put her jangly, love bangle jewelled arms around Gina's shoulders and enveloped her in a big hug.

Gina thought she might cry. The two women shared a quiet moment. Then after breaking apart, Deedee took one of Gina's hands and gave it a squeeze as she told her, 'I'm sorry he made you feel small, Gina, but the worst of it is over now. Whatever happens with your marriage, you've taken the first step to changing things by travelling solo on your dream holiday when you could have cancelled and just carried on with your life and stayed the same. You're on your way to building a bigger life for yourself now and very soon you'll be flying... Higher than you ever thought possible. You'll see.'

Gina looked at her friend, nodding slowly as the realisation of what Deedee was saying sank in and she felt the corners of her mouth lifting into a tentative smile at the prospect of considering a future where she could metaphorically fly. Full of possibilities, with solid female friendships, travelling, pursuing her passion for art, even watching *Love Island*, or reading a romance book in her own living room if she felt like it and posting pictures on her Instagram without judgement. She wanted it all. Ordinary things, that often turned out to be the best things.

But then, on remembering that message from Colin last night, she knew deep down that she did still love him and perhaps she always would, and that he wasn't all bad. Maybe he had just lost his way too. She thought of how he was at the start of their marriage, spontaneous and fun, back when he never put her down. In fact, he had built her up when she had been at a low point, and he had cared for her. They had cared for each other, they had *liked* each other and supported each other. They had been a brilliant team and some of her happiest memories were of when they did things together, just simple everyday things, like sitting next to Colin at the computer and helping him rewrite his CV. Or pinning his new suit trousers so she could hem them for him and washing his hair when he broke his arm that time from messing around in the apple tree at the end of the garden. She wondered if there might be something salvageable. If they could find their way back to each other and reignite the spark they once had in the beginning, it was the reason for booking the holiday in the first place, after all. Maybe this break from each other would turn out to be just the thing they needed, absence making the heart grow fonder and all that. But then Gina remembered the memory box and that sinking 'rug being pulled from under her' feeling returned with a vengeance. She had trusted Colin completely and if he had taken the box in a fit of jealousy or whatever knowing how much it meant to her, then she wasn't sure she would ever be able to fully trust him again. Although could she really turn her back on a twenty-seven-year marriage? It was the best part of a lifetime, certainly the majority of her life had been spent in the relationship. And then it dawned on her that she had lived more years of her life with Colin than she had without him. No wonder the thought of going it alone terrified her, she was practically institutionalised!

Shaking her head as if to banish the medley of conflicting thoughts from her mind, Gina shifted her focus to the positive, the thought of flying, of making exciting changes to her life which she was determined to do no matter what happened when she got home, and soon a floaty lightness came over her. With a renewed vigour, she put her best foot forward and carried on walking towards the taverna with the bird's eye view of the clinic, wondering what possibilities it might hold for her come four o'clock. It felt good to daydream, even if it was highly unlikely that her Nico was the doctor here. He had lived in Athens all those years ago, so it was a stretch at best, she reckoned, for him to live on this tiny island now. Plus, this was real life, not a Hallmark movie and so the chances of just bumping into him were remote. She reckoned she had more chance of winning the lottery, that she had been buying a ticket for every week for the last decade or so, without a win of any kind whatsoever.

'Deedee, can I tell you a secret?' Gina ventured, figuring it did no harm to fantasise, and even though Colin had said in that last message that he loved her, he had still been very quick to moot the decision of trialling a separation not that long ago, so was it really that bad to find another man insanely attractive and irresistible?

'Of course, nothing shocks me, darling.'

'I very nearly touched Cristos in the art class! As in stroked my fingers all over his solid chest, and I've never had that feeling before, it was like a magnetic force drawing me to him. Can you imagine if I had actually done that?' Gina shook her head. 'And there's more—' She stopped talking.

'Go on,' Deedee prompted.

Gina swallowed and then told her, 'I had a vision in my head of getting naked with him, as in, you know, having sex!' She lowered her voice and gave Deedee a furtive look. 'Clear as day, like a film, it was. So vivid, I actually had to remind myself later on that it hadn't actually happened. And I can't stop thinking about it.'

'Oh, I bet you can't, darling, and yes I can absolutely imagine, and I can tell you it wouldn't be embarrassing at all. Yes, you might have raised a few eyebrows if you had come on to him out there underneath the tamarisk tree with a full audience of eager artists. But in your hotel room, or better still in a moonlit pool with twinkling gold night lights nestling among palm trees around the perimeter, or on a deserted beach, the deck of a yacht, or the balcony of your bedroom... then it would be utterly divine and very, *very* sexy. Cristos would melt if you made that first move! You'd undoubtedly have the best sex of your life. Trust me, darling!' Deedee said, as if recalling her own experiences.

'I couldn't do that!' Gina gasped a little and then exhaled.

'Why not?'

'Because—' Gina stopped talking to give herself a moment to ponder why not exactly. All she could come up with was, 'I'm still married.'

'Separated! There's a difference. And if you want my honest opinion...' Deedee turned to look at Gina.

'Go on,' she ventured.

'You've played small for far too long! And deprived yourself of joy and living life to the fullest like I do. You deserve to treat yourself. There, I've said it.' Deedee nodded firmly. 'Have a fling! And don't be worrying about me or Rosie judging you, as I for one would jump at the chance to get intimate with Cristos. And we both know how invested Rosie is in making sure you have a happy ending on this holiday.' She winked.

After polishing off another truly scrumptious sharing platter, and a bottle of Savatiano between them, having said goodbye to Rosie several hours ago and enjoying a long, lazy meal of chatting and relaxing as they watched the world go by, Gina spotted a tall, dark-haired man wearing jeans, a striped, open-necked cotton shirt and carrying a leather doctor's bag. He was striding purposefully towards the door of the clinic. She pressed a hand on top of the table as if to steady herself and lifted her shades with her other hand. The doctor was definitely about the right age to be her Nico, and he had the same tall, athletic build and short, thick black hair. And her pulse quickened. Could it be? She drained the last of her wine.

'What is it?' Deedee asked, looking at Gina as she placed her empty wine glass on the table, and then following her gaze, she realised what was going on. 'Four o'clock!' Deedee checked the time on the screen of her phone. 'That's come around quickly, time sure flies when you're having a lovely time.'

'Four o'clock!,' Gina repeated vaguely, wondering if this really could be him. 'Do you think we should go over right away? It might be better just to get it over with, rather than me sit here getting increasingly nervous.'

'No. Let's be cool,' Deedee said. 'We'll finish off here and pay the bill and then we can saunter over to the clinic and see if we can get a close-up look at the doctor as we happen to be just passing by. It's not a good look to go all guns blazing like Rosie did in the art gallery. Oh no! And word might already have spread around the island about a trio of crazy British women racing around looking for hot men. No, definitely not a cool vibe.' She pulled a face and laughed. 'Do you think you would actually recognise him after all these years?'

'Yes. I think I would. From what I can see at this distance, it could actually be him... The height, the build, the way he walks, it's all the same,' Gina told her, inhaling sharply as her pulse quickened, the memory of her Nico suddenly coming into sharp focus.

'*Really?*' Deedee peered over the top of her shades to scrutinise Gina. She nodded. 'Oh God, Rosie is going to freak out if it is your Nico, the long-lost holiday romance, and she misses the reunion moment.' Deedee shook her head as she swallowed the last of her wine. 'How sure are you, Gina?'

'It's hard to know for definite as it's been such a long time,' Gina started, 'and Nico used to wear faded jeans and a cotton shirt too, but then lots of the Greek men here do. You know they have a cool, relaxed vibe going on. But the man I just saw walking towards the clinic over there seemed familiar and my heart is beating a little faster.'

'Right, in that case. Forget being cool. Let's go.' And Deedee stood up, flagged down a passing waiter so they could swiftly pay the bill, gathered up her handbag and taking a leaf out of Rosie's book, she dashed off, flapping one hand behind her bottom for Gina to hurry up and come along too.

13

It wasn't her Nico! The doctor had been very handsome and charming and looked a lot like how Gina imagined her Nico might look now, thirty years on from when she last saw him, but it definitely wasn't him. No, Nico the doctor was happily married to his hotelier husband, Pavlos, and he had never had a summer romance with a woman, not ever. Deedee had been the one to double check, saying, 'Well, you never know. Anything goes these days...'

They had chatted to the doctor, for a little while, and he had kindly sifted through his memory to see if he remembered any of his friends, also called Nico, ever talking about a romance with an English girl. He remembered the taverna called Toula's but he hadn't been there in a while so couldn't say for sure if it was still there, let alone if the family still owned it. His suggestion was to try the open-air market where many of the people who lived on the island would be, as someone would be bound to know more if they asked around. So, as it was Wednesday – market day – Gina and Deedee found themselves headed there.

'Wasn't he the most gorgeous guy?' Deedee said as they walked way. 'So charming and personable. Very open too. I'm not sure many men would be so attentive to two strange tourists grilling them about their love life.'

'Hmm, err... more like *one* strange tourist,' Gina laughed. 'I can't believe you actually asked him outright if he was absolutely sure he hadn't ever had sex on the beach with a woman under a velvety moonlit sky!'

'Well, you never know. Always best to clarify these things. And he didn't seem fazed, amused in fact.' Deedee chuckled naughtily. 'Plus, I have plenty of gay friends who had encounters with girls in their teenage years – or later even – when they were still figuring stuff out, before they actually came out. But I take your point, I probably shouldn't have been *quite* so intrusive with my questions.' She pulled a pensive face. 'Funny though, isn't it, how you can meet a complete stranger and feel comfortable with them right away, much like we did. I knew you were my kind of person the first moment I saw you sitting by yourself in the bar at the hotel with your cocktail and a curious look in your gorgeous, sparkly eyes. Very glamorous, poised and interesting.'

'Oh, I think that's one of the nicest things anyone has ever said to me,' Gina beamed, giving Deedee a playful nudge with her elbow. 'I saw you and thought you looked so glamourous and chic, poised and interesting too... And well, I don't see myself like that at all to be honest.'

'Well, you should.'

'Hmm, but last week, I was wearing a pink tabard and scrubbing someone else's loo! Not very glam at all,' Gina laughed, but wished she could stuff the words right back into her mouth as the magical little bubble she had created for herself here of holiday happiness burst in an instance. The smile froze on her face. 'Sorry, that was a bit crude.'

'Darling don't be sorry. Do you like your job?'

'Yes. Yes I do, actually.' Gina nodded. 'Obviously there are irritating moments like there are in all jobs, I assume, but on the whole, I do like it... enjoy it even. It can be quite cathartic, quietly working and minding my own business as I think through whatever is on my mind. And my cleaning jobs paid for me to come here.' She shrugged.

'Good. And pink tabards are very glam indeed,' Deedee said kindly, not batting an eyelid. 'There's a designer shop in London that sells them haute couture with street art sprayed on, or rhinestones or whatever for fashionistas with more money than sense.'

'*Really?*' Gina said, agog.

'Yes, really.' Deedee smiled.

'Well, I have plenty of pink tabards and could very easily give them a glow up with a bit of spray paint and some gemstones,' Gina joked.

'You could set up an Etsy shop or sell them on eBay, especially with your artistic flair! You'd make a fortune, Gina.'

'Now that is a brilliant idea!' Marvelling, the two friends nodded at each other bonding further in their light-hearted banter.

'Come on, let's get to the market and see if we can find your Nico.' And Deedee looped her arm through Gina's as they walked on along the sea wall soaking up the late afternoon sun and giggling together like a pair of teenagers.

Gina grinned, suddenly loving that she was now the sort of woman who had a friend to loop arms with as they walked along and chatted together. And musing too that her lovely new, and very well-to-do, friend couldn't care less that she scrubbed other people's loos. Gina knew that it shouldn't matter that she was a cleaner, she was proud of the work she did, always doing a good job and making sure she got paid appropriately for it, but also knew very well that people judged her for it. Like the time she'd mentioned it at one of Colin's work dos, when a pompous type in a too-tight suit had puffed his chest out like a ruffled pigeon and asked her in a very loud voice, 'And what is it that the lovely Gina does?' Colin had near choked on the miniature Wagyu beef slider he'd just slotted into his mouth when she'd replied, 'I'm a cleaner,' having forgotten his instruction to, 'just say you're a homemaker if anyone asks'.

Now she was here and had the luxury of hindsight and physical distance to look at her life in England through another lens, she could see it in such contrast. How different she felt being here in this picturesque place, where the pace of life and stunning surroundings put it all into perspective. She felt stifled at home, trapped and alone like a bird in a cage, never going anywhere or doing anything different. But that was all changing now, and better late than never and all that. And she could see the funny side too now of Colin and his apoplectic, red face back then, so worried about what his boss would think of him having a cleaner for a wife. Silly really, and she felt a bit sorry for him being trapped too, just in a different cage made up of office politics and insecurities. Oh well, he wouldn't have to worry about that for much longer if their trial separation became a permanent thing. He wouldn't have to put up with her embarrassing him any more.

Gina and Deedee walked on in silence, content in each other's company with Gina's thoughts turning to Nico the doctor now, and how he looked like a younger Richard Gere. A sudden moment flashed into her head from her teenage years of laughing around with her Nico when he had turned up at the beach one day to take her out on his sailboat wearing a white naval officer style peaked hat. Gina had thought he looked just like Zack in *An Officer and a Gentleman*. Nico had gone with the compliment and really built his part by giving her a deadpan look as he kissed her and then scooped her up off the sand and carried her into the sea, just as Richard Gere had carried Debra Winger away at the end of the film. Gina had even taken the hat off Nico's head and put it on herself just before he threw her into the sea and then dived in to be beside her. They had splashed each other, laughing, and cavorting around until swimming into each other's arms for an exceedingly passionate kiss, the sun dazzling on the sea all around them like a frame formed of a trillion tiny diamonds and Gina had never felt so alive as she had in that moment. Neither of them had even cared that the officer's hat had floated away out of reach, so wrapped up in each other as they were.

Sighing, she let the memory of that scene slip away and felt relieved, but disappointed all over again that Nico the doctor wasn't her Nico. Because even though the fear of his rejection was still very much there inside her, she realised too that the prospect of being able to see a photo of her mum's face again would definitely make any awkwardness worth putting up with. She could deal with it – a mutual politeness, a possible look of regret that she imagined her Nico would have in his eyes on seeing her if they were ever to meet up again. But she'd have her mum back, be able to see her face clearly again and that was worth so much to her. When the cotton wool head came along, and the hot mess fired up it was impossible to remember Shirley and that's when the grief turned up too and walked alongside Gina making her feel sad and invisible and a bit like a robot going through the motions of her own life.

The two friends carried on walking, and as they reached the little church at the water's edge, Gina's heart lifted on seeing in through the open, arched wooden door. She stopped walking.

'Deedee, do you mind if we make a pit stop and go into the church? I'm having a lovely déjà vu moment of being right here with my mum, standing next to her in this exact same spot. I think we went inside to light a candle for her parents, my granny and grandad. Yes, I remember feeling relieved as it was a sweltering hot day, much hotter than it is now and I had glittery pink jelly shoes on that were hurting my feet like hell—'

'Oh yes, I remember those shoes, all the teenagers wore them back then. Too chunky for me.' She pulled a face and Gina smiled to herself, unable to imagine Deedee wearing anything that wasn't 100 per cent stylish and from the pages of *Vogue* magazine or whatever. 'Maybe it was earlier on in the day when you were last here with your mum, when the sun is at its hottest,' Deedee suggested. 'It is nearly five o'clock now after all.' She glanced at her watch.

'Yes, that could be it. I do remember it being lovely inside the church with its stone interior and a refreshing breeze from the sea. Mum and I sat together and chatted, and I remember her saying she was proud of me as she pulled me in for one of her super-squishy cuddles, complete with an arm jiggle too. But I batted her away, thinking I was too old for a cuddle like that. Silly, isn't it? I'd do anything to have one of those cuddles from her again. We always used to joke about her near suffocating me.' Gina smiled and slowly shook her head at the recollection. 'It was the summer holidays after I finished senior school, having just got my exam results.'

'Ah, what a wonderful memory to have. And yes, the benefit of hindsight. But we don't care about any of that when we are young and think there's all the time in the world. Let's go inside and see.'

The two women wandered into the church with its simple wooden pews, just a couple on either side, and a beautiful starry night painted domed ceiling and Gina let out a small gasp as the same welcoming, refreshing breeze furled around her bare legs making her feel light and energised again, just as she had back then.

'Where did you and your mum sit?' Deedee asked, quietly.

'Here I think.' And Gina went to the pew on the left, behind a circular table housing a small pit of sand with several candles placed within it, glowing silently and comfortingly in reverence to the memory of lost loved ones.

'Why don't you sit for a moment and remember your mum,' Deedee suggested. 'I'm going to light a candle for my late husband, Joe.'

After smoothing down her cotton dress, Gina sat on the pew and then scooted along a little bit as if to make space for where Shirley had sat on the end, then she closed her eyes. She drew in a big breath of salty sea air as if to let it flow through her and take her back in time, then she exhaled and let her mind wander through the years to create the feeling again. The presence of her mum sitting beside her. Gina could almost feel Shirley's arm around her, pulling her in for one of those cuddles again, the scent of her perfume – vanilla and woody – Guerlain Samsara; she always wore it, often treating herself to a bottle especially for her holiday in the duty free shop at the airport. Gina's lips lifted into a smile, content in the moment, reminiscing and just being still for a while as she remembered her mum.

When Gina was satisfied that she had absorbed as much recollection as she could from the last time here in the church, she opened her eyes and, before she stood up, ran a hand over the smooth wooden surface of the space beside her on the pew and softly said to herself, 'Hello Mum, nice to have you here.'

'You OK?' Deedee asked, handing Gina a candle.

'Yes, I feel strangely calm and kind of...' she paused, searching for the right word, 'content! It's an unusual feeling and not one I've felt before when thinking about my mum. It's always been a kind of sad feeling of... well, just missing her. But I truly enjoyed thinking about her just then.'

'So, what was different this time?' Deedee asked.

'Well, it might sound daft, but I spoke to her, my mum, Shirley, as if she was sitting right next to me.' Gina glanced over at the pew.

'That's not daft! I talk to Joe all the time,' Deedee replied. 'It's cathartic, I find. Just because he's not physically here, doesn't mean his spirit isn't, his soul, essence, presence, ghost or whatever you want to call it. I feel him around me all the time.'

'That's lovely. What do you talk to Joe about?'

'Oh, all kinds of things. Sometimes I just talk through everything I have on my mind, or I might tell him something I know we would have laughed about together... that kind of thing. I can even hear his voice sometimes talking to me, saying what he thinks, or telling me off even,' she paused to laugh. 'He was very good at steadying me when I got carried away with some of my wilder ideas.'

'Really? Wow, that's amazing and must be such a comfort. I've never actually talked to my mum before; it's just mostly been sad thoughts of wishing she was still here, which seems a bit pathetic really, when she died so many years ago.'

'It's not pathetic, Gina. It just sounds to me as if you didn't properly grieve for Shirley at the time when she died.'

'You're right. I don't think I did,' Gina pondered.

'And do you ever talk about your mum?'

'No, not ever. When she died, there wasn't really anyone to talk to about her. My dad wasn't around, he disappeared after the divorce when I was a very young child. Mum's best friend moved to Australia not long after the funeral. Then, of course, I met Colin and he had never met Shirley and used to say that it wasn't good for me living in the past, that it was depressing and so I kind of boxed off that part of my life and went all in with him and getting married and looking forward to the rest of my life,' she smiled wryly. 'But I do really feel a closeness to Mum, being back here on the island.'

'Good, I'm happy for you, Gina.' Deedee gave Gina's arm a pat. 'And I'd love to hear more about Shirley and tell you more about

Joe. How about we swap stories over drinks and some more *saganaki* small plates tonight. We could meet in the hotel bar, early, to bag a table and enjoy a raspbouzo or two.'

'I'd love to!' Gina grinned. 'And I promise to pace myself this time, no more running around singing "Fernando", followed by a horrendous hangover for me,' she nodded, resolute.

'It's a date. Although feel completely free to sing "Fernando" and dance if you like, why not enjoy yourself!' Deedee shrugged. 'And if Rosie has finished with her clients, then we can invite her too.' She lifted her eyebrows in question. 'With a caveat to keep the conversation away from hunting for your Nico, or matchmaking of any kind. I have a feeling you could do with a break from all that.'

'Ah, yes, it is a bit intense. An evening off from it to just enjoy being on holiday with my wonderful new friends would be lovely,' Gina laughed.

'That's settled then,' Deedee smiled. 'And Gina, I know your original goal for coming back to Kalosiros was to try to find a spark in your relationship and feel close to your husband again, and I know how let down you've been feeling. But sometimes something can happen, that at first glance seems like a *bad* thing, but can turn out to be absolutely the *best* thing. This holiday has reignited the relationship you have with your mum... And yes, I do mean "have", as relationships don't just end when a person dies. Coming back here has brought you closer to your mum instead. And maybe, if we do manage to find your Nico, then you'll feel closer to her still. Because even if he doesn't have any photos, he's bound to have happy holiday memories too that you can chat about together.'

'Thank you, Deedee,' Gina said.

'What for?'

'For being a brilliant friend. And for being funny and very wise. Meeting you is one of the best things that's ever happened to me... and you're right, Colin letting me down and me coming here on my own has turned out to be absolutely the best thing as I wouldn't have found you and Rosie. I'm so pleased we met, and I hope we can keep in touch when the holiday is over.'

'Of course we will. We'll set up a WhatsApp group.'

Gina lit her candle and placed it in the sand next to Deedee's candle for Joe and both women walked out of the church and into the early evening sunshine, smiling and laughing together as they linked arms and carried on making their way to the open-air market.

14

'Wow! It really is just like stepping back in time.' Gina unhooked her arm from Deedee's so she could lift her sunglasses to get an even better look at the market. 'Although it's bigger and more bustling, but the atmosphere still has that happy, holiday, festival vibe.' She beamed on hearing the sound of traditional Greek music drifting in the warm air. 'The stalls, the sounds, the smells, I love all of it. I feel just like a teenager again! I can almost hear my mum's voice saying, "Ooh, which stall first, Gina?" as she used to when we arrived here for the first time of each holiday,' she laughed.

'And which one did you visit first?' Deedee smiled, scanning the rows of stalls.

'Oh, it was always the bakery stall for a big slice of juicy *portokalopita*.'

'Ah yes, the traditional Greek orange filo cake,' Deedee said, 'truly scrumptious.'

'Mmm, with the gooey orange syrup, so good!' Gina did a chef's kiss with her fingers to her lips.

'Let's see if we can find a stall selling it. All this talk of orange cake is making me want a slice.' Deedee glanced around.

'Me too.'

They walked on, taking in all the sights, sounds and smells. Gina inhaled deeply, the smell of oregano and garlic, basil and olive oil teasing her nostrils, and mingling with a sizzling sound coming from an enormous grill laden with *souvlaki*.

'You like to try?' a man tending the grill asked as Gina and Deedee wandered over to take a closer look, marvelling as he expertly twiddled and turned a row of wooden skewers crammed with cubes of spiced lamb, chicken, chorizo, peppers, onions, and mushrooms too before shaking a big silver bowl full of fresh salad next to a pile of gyros and more bowls of briny olives and crumbly feta cheese.

'Thank you, it looks delicious but maybe later,' Gina grinned, still full up from the giant sharing platter they had enjoyed earlier and figuring if she was going to have more to eat this evening, then it was going to be a slice of the very best orange cake.

'I wonder if you might help us, please? We are looking for a man called Nico,' Deedee said, moving closer to the grill so as to be heard over the sizzling sound, the music and chatter of the market crowd, which was building now into a buzzy, vibrant throng full of multigenerational families with children, tourists strolling and local fishermen and stall holders dashing around with baskets and trays full of produce.

'What do you say?' The man on the grill grinned, cupped his ear and leaned forward. Deedee stepped in even closer and had just opened her mouth to ask him again when Rosie appeared behind them and standing on tiptoes, with her hands to the sides of her mouth, bellowed over their shoulders:

'MY FRIEND IS LOOKING FOR HER FIRST LOVE, IT'S VERY ROMANTIC. HE'S CALLED NICO.'

The music stopped at precisely the same moment.

Gina wanted the ground to open up beneath her, as they were suddenly plunged into silence. Everyone around them stopped talking and moving to stare at her, the tourist woman hunting for a lover and standing underneath Rosie's raised arm, high up in the air with an index finger pointing straight to the top of her head. She might as well have a flashing neon sign there saying, 'desperado right here'! Gina swallowed hard as her face reddened, and she instinctively crossed her arms over her midriff area in case the flaming map of Australia gathered again, and made it ridiculously obvious she was having a mid-life moment, crisis even, searching for her first love, and her body deciding to crank up the thermostat whenever it blooming well liked and without any good reason.

'Um, he's an old friend,' she muttered to nobody in particular, shrugging apologetically as she turned in a circle wishing the small crowd gathered around the grill weren't all staring quite so intensely at her. 'And I'm sorry I don't remember his surname, but his family used to own a taverna called Toula's...' Gina added lamely, but the music had started up again and so she assumed the guy hadn't heard her after all as he went back to twiddling and turning his skewers. Fortunately, the crowd soon lost interest and carried on chatting and mingling as they had been before Rosie's outburst.

'*Rosie!*' Deedee exclaimed, turning on her heel to face their hopelessly romantic and permanently frazzled friend. 'What are you doing here?'

'I'm back to resume the search, of course.'

'But how did you know we were here?' Gina asked.

'Well, my meeting was a breeze, and my clients love the venue, a gorgeous little blue-domed white church on a hillside with a private garden full of pink bougainvillea and breathtaking views of the island so they signed the contract right away, and their search for the perfect place to get married is now complete. Which means that I'm free to fully focus on the search for your Nico and so my first stop was the clinic. I popped back to the taverna by the harbour but you had already left and so I thought why not go alone? So I went to see that gorgeous doctor, Nico, and he knew all about our hunt for *your* Nico and said I might find you both here. And well, ta-da! He was right.' She clapped her hands together in glee before rummaging inside her big tote bag. 'I have made us that map I mentioned earlier! My sketching skills aren't up to very much, mind you, nowhere near as good as yours, Gina, so you'll have to bear with me, but here it is. Our very own hidden treasure map... Actually, hidden Nico map, I should really say, but you get the gist.' And she stretched out a long concertina of several A4-sized pieces of paper sellotaped together and waggled it all up in the air.

'You actually made a map!' Gina and Deedee chimed in unison and mutual flabbergast.

'Of course!' Rosie shrugged, bringing the handmade map down to eye level and shaking it out a bit. 'I never break a promise. And this treasure hunt, sorry, *Nico* hunt,' she paused to take a big breath and nod her head making her curls bob about enthusiastically, 'needs doing properly. I found out where Toula's taverna is. See, it's right here, and still called that.' Rosie rapidly bundled up the map until she could hold it in one hand and point with a free finger from her other hand to tap at a big red heart that she had drawn in the middle of what looked like a sandy beach of yellow felt-tipped swirls with some blue wiggly waves beside it. 'It's not actually that far away, so let's go!' And after tucking the map under her arm, Rosie once again hoisted her tote bag bulging with all her work planners and paraphernalia over her shoulder and went to hotfoot it away. Deedee caught hold of Rosie's arm and she stopped moving, turning back to look at Gina and Deedee over her shoulder with a baffled look on her face. 'What's the matter? This is the best lead we have, given that we know for sure he's linked to the taverna,' she said, sounding like a sleuth on one of those Netflix true crime cold case series.

'There's no rush,' Deedee said gently, looking at Gina who was still feeling bamboozled and a bit embarrassed after being under Rosie's pointy index finger. 'It's been thirty years so I'm sure another day won't make much difference.' Gina let out a sigh of relief. Yes, she did want to find her Nico, and was prepared for whatever reaction she received, but not like this, in a panicked state and potentially in the middle of Toula's busiest time when it would be jam-packed with tourists tucking into delicious Greek food or dancing on the sand having the time of their lives. No, a big audience would only make it even more awkward if by some chance her Nico did just happen to be there.

'But what if he's... um, I don't know,' Rosie paused, seemingly searching for a plausible reason to go to Toula's right now, 'here on holiday! Yes, didn't you say that he lived in Athens, Gina? Well, what if he's visiting and going home tonight? We'll have missed him, and it will be like that film, *Serendipity*. Another missed chance and—'

'Rosie!' Deedee said firmly, jumping in and putting her arms around their friend who was clearly in danger of working herself into a full-blown panic attack. 'Take a deep breath, darling. In and out. In and out. That's it. Do it with me.' Deedee smoothed the heel of her hand over Rosie's back to help her calm down. 'It's not going to be like that film *Serendipity*. We will go to the taverna tomorrow and if Nico still has a connection to it then we will find out and ask whoever is there to contact him. But please do bear in mind that it is extremely unlikely that he is going to be there simply waiting for

Gina to turn up. And if you don't mind me saying so, Rosie, you look very tired, and like you could do with an evening off. It's been very full on for you here, with looking after your wedding clients and all the activities we've enjoyed together. And now with your mission to try to find Nico.'

Gina and Deedee both gave Rosie a sympathetic look as she pushed her shades up onto the top of her head, revealing blood-shot eyes ringed with dark circles. Rosie let out a long puff of air. Silence followed.

'Hmm. I guess I have been a bit intense,' Rosie said eventually. 'But I just want you to be happy, Gina, to have the photos of your mum so you can see her face again, and you never know... rekindle a romance, and with your first love it would just be so romantic. The perfect happy ever after.' She lifted her shoulders in a sheepish shrug.

'I know you do, and it's lovely of you to care, Rosie,' Gina said softly, giving her friend's arm a stroke. 'But Deedee is right, the taverna will still be there tomorrow and if there is a link then there will still be a link tomorrow too. Plus, don't they find each other again at the end of *Serendipity*?'

'Yes, they do.' Rosie jigged her head in agreement.

'So you agree to take an evening off from your search for Nico? We can stroll around the market and soak up the holiday atmosphere. We can buy some souvenirs and just be tourists having a nice time,' Deedee suggested. 'And then Gina and I thought it would be nice to have another night of chatting and cocktails in the hotel bar later on, if you're up for that?'

'And I'd love to find a floppy sun hat just like yours, Rosie, and a tote bag too, if I can. Plus a fan for my flaming hot flushes. What do you reckon?' Gina asked.

After a short while, Rosie nodded and folded the map back into her bag which she let slip from her shoulder and onto the ground at her feet. 'OK, OK, I suppose cocktails and chat will be fun, and market shopping,' Rosie grinned, lifting her eyes, and bobbing her head around in defeat.

'That's our girl!' Deedee said, closely followed by Gina. 'Or should we say our romance queen?'

'Err... Queenager! Thank you very much,' Rosie corrected and the three of them laughed. 'But on one condition, well, two really?' she said, tentatively, and Gina and Deedee shook their heads in faux exasperation.

'Go on...'

'Can we go to Toula's tomorrow morning then? Early?' Rosie asked.

'Well, let's have breakfast at the hotel first,' Gina suggested. 'I was hoping you might be able to help me set up my Instagram account and load up some photos.'

'Oh yes, please. I'd love to do that for you, Gina.' Rosie's eyes widened in anticipation of having another project to help with.

'Thanks. Now, what's the other condition?' Gina smiled.

'That you let me find you the perfect sun hat and big tote bag? I'm sure I saw a stall on my way here that was selling lovely hand-painted paper fans with pretty wooden frames. Come on, let's go there now before they sell out...' she said eagerly, and they all laughed. Rosie really couldn't help herself!

After finding the stall and discovering that there were plenty of fans and no need at all for Rosie to panic, they each chose a selection and wandered on to the next stall where there were lots of lovely floppy sun hats.

'This one will suit you, Gina.' Rosie plucked a white, straw sun hat with a wide rim and a raffia trim decorated with small shells and beads from the display rack. Gina tried it on and looked into the mirror handed to her by the woman running the stall.

'You like this one?' the woman asked. 'My son makes them.'

'Ooh, does he? And what's your son call—' Rosie started.

'NO!' Gina and Deedee quickly jumped in, each shaking their heads in mock despair.

'OK, OK. Sorry. But you never know.' Rosie laughed, holding up her palms in surrender.

'I'll take the hat.' Gina turned back to the woman and pulled out her purse to pay. 'And one of these beach bags too, please,' she said, choosing a white raffia one to match the hat.

Happy with her purchases, Gina looped the bag over her shoulder and the three of them carried on meandering around the market admiring the stalls selling all kinds of things – rolls of colourful fabric, leather sandals, wicker baskets full of giant green peppers and red chillies, dried herbs – marjoram and thyme – and every type of fresh fruit you could possibly want. They even found the bakery stall and Gina bought three big slices of the traditional orange filo cake for them to enjoy when they got back to the hotel.

Gina had just stopped to admire a selection of delicate lace tablecloths when a man came over to her.

'You say you look for man called Nico,' the guy said in heavily accented English.

'Err... yes,' Gina managed before Rosie overheard and added, 'Oh yes, we definitely are,' giving Gina and Deedee a wary look.

'Come, I know him.' And before she could protest, Gina found herself trotting alongside the man, with Rosie and Deedee too, as he strode off towards a stall selling fresh fish packed in large trays of ice. The craggy fisherman with his weather-worn face wasn't her Nico. 'The taxi driver, he called Nico too, I show you.' The man from the market wasn't giving up. 'And the doctor in the harbour. And the chef over there...' He pointed towards a little food truck with a blue and white striped awning selling gyros and squares of moussaka.

'Ah, we've already spoken to the doctor, so thank you,' Deedee intervened.

'But not the taxi driver! Do you know where he works or lives by any chance?' Rosie asked, whipping out her notepad with her fluffy pom-pom pen poised ready to make a note. The man shook his head. Gina opened her mouth to speak but found herself looking over to the food truck just in case. The guy at the serving hatch was about twenty-five years old and so very clearly not her Nico. 'Thank you,' Rosie said to the man and turned to go over to the food truck, presumably to interrogate the poor guy who was very busy packaging up generous portions of moussaka for his waiting queue of customers.

'It's not him,' Gina quickly told her.

'Oh, are you sure?' Rosie asked, reluctantly slotting her pad and pen back into her bag.

'Yes, definitely.'

'Come on, let's go and find a taxi to take us back to the hotel. We can ask the driver if he's called Nico or knows of any other drivers that are,' Deedee said, swiftly shepherding Rosie away.

They walked back through the market towards the square where the taxis waited, chatting about their purchases, and resisting Rosie's attempts to persuade them to change their minds and, 'pop by Toula's now after all... just in case!' when suddenly a female voice with an English accent called out behind them.

'Shirley? Shirley... is that you?' Gina didn't register at first, but the voice called again, and it was Deedee who made the connection.

'Gina, I think the old lady behind us is talking to you, she's waving and calling out for Shirley, your mother's name.'

'Oh!' Gina stopped walking and turned to see an elderly woman wearing a headscarf and a cotton apron over a floral dress and carrying a wicker basket laden with oranges and lemons and loaves of bread in the crook of her elbow.

'Maybe she knew your mum and is mistaken; you did say that you looked very alike,' Deedee said.

'Shirley Gilmore... is that you?' the woman called out again with a wide smile on her wrinkled face as she lifted an age-spot-mottled hand to shield her eyes from the still shining evening sun. Gina started walking towards her.

15

'So let me get this straight... because, unlike you, Gina, I wasn't the sensible one last night and had far too many raspbouzos, so my recollection of what we talked about is rather hazy,' Rosie groaned, pouring herself another cup of strong Greek coffee. 'The elderly English woman who owns the apartment complex where you used to stay when you came here on holiday, who thought you were your mum – she's Meryl, right?' she recapped as the three of them enjoyed their breakfast of Greek yogurt with chopped nuts and swirls of honey with a selection of flaky pastries.

'Yes, that's right,' Gina smiled. She was delighted to have bumped into Meryl, not just to discover that she was still alive but that she was still running the holiday apartment complex. Although Gina privately wondered how she was coping, because she must be in her late seventies or even her eighties by now. They'd had a lovely few minutes reminiscing, but Gina wasn't sure if Meryl really believed that she wasn't Shirley as she seemed confused and kept calling her by her mum's name, and getting muddled over dates and details from back then. Gina didn't have the heart to tell her there in the street that Shirley had died. In fact, she wasn't even sure if Meryl was ever told – she knew about the breast cancer as Gina had a memory of her mum calling Meryl to let her know they weren't going to be able to come on holiday for a while. It was a sad moment as they had been staying at Meryl's every year since Gina was a little girl. And she had wanted to update Meryl, but the days and weeks after Shirley died were all such a blur. Gina had gone through the motions sorting out the funeral and the solicitor had dealt with the will.

'How wonderful,' Rosie said, putting her cup down to pick up her pen and add this important detail to her 'Gina and Nico's Reunion' page in her notepad which she had open on the table next to her.

'It is! And it was great to see her again, but I can't believe she thought I was my mum.' Gina bit into a deliciously gooey square of baclava.

'How do you feel about that?' Deedee asked.

'OK. It's nice in a way,' she started, wiping her mouth and fingers on a napkin, 'if a bit unsettling. But it felt strangely comforting at the same time, and I'm looking forward to visiting the holiday place again. We had a lot of fun times there.'

'And will you try again to see if Meryl remembers Nico?' Rosie asked.

'Yes, but you saw how she was yesterday. She didn't seem to know who I was talking about when I mentioned his name, or his grandparents, and I was sure she was friends with them. I have a vague memory of it being how Nico and I first met... when his grandparents came to visit her – maybe I was playing ping-pong with my mum – there used to be a table in the courtyard, and... yes, I think they asked if Nico could join in, as he was keen to learn more English words.'

'Hmm,' Deedee nodded, 'Meryl might not remember Nico, but you never know, Gina, if she does remember your mum, as she seems to, then she might have some photos of Shirley to share with you. You could get your phone out of the safe and take it with you just in case. Snap some pictures of her photos if she doesn't want to part with them.'

'Oh yes, good idea,' Rosie said, writing 'remind Gina to take her phone' on the page of her notepad. Gina smiled to herself thinking how lucky Rosie's brides were to have her as their wedding planner with such meticulous attention to detail.

'Actually, she might well have some photos from our holidays as I have another patchy recollection of there being a big pinboard behind the desk where Meryl used to give out the keys and bundles of fresh towels when we arrived each year,' Gina told them. 'The pinboard had lots of polaroid photos on it, of guests who had stayed in the apartments over the years,' she added, very keen to take a look now.

'Ooh, there could even be a picture of Nico, so do point him out to Meryl if there is. A visual reminder might help jog her memory,' Rosie suggested, quickly following this up with, 'Are you sure Deedee and I can't come with you? I could tone it down... you know, the enthusiasm, and just be a *bit* more discreet.' She shrugged.

'I think Gina really needs to do this by herself, so she can talk to Meryl properly and break the news about her mum's death. It's going to be an emotional conversation,' Deedee jumped in, 'and Rosie, you're going to be busy visiting the taxi ranks and talking to all the drivers until you find every single one named Nico.' Deedee exchanged a quick look with Gina who smiled and mouthed, 'Thank you,' as she dipped her head and busied herself with eating the rest of her breakfast.

'Yes, good point!' Rosie said. 'And there are quite a lot of taxis on the island. I also thought we could call into all the hotels, cafes, and the shops too... might as well widen the search if we can and make a note of all the leads, however big or small,' she added, sounding like the Netflix sleuth again. 'But please do let us know when you're ready to go to Toula's. We can always meet you there.' Rosie widened her eyes in anticipation. 'If you are still sure you don't want to go to Toula's now and then go on to see Meryl later?' she suggested, her persistence shining through.

'Ah, Rosie, I'm sure.' Gina looked up. 'I want to see Meryl right away and make sure she's OK. She used to be so vibrant and lucid and yesterday it was as if her light had dimmed and she was anxious about being in a muddle. So why don't you take a break, and nurse your hangover? There's no rush to race off to taxi ranks and cafes. You're on holiday now,' she smiled gently. 'And Meryl said this morning was better for her as she likes to take a nap in the afternoon. But I will message you, I promise. We have our WhatsApp group now so I will contact you when I'm on my way to Toula's.' Gina figured it best to get it over with as Rosie was never going to let it go, and strangely, bumping into Meryl seemed to have softened Gina's fear of Nico rejecting her. Maybe it was the connection with the past, it somehow made it feel like less time had passed, as though it was only yesterday since she and Nico had seen each other. Gina hoped so, but remembered too that he had stopped writing and might not want to see her again.

Meeting Meryl had been marvellous and had made her feel a little bit like the young woman she was back then, and she was looking forward to talking to her again... someone who had known her mum and could share the memories of the good times they'd had together, even if she did think that Gina was Shirley. Meryl had talked with crystal clear clarity about some of the lovely things they had all done together back in those days, like the time she had laid on a buffet of delicious Greek foods on a long table in the garden for all her guests to enjoy together. There had been music, and candles and wildflowers in jam jars on the table and Gina remembered being around ten years old and trying a fresh fig for the first time, still warm from the Greek sun as she picked it straight from the tree and bit into it, savouring the sweet juice as it trickled over her fingers.

'So, shall we get on with this Instagram account then, Gina?' Rosie asked. 'Why don't you go and get your phone now and then you'll have it with you to take to see Meryl?'

'Sure.' And Gina finished her breakfast and went to retrieve her phone from the safe in her room.

Arriving back at their breakfast table, Gina grinned and waggled her phone in the air.

'I think Colin has curbed his million-messages-a-day habit. I just turned my phone on and absolutely nothing has pinged up on the screen,' she told them, the tautness in her shoulders that she had felt when switching the phone on in her room fading now.

'That's good, isn't it?' Deedee asked, pouring more coffee for them all. Gina hesitated as she contemplated this new development into uncharted territory of wondering if Colin really had backed off and if she could trust it to continue, because this had happened before... He had once previously eased up on the messages, after she had explained that it put her in a difficult position when she was working, only to resume it all a few days later.

'Yes... yes I think so.' She lifted her cup in a gesture of thanks towards Deedee as she passed her phone to Rosie. 'But strange too, in a way,' she paused, trying to unravel why she felt this way, 'I guess I'm just not used to it.' And hope I can trust it, she thought to herself.

'Well, that's understandable, you've been married for a long time so there's bound to be a period of adjustment to get used to, if the separation becomes a permanent thing,' Deedee said. 'And please go easy on yourself. There's no rush, you must do what's best, and go at the right pace for you.'

'Absolutely,' Rosie added, 'although if you do make the trial separation a permanent thing then please don't give up on finding love again, or just passion. You're only young and there's an incredibly nice and very handsome man, and art teacher too, right here, and you know what they say about a shared interest being very important, plus we might still find Nico—'

'Oh, Rosie,' Gina laughed and shook her head. 'I promise I won't give up on anything.'

'Good!' Rosie seemed satisfied.

'But I'm not sure if Cristos is the answer, I've heard he's a bit of a player.'

'There's a lot to be said for a player, a holiday romance could be just the thing you need, Gina,' Deedee chipped in, naughtily, and Rosie nodded in agreement.

'We'll see,' Gina laughed, shaking her head again.

'So what's your email address, Gina?' Rosie said, turning her attention back to setting Gina up with her own Instagram account.

'Um... it's a shared one with Colin, will that work?' she asked, realising it would mean that Colin would know she had joined the millions of people 'with too much time on their hands'. A short silence followed, and Gina saw Rosie and Deedee share a look. She swallowed and conceded, 'I need my own email address, don't I?'

'Oh yes, darling, you most definitely do,' Deedee said. Rosie nodded too.

'OK, can you help me with that too then please?'

'Yes! I'm all over it,' Rosie said, efficiently tapping the screen on Gina's phone, 'Right, what name would you like for the email address?'

'Gina Bennett,' she started, but then stopped, 'actually, no, can you make it Gina Gilmore? That was my name before I was married. It feels more appropriate given that I'm separated, and after seeing Meryl yesterday and being here on the island, all of it is making me feel very much like that Gina again.'

'Good for you!' Deedee said, raising her coffee cup towards Gina's in cheers.

'So, here's your email inbox, I've put a shortcut here for you.' Rosie tapped the phone's screen to show Gina where it was. 'And here is your Instagram account! The log-in details will be in your inbox, I've given you "Fernando" as your password seeing as you love that song.'

'Oh yes, don't remind me.' Gina shrugged, shaking her head and they all laughed as she recalled her frolic across the beach on her first night here.

'And I do have a picture of you, Gina... mid-frolic! And can easily add it for you, if you'd like the memory?' Rosie offered.

'Oh no,' Gina groaned.

'Why not?' Deedee asked. 'See how glorious you look,' and she passed Rosie's phone across so Gina could see the photo.

'I agree, Gina,' Rosie added, taking her phone back after Gina had studied the picture for a little while, surprised at how different she looked and barely recognisable as the woman with the grey roots, crying in her car that day outside Anne's house. 'See how lovely this image is with the moonlit beach backdrop. Now, if you were one of my clients and I was advising you on which wedding pictures to pick, then I would be telling you to notice the dress swathing your incredibly toned body and your hair floating back from your face in the breeze. But the best bit of all is your smile and the sheer joy captured in your eyes. Yes, this one is perfect! You could actually be flying.' Gina saw Deedee's tilted head and smiling face, presumably recalling the conversation they had when walking on the harbour arm, and so she decided to go for it.

'OK, please add the picture,' she said.

'Brilliant. What would you like as a caption?' A short silence followed as Gina contemplated, and then it came to her.

'*Learning to fly…*'

Gina smiled back at Deedee and the two friends nodded in unison as if to mark the special moment.

'Love it!' Rosie clasped her hands together in glee. 'And congratulations, you are now up and running. And you have one follower… yours truly,' she added, giving Gina a gentle nudge with her elbow. 'Oh, and I've taken the liberty of making sure you're following my wedding and event planning account and a few other people I think you'll like.'

'Rosie, you are a genius! Thanks so much,' Gina said, a surge of excitement darting through her as she scrolled through and saw all the beautifully escapist pictures on Rosie's account. Then, with Rosie guiding her, Gina went to her own grid and saw the pictures she had taken of her hotel room, the view from her balcony, the beach and the lemon orchards – all loaded onto her grid, with the hotel tagged and lots of relevant hashtags too. 'Ah, you've made my pictures look great,' Gina said, admiring the filter Rosie had chosen, 'and this one's caption… "having the time of my life" is absolutely true,' she grinned, turning the phone to show Deedee the picture Rosie had got of Gina holding her painting on the beach with Cristos standing behind her and tagged to the hotel.

'Love it. You and Cristos look so good together.' Deedee gave Gina a surreptitious wink.

'Yes, thank you Deedee,' Rosie said, lifting her shades to scrutinise Gina. 'My thoughts entirely, and my offer to set you up with Cristos still stands, by the way, if… you know… we don't manage to find your Nico. Doesn't have to be for sex if you're not ready, it could just be a date to dip your toes back in the dating game, as it were. And remember, he fancies you, so no nonsense about him not being interested in someone like you. You're a hot stunner and that's the end of it!' Rosie said firmly.

Gina swallowed and after clearing her throat and exchanging a quick look with Deedee, she told Rosie, 'We'll see. It feels naughty, with me still being married.'

'Separated! And it would just be a little holiday drink together,' Rosie assured.

'Mmm, maybe,' Gina replied. 'Let's just say that I don't think I'd be too mad to have a holiday drink with him.' She busied herself with lifting the coffee cup up to her face where a smile was dancing at the corners of her lips, the feeling taking her by surprise.

16

Gina paid and thanked the taxi driver before stepping out of the car. After slipping her purse into her new white, raffia tote bag, she pushed it over her shoulder, pulled her sunglasses back over her eyes and went into a little flower shop at the foot of the winding, cobblestone-paved street leading up to the apartment complex.

'*Efcharisto*,' she said in thanks to the young Greek girl after buying a big bunch of beautiful flowers for Meryl, and she started walking and relishing the sights. The quiet little cove was behind her where she had spent many happy days as a child, swimming in the sea and building castles in the sand, watching with fascination as the fishermen brought their catch of the day ashore in nets before cleaning and packing the fish into ice-filled boxes, the seagulls swooping for scraps.

Ahead of her, Gina could see the same pretty, whitewashed, higgledy-piggledy houses with front doors and matching window frames in vibrant colours – pastel pink, blue and there was even a house with an orange door and an enormous arch of matching flame-coloured bougainvillea growing up and over the flat roof. It was stunning, like a painting, Gina thought as she pulled out her phone and after carefully resting the flowers on a nearby wall, took a few pictures, capturing the traditional Greek scene. She made a mental note to try painting the scene too when she got back home. A canvas that could hang in her hallway to remind her of this moment. She stopped moving and, after closing her eyes, she tilted her head to the sun, letting the warm rays bathe her and lift her.

Feeling rejuvenated, Gina opened her eyes and walked on, smiling as she saw a grey-haired cat dozing in a sun-dappled court-yard; it was as if time had stood still. The same old ladies in flowery dresses and headscarves sat in the shade chatting. Gina waved as she went by and smiled to herself when the women gave her gummy smiles in return. There were even the wicker baskets, leather belts and bunches of cinnamon sticks still hanging from hooks on the walls, ready to be taken to the market, that she remembered seeing as a child. It reignited her love for the island all over again.

After walking for a while, Gina recognised the opening at the top of the hill which meandered into a rustic track road where the holiday apartments were located, the old sign, all weather-worn and hanging tentatively from one corner of a post, confirmed it. She touched a hand to the post to see if she could put it back in place, but it tilted again and so she made a mental note to see if Meryl knew about it and if she might have a hammer and a nail, so Gina could fix it on her way back down the hill.

Checking the flowers and tidying the pink paper the florist had wrapped around them, Gina turned the corner and stopped. The smile of anticipation froze on her face. And her heart sank. The four little two-storey white houses were a shambles and nothing like Gina remembered them being. Crumbling plaster covered each house, the paint on the doors flaking, the flourishing flowers that once curved beautifully up the front of the houses, now wild and overgrown, full of weeds, and surely blocking the sunlight that had once streamed in through the windows. Chickens were roaming free, a donkey too. Plus, a dog without a collar came jaunting over to her, and Gina went to pet it, but thought better of it as she spotted what looked like a patch of mange behind its ear. She added another mental note to let Meryl know about this too and ask who the dog belonged to, so they could get some treatment from a vet.

Gina walked over to the small white building where she remembered Meryl worked and lived in at the back. She pushed open the door.

'Meryl?' she called out, on seeing the place empty. Maybe she was in the garden at the back hanging sheets or towels up to dry in the hot sun. A wave of déjà vu came over Gina as she walked over the dusty, tufty, arid grass around to where the garden party had been all those years ago. Smiling, she spotted Meryl sorting wooden pegs, bent over a wicker basket on a table. 'Meryl, it's me... Gina. How are you?'

The old woman looked up and smiled. 'Who are you?' The smile faded, replaced by a cloud.

'Meryl, it's me, Gina, we met yesterday, remember? I used to stay here on holiday with my mum, Shirley,' she tried again. 'And these are for you.' Gina placed the flowers on the table.

'Shirley died.' Meryl looked up with sadness in her eyes. Ah, so she was told. Gina let out a slow sigh of relief which was swiftly replaced with a wave of fresh concern. Meryl was clearly struggling, and not just with her memory. The whole place was falling apart. Even the pegs were broken, no wonder Meryl was sorting through them, Gina could see from here that only a few remained intact, the rest were no use at all.

'Here, let me help you with this.' Gina took the basket of pegs and found enough good ones to double up on pegging the napkins to the washing line. Then she took the pile of threadbare towels that were lying on the grass and turned to Meryl. 'How about we take these towels inside and put them away. And find a vase for the flowers too?' To her surprise, Meryl pulled herself up from the chair she was sitting in and silently followed Gina into the office area. 'OK, which way is the kitchen, Meryl?' Gina couldn't remember.

'Here it is, dear.' Meryl pointed a spindly arm towards a door where Gina found a vase in one of the cupboards. After filling it with water and arranging the flowers, she placed the vase on the desk back in the office and opened the double wooden doors to let some air into the stuffy area, wondering when the floor had last been swept. The beautiful blue and white patterned ceramic tiles were covered in grime and dust from the track outside and were in desperate need of a bleach and a scrub. Possibly a re-grout too to get them back to some semblance of suitability for a welcoming holiday home reception area – the professional cleaner in her could see it right away.

'The flowers are beautiful, thank you, Gina. And I was so sorry to hear about your mum. And very sorry that I got in a muddle yesterday... please will you forgive me?'

'Oh, yes, of course, Meryl, it's all fine, I was thrilled to bump into you,' Gina said tentatively, taken aback at Meryl's sudden sense of clarity. 'How are you?'

'Not so good, dear. I've been poorly and then...' Her voice petered out. 'But it's marvellous to see you. Can I make you a snack?' Meryl pottered into the kitchen.

Gina quickly followed her. 'No, thank you,' she said, having seen the grimy worktops and piles of washing up too. 'But how about you take a rest and I'll put the kettle on to make us a nice cup of tea. I'd love to have a proper catch up, if you'd like to?' And Gina gestured to a white wicker chair by the desk where Meryl went and sat down, her body seeming to sag in relief.

'That would be lovely, Gina. Thank you.'

In the kitchen, Gina filled the kettle with water to boil and pushed up the sleeves of her cotton shirt ready to get stuck in. Stacking the dirty dishes in the sink, she found a bottle of washing up liquid in a cupboard and after pouring hot water over them, left them to soak while she filled a bucket with hot soapy water too and with a mop from the same cupboard, she quickly mopped the floor until the tiles shone and she was satisfied they were up to her high standard as a professional cleaner. Then, Gina wiped down the worktops and opened the windows, and after scrubbing two mugs she made herself and Meryl a cup of tea, immediately realising they would be having it black, as the fridge was empty apart from a packet of mouldy feta cheese and a tray of eggs, presumably from the coop at the end of the garden, if the feathers still stuck to them were anything to go by.

Gina went to give Meryl her tea and was surprised to find her sleeping, so she left her mug on the corner of the desk ready for when she woke up, figuring it best to let her rest. The woman was clearly exhausted and so frail, Gina wondered if she had any help at all with the work involved in running a holiday apartment complex. It didn't look like it, and this filled Gina with a sadness, to see the once vibrant, happy holiday home now little more than a dusty relic of days gone by.

She was just about to tackle the floor in the office when she heard voices and what sounded like wheelie suitcases being dragged across the uneven, gravelly ground outside. Gina went to take a look.

'Do you speak English?' a middle-aged, red-faced man puffed in her face.

'Um... yes?' Gina started but was quickly cut off by a weary looking woman with an incredibly sweaty top lip and a mottled heat rash radiating across her neck.

'Thank goodness for that. The taxi driver had no idea what Dave was saying when he tried to explain the address of where we were staying. But we are here now, and it looks lovely.' The woman smiled, her eyes flicking towards Dave, her husband presumably, as if for reassurance.

'Lovely?' Dave boomed. 'A shambles more like. Nikki, it's nothing like the pictures you showed me on the website. I could have you for false advertising,' he said, turning back to Gina with a menacing look in his eyes. A short silence followed. 'Only joking!' he eventually caveated, before nudging Gina and throwing his big head back and laughing like it was the funniest joke anyone had ever told. The woman fidgeted with her hair and Gina instantly felt sorry for her as the rash intensified and she pulled a mini hand-held fan from her pocket in an attempt to cool herself down. 'So, lead the way, love. We're booked in for two weeks.' It took a few seconds for Gina to realise that Dave thought she worked there.

'Oh no, I'm...' she started, but on seeing the sudden look of anguish in Nikki's eyes, Gina changed her mind and instead said, 'Sure, follow me,' and quickly marched on ahead to see if Meryl had woken up and could help her with the check-in process for these new guests. Her heart sank all over again on thinking of Meryl having to deal with the likes of Dave on her own. But Meryl wasn't in the office so there was only one thing for it, Gina was going to have to do the check-in. She quickly scanned the reception desk, opened a drawer and to her relief found what looked like a ledger. Thumbing through the pages as fast as she could, Gina found the one with today's date on and there in the 4 p.m. slot were the names *Dave and Nikki Jones, two weeks, number 4*. Right, I need to find the keys, thought Gina, opening the drawers again, and then remembered the pinboard behind her. Four keys were lined up on little hooks in a corner and she was just about to take the fourth one when she stopped, her hand in mid-air as she saw a polaroid picture of herself as a little girl. Her eyes scanned, as her heart rate raced, it was as if time had stood still for a moment until she saw her. Shirley. There she was. Her kind eyes and curly hair that Gina had inherited, gazing back at her with a big smile. In another picture, Gina was standing next to her mum, probably about sixteen years old, and she couldn't believe it, the jelly shoes she remembered were there on her feet. Gina swiftly blinked back the tears smarting in the corners of her eyes as she gently touched a fingertip to the face of her mum.

'Chop, chop! Let's be having you!' Dave's voice and the ding of a little bell on the desk startled Gina from her reverie. Grateful to still have her sunglasses on, she swallowed hard, and after inhaling through her nose, she took the number four key and gripped it in her hand as she let out a long calming breath. She was just about to turn around to hand the key over and try to check in Dave and Nikki when a sudden memory sprung to mind.

'Oh, check-in is actually at four,' Gina said, in her best breezy voice, letting the words hang in the air as she held Dave's gaze and tried to keep a straight face while he seemed to be working out where to go from here. 'Sorry,' she added, insincerely, for good measure, taking a quick look at Nikki who was still fanning herself. 'Tell you what... I could let you in early, if you like, but not till...' she paused to glance at the wall clock behind them. It was only twelve o'clock now and Gina wondered what state the apartments were actually in. As far as she could see, there weren't any other guests staying here, all the keys were on the board and the shutters at the windows of every one of the four buildings were closed up. And she needed to find Meryl, and then see if the apartment needed cleaning before she could let Dave and Nikki go in there. It was obvious that Meryl needed the money from the booking and so Gina made a snap decision to help her. 'Yes, I could probably let you in at two-ish. How does that sound?' She put a hand on her hip and tilted her head to one side to see if Dave would go for it, the favour he might think she was doing for him.

'How does that sound?' Dave harrumphed in repetition, his whole head getting even redder. 'It sounds bloody awful. What are we supposed to do in this heat while we wait around for two hours? Is there even a pub nearby or are we expected to die from dehydration?'

'Err, yes there's a lovely little taverna but it's back down the hill and a walk along the beach,' Gina said, thinking of Toula's and very much doubting that Dave would die of dehydration any time soon given the size of his beer belly, like a camel with a hump, but on his front. With that, he could probably sustain himself for a pretty long time. 'I could call a taxi to take you there, if you like?' and she pinned a big smile on her face.

'Oh Dave, I don't fancy going all the way back to the beach,' Nikki puffed.

'You can stay here if you like,' Gina grinned at her. 'There's a gorgeous garden out the back, if you want to wait there in the shade,' she added kindly, to which Nikki mouthed, 'Thank you,' before exhaling in relief.

'Done. Better call me a taxi in that case.' Dave slapped a hand on the desk as if sealing some kind of deal. 'Here, you keep an eye on the cases, Nikki, and don't let them out of your sight. You can't be too careful in these foreign places,' and he rolled his wheelie suitcase away sideways towards his poor wife who deftly caught it just in time, so it didn't career into her legs. Gina found a card for a taxi firm, called it, and then led Nikki out to the garden to find a comfortable spot, planning on bringing her a pitcher of iced water once Dave had disappeared. Dave pushed his hands in his pockets and went to wait out the front under a tree for the taxi to arrive.

Satisfied that she had it all under control, Gina organised the pitcher of water for Nikki and went in search of Meryl.

'There you are!' It was Meryl who found Gina, as she came walking across the courtyard area outside the four apartment buildings. 'I woke up and you weren't there. Are you OK, dear?'

'Oh yes.' Gina explained to Meryl about Dave and Nikki arriving and asked where holiday home number four was. After unlocking the door, Gina saw to her horror that it was just as she feared it might be. Musty and drab and was that a cockroach she saw out of the corner of her eye? Either way, it had definitely seen better days, so once again, Gina pushed up her sleeves and put her expert cleaning skills to good use to help her elderly friend out, figuring the catch-up chat and a proper look at the polaroid pictures on the pinboard would have to wait for now.

Once the apartment was spotlessly clean, and Gina was satisfied there weren't any cockroaches – it was a dead spider she had seen – she soon realised that it wouldn't actually take too much to do a mini makeover, and so she turned to Meryl.

'Where do you keep the bed linen?'

'Let me show you, dear.' Meryl went back to the office and Gina followed.

After sorting through a pile of fresh linen, and selecting the best-looking set, Gina found a washing basket to load it into, together with a bale of clean towels and then thought of another idea. Turning to the fresh flowers she had brought for Meryl, she lifted a few stems out and made them into a small arrangement, figuring they would be nice for the bedroom in the little ceramic pot she had spotted in the kitchen. With visions of how the apartment could look, rustic and traditional, with the crisp white linen on the beds and the windows flung open to let in the warm, salty sea breeze, Gina hitched the basket onto her hip and went back over to make a start on creating her vision.

'Oh, Gina, it looks marvellous,' Meryl said, a little while later, seeing what Gina had achieved. The apartment now smelled fresh from the pine-scented cleaning spray Gina had used, and the bed was made up simply with a couple of white cushions arranged by the pillows and a hand-embroidered throw across the foot of the bed. It looked traditional and homely, but light and airy too. The perfect place to relax after a day of exploring the island. The breeze from the open window was welcoming, now that the drab, worn curtains had been removed and the white wooden shutters were sparkling clean. And the vivid flowers added a lovely dash of colour on the cabinet by the bed. In the now-pristine little kitchenette, Gina had washed some of the fresh eggs and popped them in a basket, next to a plate of figs picked from the tree outside.

'Thank you, dear.' Meryl gave Gina a hug.

'It's been a pleasure,' Gina said, stepping back to take a good look. She smiled, pleased with the result, because even though she was here on holiday, she had enjoyed doing the makeover and making a difference. And feeling appreciated.

17

Later the same day, on their way to Toula's, after walking across the sand with a warm breeze from the sea, the three friends fancied a pit stop at a beach bar serving refreshing cold drinks in copper mugs with straws. Shaded from the blazing sun under a bamboo pergola with driftwood furniture and giant cacti in terracotta pots, Gina finished relaying to Deedee and Rosie what she had discovered when she went to see Meryl.

'Oh, that's heartbreaking,' Rosie frowned, taking a big slurp from her straw.

'But lucky you were there when the dreadful-sounding Dave, and his wife arrived,' Deedee said.

'Yes, I'm glad I was,' Gina sighed. 'Meryl told me, as we were cleaning up and doing the mini makeover, that she had completely forgotten dreadful Dave, and his wife, Nikki, were coming. I don't think she has had many bookings over the last few years – the ledger I found was practically empty and I took a quick look at her website and it desperately needs updating, as the photos they've used on it look like they were taken when I stayed there as a child.'

'That's a shame, but maybe I can help her if she wants to turn things around?' Deedee offered. 'I have many clients coming into my travel agency, looking for a secluded, self-catering place to stay on a gorgeous Greek island. Did you not consider booking with her for your holiday here, Gina? Mind you, I'm glad you didn't, or we would never have met.'

'To be honest, I didn't,' Gina said, stirring her drink with the straw. 'I couldn't remember the name of the apartment complex and guess I'd assumed that Meryl might have retired by now. I'm surprised she hasn't actually; she told me today that she used to think about going back to England, but she doesn't have any ties there any more. Her father was in the army and so she grew up living in lots of different countries and not ever managing to put down roots. It's why she moved to Kalosiros in the first place, to set up the holiday apartments and meet lots of lovely people, and she now feels too old to relocate all over again.'

'Yes, she is very elderly, guessing in her late eighties, and has done remarkably well to have kept it going all this time... did she say what her plans are? Surely, she can't keep on running the place all by herself?' Deedee asked.

'She didn't, no,' Gina replied, 'but I'm going to visit her again and will ask her, because she can't carry on the way she is. She was clearly struggling, and it was sad to see, and I didn't get the impression that she has any friends to call on so I'd like to try to help her if I can, somehow. She was there on her own and seemed sort of lonely, if you know what I mean.'

'Hmm, that's not a good sign.' Rosie shook her head, looking concerned. 'Wasn't Meryl friends with Nico's grandparents?'

'Yes, that's right,' Gina nodded.

'So I wonder if they are still around in that case. Though surely they would help her out if they were and knew she was struggling,' Deedee said, solemnly.

'Well, they were elderly, or seemed so at the time to my teenage self, when I last saw them thirty years ago. So it's likely they might have died. That could explain why Meryl didn't remember them when I mentioned Nico's grandparents and Toula's taverna, if she hasn't seen them, or indeed him, in a long time.' Gina frowned in thought.

'Poor thing.' Deedee shook her head. 'Will she be OK on her own dealing with dreadful Dave?'

'I hope so, and she has my phone number now, so she can call me anytime if she needs to,' Gina told them, growing concerned about what would happen to Meryl when she went back home, if there really was nobody else here on the island to help her. Deedee could book holidaymakers in but there was a lot of work needed to get the rest of the holiday homes up to scratch and, even then, Meryl would need help with the cleaning and catering and keeping the business running properly.

'That's nice, but hopefully dreadful Dave will behave,' Rosie said. 'Talking of Meryl's business though, did you – by any chance – find pictures of your mum?'

'Oh my God, I can't believe I didn't already say! Yes, I did,' Gina beamed. 'We had a marvellous chat while we were cleaning, and there were some lovely pictures of Mum on the pinboard which seemed to help Meryl remember, and I have copies here.' Gina swiped across the screen of her phone to show them the photos. The three women came in close together to take a look.

'Oh Gina, your mum was beautiful, and you do so look like her. In fact, if I didn't know differently, I'd have said this was you in the picture,' Deedee said, putting her arm around Gina's shoulders and pulling her in even closer for a hug.

'Gina, I'm so happy for you being able to see your mum again,' Rosie added, running a finger underneath her sunglasses to the corner of her eye. 'And sorry, I know I shouldn't get emotional, but this is so romantic, in the true sense of the word, as in "love in all its forms and with a happy ending" way. You getting to see your mum's face again is just, well... it's just pure lovely, that's what it is.'

The three women looked through the rest of the photos that Gina had taken of the polaroids on the pinboard and came to the one of Nico and her, on the beach, the golden glow of the sun like a halo all around them as they stood side by side, hand in hand, smiling to the camera. Another picture of them gazing at each other and so clearly in love. Gina's heart skipped a beat as she remembered the moment – in that new stripy bikini she had bought from the market and feeling so deeply in love with Nico, as his hand had felt like fire in hers, sending sparks flaming and flickering within her. The memory was so clear, it felt like only yesterday.

'OMG,' Rosie breathed, taking her sunglasses off now to scrutinise the photo. 'Look at you two! Adoring each other. And both so gorgeous. Nico is so incredibly roasting hot with his kind-looking eyes and model-like cheekbones and jawline, and the way he's smiling, right up to his long-lashed eyes. He looks like a really nice guy. Not to mention the messy curls and the washboard abs,' she gushed, using her thumb and index finger to enlarge the picture on the screen so she could scrutinise him further. 'And I wonder if he considered modelling, with looks like that. He'd be perfect in a tuxedo on a wedding-event shoot, or snug-fitting shorts in a beach-wedding-venue catalogue.' Rosie went to whip out her notepad, presumably to make another list of some sort, centred around making Nico a model... if they ever found him. Deedee quickly and gently placed her hand over Rosie's to calm her down and the notepad went back inside the bag. They all laughed. 'But we absolutely do need to find him now,' Rosie added, fanning herself over dramatically with her hand.

'Well, shall we still carry on with our plan of going to Toula's,

even if it's fairly unlikely Nico's grandparents are still there?'
Deedee asked, looking directly at Gina for confirmation.

'Um... I'd like to, if that's OK?' Gina said tentatively, before
adding, 'I do really want to find Nico now, and not because he's so
incredibly hot, as you clearly saw, Rosie,' she laughed. 'Well, he
was hot back then as a teenager, he may of course be completely
different now,' she shrugged. 'But I need to see him because
Meryl's place has brought all the memories back. The shared
history. And he's the only one I really have that with.' Gina nodded
more resolutely as she had made her mind up. Seeing Nico's face
again in the picture pinned to the board had also brought all the
feelings she'd had for him rushing back into her head and her
heart. She couldn't stop thinking about him now, just like she
hadn't been able to as a teenager. And she was prepared to risk
rejection, if there was any chance at all of finding out if he remembered her. She just knew deep down that she couldn't leave
Kalosiros again without doing all that she could to find her first
love. She needed to talk to Nico, to explain and to say sorry for
letting him go, for not keeping in touch. And she would tell him
she didn't blame him either when he stopped writing to her. He
moved on, just as she had with Colin, she assumed. But still, there
was unfinished business and she needed to know if it was the same
for Nico. Plus, she would love to talk to him about the times they
had shared together, his memories of her mum and his grandparents. She had been fond of them too, always welcoming her with
open arms every summer when she arrived, followed by an enormous hug and a hunk of still warm baclava straight from the
kitchen with a can of Fanta to follow.

'It most definitely is OK,' Rosie exclaimed, swivelling her head
to look at Gina first, and then Deedee. 'Drink up, ladies, and let's go
and find your gorgeous Nico!'

They had been walking along the beach for a while and could

see the taverna with Toula's signage in the distance when Gina felt her phone vibrating in her beach bag.

'Oh, it's Colin,' she said, on seeing the screen as she pulled the phone from the bag and stopped moving. Her pulse quickened, and not in a good way.

'Are you OK, Gina?' Deedee asked and stopped walking. Rosie did too. 'Your hands are shaking, darling.'

'Err, I'm not sure. He never phones me... he only ever sends text messages,' she mumbled, trying to fathom out what was going on. 'Could it be an emergency, do you think? Maybe something has happened to Pam, my mother-in-law.' The three women stared at the phone, still buzzing as Colin's call kept ringing out, none of them knowing what to do. 'I should answer it, shouldn't I?' Gina muttered gingerly, really not wanting to talk to him, not here on the beach, in this beautiful setting, with her new friends by her side. She could feel her buoyant, happy holiday mood slowly sinking away to one of horribly familiar, continuous, low-key dejection and anxiety, the default setting of her life back home. But before a decision could be made, Colin's call cut off and Gina let out a long breath of air that she hadn't realised she was holding in.

'Come on, let's carry on to Toula's. He'll phone back if it is an actual emergency, I'm sure,' Deedee said lightly as if trying to lift the mood. But as soon as they started walking on, Gina's phone vibrated again.

'I had better answer it,' she said, reluctantly, and both women gave her a look of understanding, nodding, and patting the side of her arm in support before they walked ahead to give her some privacy.

18

Gina took a deep breath and lifted the phone to her ear.

'Where are you?' Colin said to open the conversation.

On autopilot, Gina opened her mouth to tell him right away as she usually did, part of her wondering what the trick was as he could easily look on the tracking app, but something inside her had changed and so she stopped herself. Instead, she momentarily closed her eyes before saying, 'Colin, we are trialling a separation. You can't just call me and demand to know where I am.' Silence followed and Gina could feel her skin prickling in anticipation of his response. She wasn't used to standing up to Colin, but in this moment, she could suddenly see with such clarity, as if she was someone else, or perhaps another part within her, that after lying dormant for however many years was now showing up and definitely not putting up with it any more. 'Are you still there, Colin?' she asked after a while, wondering if he had hung up. She checked the phone to see. Yep, still there. She put the phone back to her ear and decided to sit it out. She wasn't going to cave in and say sorry or whatever like she would have done in the past. The way he had started the conversation was rude.

'Yes, I'm still here. And you're still my wife... in case you'd forgotten.'

'No Colin, I hadn't forgotten.' Gina kept her voice measured, until she knew where he was going with this.

'Are you sure about that?' he asked, his voice low and surly.

'What do you mean? Please Colin, don't play games, what's up?'

'What's up? I'll tell you *what's up*, as you so casually put it. You taking me for a fool, that's what's up!' he said, ending with a self-satisfied sounding harrumph.

'Colin, I have no idea what you're talking about. You were the one who didn't come on the holiday, and who said you wanted a trial separation,' she reminded him.

'Yes, well that was before I found out why you were so keen to go on holiday without me... And yes, I did see your silly "Gone to Greece" note on the fridge. So I do know where you've gone and didn't need you to spell it out to me,' he said, with more than a hint of sarcasm in his voice. 'Did you really think I wouldn't work it out?'

Gina inhaled again and breathed out slowly to steady herself, she could tell that he was furious, and it made her feel uncomfortable, even now, all these miles away.

'Work what out, Colin?' she asked, racking her brain to figure out what on earth he could mean.

'You wanted to hook up with your Greek guy! And it wouldn't surprise me if this is why you wanted some time apart in the first place. I know all about it.' She could hear him breathing heavily as if pacing around and working himself up.

'About what?' Gina tried again to get to the bottom of this, a sudden sensation swirling within her, a cold chill making her tremble despite the blazing, beachy sun beaming down upon her.

Seeing a trio of large tamarisk trees, Gina went and sat underneath them in the shade.

'You and whatshisname... that holiday romance bloke, Nico, wasn't it?' Colin kept on.

'Nico? I haven't seen him in years,' Gina said, her pulse speeding now.

'You're lying, Gina. You were showing off about having the time of your life with him. You didn't even bother trying to hide it.' Another silence followed.

Gina could feel beads of sweat marshalling into the map of Australia over her midriff. She pushed off her dupe sandals and pulled her knees up, wrapping her free arm around her legs to comfort herself. She didn't want to do this. She didn't want this moment to ruin her dream holiday, where she had indeed been having the time of her life. Until now.

'Colin, listen to me... I am not here with Nico—'

'Stop lying, it all makes sense, and to think you were expecting me to come with you to Greece while you met up with him. What was the plan? To fob me off with a beer on the beach or whatever and then sneak off to meet him? Bet you were overjoyed when I couldn't make it.'

'Colin, you've got this all wrong. I'm not here with Nico,' Gina told him again.

'Who is he then?'

'I have no idea what you're talking about. What it is you think you've seen?'

'You, on Instagram, all cuddled up with him. And since when did you even *have* an Instagram account?' he huffed, accusingly. And the penny dropped; Gina knew what he thought he had seen. Her with Cristos holding her painting of the sunset and Rosie's caption.

'Having the time of my life.'

Gina's cheeks flamed as she recalled the moment, standing with Cristos, with that all-consuming urge to touch him. The monumental return of her libido. Despite it all, in this moment she still felt guilty having thoughts like that for another man.

'I went to an art class run by the hotel. Colin, he was the art teacher. He's called Cristos,' she told him, suddenly hating herself for feeling the need to placate her estranged husband and explain herself.

'Yes, I saw you had tagged the hotel, but do you expect me to believe that's all it was, an art class?' he said. Then he demanded to know again, 'When did set yourself up with Instagram?'

A longer silence ensued, and Gina dipped her chin on top of her knees wondering what would happen if she ended the call. Just cut Colin off and didn't talk to him ever again. She felt cross now, with him, but with herself more, she didn't want to answer to him, to be in his shadow for a second longer, so after taking a deep breath and exhaling hard, she told him, 'Look Colin, you can believe what you like. If I want to have an Instagram account then I will do, I'm an adult.' She then remembered Anne's words on that day in her drawing room. 'And a woman of substance! Yes, so I am perfectly capable of going on holiday by myself and having a jolly good time, which is exactly what I am doing!' she added, a little devilish part of her wanting to wind him up just a teeny tiny bit as payback for all the times he had wound her up on purpose.

She could see him now, most likely pacing up and down the hallway, stabbing a finger on the mouse to make their shared computer screen come to life where her Instagram grid would be in full view and crammed full of beautiful pictures of the dream holiday he had baled on, right there teasing him. She guessed he had been looking at the hotel on Instagram and had spotted her pictures via the tag which would then lead him to see that she had her own account. And he'd have a red face, like dreadful Dave, and be no doubt fuming at her audacity. But she had deferred to him for far too long, relegating her own happiness and going along with his joyless ways and wasn't prepared to do it any longer.

The silence continued until Colin eventually said in a sneering voice, 'Who have you been talking to?'

Gina stared at the screen of her phone, wondering what his point was. Did he think so little of her that he assumed she could only function under the influence of somebody else? But then she supposed that was exactly what she had been doing, denying herself even an Instagram account because her husband thought it was for idiots with too much time on their hands. Which, come to think of it... why was he even looking at Instagram if he felt so strongly about its time-sucking capabilities?

'I haven't been "talking" to anyone, as you put it, apart from my new friends – yes, I've met two wonderful women and will be keeping in touch with them – but like I said, I wanted an Instagram account and so now I have one. The question is Colin, how do you know about it? Have you been spying on me? Have you been looking at the hotel on Instagram? Or searching my name on social media channels to see what comes up?' she asked him directly.

'Don't be daft! Why would I spy on you?' he said, far too quickly and there was a wariness in his voice. 'Now I know you really have gone completely bananas. That Greek sun has gone to your head. Wish I hadn't bothered calling you now... That'll teach me for being a fool and still loving you like I did on the day we got married.'

'Oh Colin, you don't still love me like you did on the day we got married, neither of us feel the way we did then,' Gina said, quietly. 'Let's not pretend any more.' Smarting, she tightened her arm around her knees, and bizarrely, the older woman with the pink-framed glasses she had met on the aeroplane sprung to mind, bringing a sense of now-or-never surging through her veins followed by an overwhelming flood of calm. As the words tumbled out, Gina knew it had to be done, or she too would end up being another unhappy older woman with pink-framed glasses still living in hope of having her Shirley Valentine moment. 'Colin, this trial separation needs to become a permanent thing.'

Silence followed.

Twenty-seven years together coming to an end and Gina knew there would be no going back now. Colin wouldn't have it; she knew him well enough to know that his ego would always prevail and there could never be any kind of reconciliation if she was the one to end it, not that she wanted it any more anyway. But it was OK, and she could almost hear the snap of the spindly thread that had been holding their marriage together.

'So that's it then, is it?' he eventually said, his voice like ice.

'Yes, I think it is, Colin.'

'Well, we will see about that when you get back home, because you've got another thing coming if you think me and Mum are moving out, and you're keeping the house when you're the one that has done this.'

After pressing to end the call, Gina sat perfectly still for a moment, and then the trembly feeling flooded through her again. *Did that just happen?* It felt surreal. Here she was sitting on one of the most breathtakingly beautiful beaches in the world, having ended her marriage. The same beach that she and Nico had sat on all that time ago... and the irony wasn't lost on her.

'Are you alright, Gina?' Deedee had come back to check on her. 'Only you look a bit shellshocked. What's happened, darling? Was it an emergency?' She sat down next to Gina on the sand and placed her hand on Gina's trembling back.

'Um, no, not an emergency, but I'm not entirely sure how I feel right now,' Gina mumbled, still hugging her knees, and pushing her toes deeper into the sand.

'Do you want to talk? Rosie has gone ahead to Toula's, but I thought I'd wait here with you. She's going to ask about Nico when she gets there and then start walking back to us if we haven't got to her by then. The call looked serious, so we weren't sure if you would still want to go on to Toula's. Gina, darling, are you OK?' Deedee's voice faded away.

'I just ended my marriage!' Gina gasped, in a daze.

'Oh.' Deedee turned sideways to face Gina and wrapped her arms around her, hugging her tight. Gina felt her taut body softening into her friend's embrace and no matter how hard she tried; Gina found it impossible not to cry a massive river all over Deedee's shoulder.

'I'm so sorry,' she managed, in between big sobs as she lifted her head to look at Deedee and tried to wipe the tear stains off her friend's beautiful silk kimono. 'I'll buy you a new one.'

'You will not!' Deedee said, sternly. 'Now cry away... It's just fabric, and trust me, it's had worse on it – red wine, lipstick and all sorts, so some hot tears won't hurt,' she added, glancing to her shoulder, and smiling gently at Gina.

'I don't even know why I'm crying when it was me that ended it. And I *wanted* to end it, not because of Nico or my mad, lustful thoughts of wanting to touch Cristos, but because it was long overdue. I've been unhappy for years if I'm honest, and Colin has too to be fair, but it was good in the beginning, it really was. And I tried really hard to be happy and to make him happy.'

'Oh Gina, you're allowed to be sad. How did he take it?'

'Not well. He thinks I'm here with Nico. He saw the picture of me with Cristos and...' Gina explained. 'But I think he cares more about my house than he ever did for me.'

'I hope not,' Deedee said, sounding fierce now. 'Did he actually say that?'

'Well, not those exact words, but he was very quick to tell me he and Pam – that's his mum – won't be moving out. I think he's forgotten that the house is actually mine, that I inherited it from my mum.'

'Hmm, but surely he knew that when he first moved in?' Deedee raised her eyebrows.

'Yes, that's right, and he said it made sense for the three of us to live there though, seeing as there was no mortgage to pay. Mum's life insurance paid off the mortgage when she died.'

'I see,' Deedee said quietly as if processing all that Gina was telling her. A short silence followed. Gina caught her breath and after pushing her hair back from her face, she wiped at her eyes and thought about it all, not wanting to contemplate if Colin really had been more interested in her house than her, because, to what end? It was too late now to change it all, the past was gone, and she had wanted him to move in – Pam too following the hysterectomy – so it felt like she had a proper family again. It had worked for them all. 'Gina, maybe don't try to figure it all out right now? It's still raw,' Deedee added, interrupting her thoughts. 'But when you're ready, I can put you in touch with a very good divorce lawyer. The best. She won't let him take your house.'

'I can't afford it on my own in any case,' Gina said, a panic prickling within her now. 'What I earn from cleaning would barely cover the household bills.'

'It will be OK, darling. Try not to worry. Everything will work out the way it is supposed to, you'll see. And you're right, from what you've shared with me, the separation was long overdue so I'm not sure you could have carried on the way you were, in any case.'

'That's true,' Gina nodded, 'it couldn't carry on, not for me, or for him actually.'

'Right! And well done you for recognising this and doing something about it. So, what would you like to do now?' Deedee asked, pragmatically.

'Can we just wait here for Rosie? And maybe call in at the

beach bar on our way back for a cocktail or ten trillion?' she laughed wryly. 'I'm not sure I want to be on my own in my hotel room this evening.'

Gina also didn't want to go on to Toula's now. It just didn't feel right, she needed time to process all that had happened. With Colin's rapid response comment about the house, she was even more convinced now that he had taken the memory box containing all her holiday photos and the letters from Nico. Maybe he still had the box though, because it seemed odd that he had remembered Nico's name from twenty-seven years ago. Plus, she wanted to know for sure how he had found out that she had an Instagram account? Maybe Rosie might know.

'Of course we can, darling. Rosie won't be long. In fact, here she comes now.' Deedee lifted her hand to wave and Gina stood up.

'Another dead end, I'm afraid,' Rosie said, catching her breath. 'I spoke to a lovely guy who owns the taverna, but he doesn't know Nico and from what I can gather there's no connection to his family there any more. I'm so sorry, Gina, but it's as we thought, Nico's grandparents died over a decade ago, one of the waiters remembered them and said the taverna was sold to someone else and then on to the guy who owns it now. But we can keep trying, can't we?' she added, brightly. 'Someone on this island is bound to remember your Nico and we've barely scratched the surface. We have more taxi drivers to talk to, I only spoke to a few, and there are cafes, hotels, the fishermen in the harbour. Our Nico hunt has only really just begun.'

'Sure,' Gina said, trying not to cry again. She bit into her bottom lip and nodded, not sure of what to say, but felt sad on knowing that an era had come to an end. The holiday memories of sitting on the steps of the taverna with Nico eating homemade houmous and pitta bread that his grandmother had made, and now Gina knew for sure that the lovely, kindly, generous Greek woman who Nico adored, and had felt like a surrogate grand-parent to her too, was no longer here. Those days were gone forever.

'Oh Gina, I really am so sorry,' Rosie said, assuming Gina's sadness was only for the news of Nico not being at Toula's and his grandmother dying. Silence followed. 'Have I missed something?' Rosie asked, realising, and looking at Deedee and then back to Gina. 'Was it the phone call?'

After updating Rosie, Gina turned to her and asked, 'How would Colin know that I had an Instagram account? Is it possible that he has one too and that we would somehow be linked?'

'Um, possibly, I suppose, but we used your new email address so I'm not sure. I guess the algorithm can be a mysterious phenomenon so you might be in his contacts, linked by mobile numbers. Or if he has an Instagram account and has been looking at your location here on the island, or the hotel perhaps – we tagged them and used hashtags in all your pictures – so maybe it wouldn't be hard to spot you if he's been searching. But let's find out.'

They had made it back to the beach bar by now and after ordering more drinks, the three of them sat down under the shade of the bamboo pergola and Gina took out her phone and showed it to Rosie.

'So what's his full name?' Rosie asked.

'Colin Bennett.'

'OK, so search that name and see if he comes up.' Gina did as Rosie instructed.

'Hmm, there are four people with that name, but none of them have their face in the profile picture,' Gina said, tapping on each one. It was the third profile with four followers that stopped her in her tracks. 'La-Z-Boy!' she said out loud, it was in his bio. 'That's him. Oh my God.' Gina stared at the grid full of pictures of what looked like Colin's socked feet! She recognised the blue and white striped sliders he wore around the house over his socks.

'Is it him?' Rosie and Deedee chimed, leaning in from either side of Gina to get a better look.

'Yes! It is. Hundreds of pictures of him with his feet up on the lazy boy section of the sofa, with various different images beyond the blue and white striped sliders of what he's watching on the telly, mostly.'

'And you didn't know?' Rosie asked.

'I had no idea,' Gina managed, stunned as she scrolled on through, her face flaming when she landed on one with an image of the *Love Island* logo on the telly. 'And he hates *Love Island*, I always had to watch it in the bedroom because he wouldn't have it on in the lounge.'

'Well, it looks like Colin enjoyed it plenty!' Deedee tutted on seeing the caption.

Bring on the bikini bottoms.

'Ugh. I don't know whether to laugh or cry!' Gina shook her head in dismay, but inside felt hurt and humiliated because all this time he had been laughing at her behind her back. 'And I can't believe this,' she added, her finger hovering over a picture of a plate of custard cream biscuits balanced on Colin's knees. A similarly inane caption below it.

Why get up when the missus will bring the biscuits? LOL

'I've seen enough.' Gina let out a long puff of air and pushed her phone away across the table top.

The three women sat in silence for a while, sipping their drinks and shaking their heads in mutual aghast at Colin's carrying on.

'Are you OK, Gina?' Rosie eventually asked, having finished her drink.

'Yes, I think so,' Gina muttered to herself, still feeling bamboozled by Colin's ridiculous Instagram posts, and foolish too for being taken in by him and his fake dislike of social media users. What a hypocrite! And it seemed that he had been doing this as a control tactic to stop her from having any kind of social life of her own, even if it was only online.

Gina finished her drink too and picked her phone back up. As she swiped off Colin's account, still visible on the screen and back to her own, she was just about to close down the app when Rosie reached across her arm and pointed to something on the screen. 'What's that? Looks like you have a direct message,' she said. Gina stopped, her index finger hovering in mid-air over the tiny red dot in the top right corner of her screen. After following Rosie's instructions on how to accept the sender – a woman called Karen Julia Jarvis, wearing a pink beanie hat over long blonde hair – into her General message box, Gina clicked and read the words.

You don't know me, Gina, but I know a lot about you and there was a time when I used to wish I was you. But I feel sorry for you now, as Colin has shown his true colours to me too. You see, I know now that he's been using me for sex for the last five years. It's not something I'm proud of and I feel like a fool for being taken in by his promises. He just called me and said that he's ended it with you and instead of saying we can be together properly now, he's dumped me, claiming that it won't look good in the divorce if it comes out that he was having an affair with me for all this time, so that's the end of it. He also ranted about you being on here now and so it wasn't hard to find you to let you know what's been going on. I'm not going to be treated second best by him any longer just so he can keep his house,

which I realise now is worth more to him than me as he had a
rant about that too, saying if you found out about me it could
ruin his claim on the house. No hard feelings and if you want the
truth, I reckon you're better off without him too, as am I.

Ps. – the team-building away-day was a lie! He was with me
on a mini-break and here's a copy of the hotel receipt, which I'm
sure you'll find a use for in the divorce proceedings.

'Gina, GINA, are you OK...? Oh my God, has she fainted?' Rosie
yelled as Gina's head free-fell down in front of her until her forehead was resting on the smooth surface of the driftwood table in
front of her. She was aware of her fingers freeing the phone from
her hand, but it didn't seem to matter as it tumbled to the floor
beneath her feet, and she listened to the sound of the sea shushing
back and forth on the sand nearby, soothing and comforting as she
let Karen's words sink in. Muffled voices now getting louder and
louder until she opened her eyes again and lifted her head
back up.

'Gina, darling... please, say something. What day is it?' Deedee
asked, and when Gina didn't reply because she was still processing
what she had just read, Rosie appeared in front of her face with her
hand hovering in the air.

'How many fingers?' Rosie asked urgently, waggling her hand
back and forth like Beyonce in her 'Single Ladies (Put a Ring on It)'
song. Back and forth, back and forth, again and again, with an
ever-increasing crazed look in her eyes that were now the size of
dinner plates. 'It's not working. She's in a trance. Is she having
some sort of seizure? She might die. Right, can we get an ambu-
lance, please? What's the Greek word for emergency? Or a doctor!
Is there a doctor in the house? Err... beach bar? Yes, yes, that's it, we
need a doctor... shall I run to the harbour, Dr Nico, he might be
there. What time is it?' Rosie paused from panting to draw breath

and glance at her watch. 'It's after four o'clock. He'll be there, let's go!' And she practically catapulted herself off her chair and gathered her long dress up, presumably to give herself a better chance of not tripping over and wasting precious time as she raced across the sand.

'What are you doing?' Gina heard Deedee say loudly as she took hold of Rosie's arm, so she had no choice but to sit back down. 'Rosie, get a grip, darling. Gina isn't having some sort of seizure, she's not in a trance, she's in shock. It's been a lot for her today. Get her a cocktail, a strong one,' Deedee ordered. Rosie nodded and did as she was told, sprinting off and arriving back a second or two later with a very strong concoction; something ouzo-based with blackcurrant juice mixed in, Gina discovered on taking a sip, as Rosie held the copper mug to her mouth like she was a delirious, newly found castaway on a desert island who hadn't had a drink in several days. Gina gasped as the liquid hit the back of her throat and felt like fire as it trickled down inside her.

'What *is* that?' Gina managed, pulling a face as the shock wore off and she came to.

'Never mind about that, you're alive!' Rosie said, trying to get Gina to take another sip, but she pushed the mug away instead.

A stunned silence followed as the three women looked at each other shaking their heads in dismay for various different reasons. Rosie clearly relieved that Gina wasn't actually dead, and Deedee and Gina speechless at Rosie's reaction – their bonkers, but utterly lovable fruit loop of a very dramatic friend.

'And I'm fine,' Gina eventually said. 'Fuming, and a bit bamboozled, but fine, and it's actually funny in a weird, sad, whatever way. The message was from Colin's mistress! Seems he's been having an affair with a woman called Karen, or "using her for sex" as she put it, for the last five years,' Gina told her friends. 'Which ties in with when the cracks really took hold in our marriage.' And to think

that she had harboured so much as a single shred of hope in
thinking they might rekindle their marriage, that there might have
been something worth saving. That she had actually felt sorry for
Colin, thinking he was trapped in a different cage or whatever
philosophical rubbish she'd had going on inside her addled head,
thinking that he had lost his way too. He hadn't lost his way at all...
he had found another way, a silly double-life full of secret *Love
Island* binge fests and ridiculing her for bringing him biscuits, and
worst of all, an affair that had been going on for five flipping years!
FIVE YEARS.

And she was angry. Furious, in fact. With herself. With him. For
being his beck-and-call fool for all those years, because that's what
she had been... She had done everything for him, right down to
putting his biscuits on a plate because he was 'peckish' and
couldn't be bothered to move himself from the La-Z-Boy section of
the sofa.

But the worst of it was that she'd had hope – during those five
years when Colin had checked out, she now knew – she had still
hoped, tried in fact, to fix things between them when there really
had been no point. Well, no more. Her eyes were well and truly
wide open now and she could see that he had a flaming cheek
telling Karen it was his house. There was no way he was having *her*
house. Shirley's house!

19

Since seeing the message from Colin's ex-mistress, Gina had spent the next few days helping Meryl with the apartments in the mornings when the weather was cooler. Cleaning could be very therapeutic when you had lots of rubbish thoughts inside your head to dispose of, Gina had remembered. It had given her a chance to think about Colin's phone call and the message from Karen and she had come to the realisation that it was around five years ago when her marriage had really started falling apart and supposed it fitted the timeline of when his affair started. It was when the push and pull dynamic of their marriage had really taken hold. The more Gina had tried to make it work, the more Colin hadn't, and there had been many moments when it felt like he was punishing her for something she hadn't done, taking his bad temper out on her, and she wondered if this was his guilty conscience at play. Blaming her to somehow convince himself that it was all her fault, and he was therefore justified in having his affair. But being here had given her a distance from it all and she was thankful for that, having decided to put it out of her mind for now and not let it ruin the rest of her holiday. The revelation of the affair hadn't actually come as a massive surprise, to be honest... The marriage had cracks in it long before the affair started, she just wished they could have worked together to try to fix things, or even mutually agreed to go their separate ways, amicably like proper grown-ups, instead of Colin taking matters into his own hands, as it were. Anyway, it was done now, all out in the open and – she realised – it was a relief. She was free.

And so it was nice keeping things simple and just pottering around the apartment complex, putting together welcome baskets for the other new guests that had turned up unexpectedly too, with fresh figs from the tree and oranges from the market. Gina enjoyed chatting to Meryl in her more lucid moments about the happy holiday memories and keeping her company as they pegged towels and sheets on the washing line to dry in the hot Greek sun, then sat together with a well-earned cup of coffee, before Gina went to meet up with Deedee and Rosie later on. She'd fallen into a routine, and it was healing and fortifying. Dreadful Dave had chilled out too and was now calling his own taxis and taking Nikki all over the island to see the sights, treating her like a queen, so she was having the time of her life. They were even talking about renewing their wedding vows which made Gina smile. It seemed that Nikki and Dave were putting the spark back into their marriage just like Gina had hoped would happen for her when the holiday was booked two years ago.

Dave had even taken to bringing fresh supplies back for Meryl to help her out, saying, 'It breaks my heart to see an old dear doing it all on her own,' now that he knew she was the owner and Gina was actually here on her holiday. Dave had had a few choice words to say about Colin too, after overhearing Gina talking to Meryl, and Nikki, when she had joined them for a coffee in the garden, saying, 'He's an idiot for letting a looker like you go.' Gina had managed to hide her smirk, or had it been a smile? Plus, it turned out that

Nikki was a veterinary nurse and, after taking a look at the dog that roamed around free, had said he was fine and just needed a good bath. He was nourished and happy and could be great company for Meryl, who had called him Kip, short for Kipros, after a Greek fisherman she had been friendly with until he died last summer.

'So, what shall we do for the rest of this evening?' Rosie asked as the three friends tucked into a delicious dinner of grilled fresh fish straight from the sea with tangy tzatziki and a feta salad as they sat on the deck of a taverna that Meryl had told them about, on a quiet stretch of the beach not far from the Hotel Mirabelle.

'I'd love to go swimming,' Gina surprised herself by saying, but she had been talking to Meryl this morning about learning to swim in the sea here as a child and so it had been on her mind since. 'A sunset swim,' she clarified.

'Then let's do it,' Deedee said, putting her knife and fork together to end her meal and wiping her mouth with a napkin. 'Mmm, that was delicious.' She finished her glass of wine.

'What, *now*?' Rosie asked. 'But I haven't got a bikini with me.'

'Then go without one!' Deedee waved to the waiter and after they had split the bill, the three women stood up and wandered across the sand under a perfect peachy-pink sky as the sun started to sink.

'Do you mean go skinny-dipping?' Gina checked, turning to Deedee, a mixture of fear and thrill building inside her.

'Why not?' Deedee shrugged and stopped walking. 'There's nobody around, and if we carry on walking, there's a quiet little cove just around this corner. I've been to it before. I spent a whole day there in fact with my friend, Yiannis, when we went sailing on his boat and then moored up for an afternoon of swimming and sunbathing. It was bliss, and we didn't see another soul for the entire time we were there.'

'I don't know,' Gina said, the fear taking over now. 'I've never been skinny-dipping. What if someone sees us? Is it even legal here?'

'And what about our stuff?' Rosie made a good point. 'Our clothes and our phones, bags, what will we do with them?' She glanced around the deserted beach.

'We could take it in turns to mind the stuff,' Deedee suggested. 'Two go in and one stays behind, and then we rotate. Come on, it will be fun. Trust me. And you said yourself over dinner, Gina, that you want to try new things now that you're a single woman and starting a new chapter.'

'Hmm, that's true, I did,' Gina agreed, 'but I was talking about taking up art classes again, trying out TikTok, wearing new make-up instead of keeping the same old look I've had for years, going on trips, watching whatever I want to on TV without having to hide in my bedroom... Those kind of new, but fairly ordinary, things. Not gallivanting on a Greek island beach completely naked with my jelly belly wobbling like a trifle!' She groaned and shook her head.

'I love trifle!' Rosie said, and they all cracked up.

'So, what do you say?' Deedee was the first to recover. 'How about we walk on round to the cove, and you can see how quiet it is and then decide if you want to join me, or not?'

'I'm in,' Rosie said, and they both looked at Gina as she mulled it over.

'OK, OK... guess it won't hurt to take a look,' she eventually said, lifting her hands in surrender.

Ten minutes later, and Gina was hiding behind a trio of tall rocks near the water's edge with her arms folded around her bare boobs unable to believe that she was actually going to do it. Run into the sea absolutely naked. Deedee, with no such inhibitions, was already stripped bare, and Gina was in awe of her friend's beautifully tanned and toned body, with a glorious, flowering red rose tattoo climbing up from the small of her back.

'Ooh, look what I've found?' Rosie exclaimed, rummaging around in the cloth book bag that she had brought out with her today now that she was no longer working and didn't need her big tote bag to lug around all her work paraphernalia. 'It's my waterproof bumbag. I probably left it in here from when I last went open water swimming in the lake near where I live.'

'Is it big enough for all our valuables?' Deedee asked. 'Mind you, I only have my phone, that's the beauty of Apple Pay, no need to carry cards around these days. And I'm not bothered about my beach bag, it's easily replaceable if someone was to take it, although highly unlikely on this secluded beach with nobody else around.'

'Should be big enough,' Rosie said, unzipping the bumbag. 'Give me your phones and let's see.' And sure enough, their three phones, plus Gina's bank card (she had yet to embrace contactless payments and made a mental note to add it to her list of new things to do) neatly fitted into the bag.

'Fabulous! Now we can all go skinny-dipping together,' Deedee said, reaching out a hand to Gina as Rosie secured the bumbag around her naked waist. 'Shall we run in together?' Deedee gave her other hand to Rosie. Gina hesitated, she still had her knickers on, and arms crossed over her boobs.

'I'm not sure,' she whimpered, the kiss of the still warm, evening sun on her bare back making her shiver in anticipation mingled with nerves.

'What are you worried about, Gina?' Deedee smiled, kindly.

'Um... being naked, I guess, and, well, to be honest, I don't look like you two.' She glanced down at her big, waist-high comfortable knickers, knowing too that the pile of autumn leaves down there could very well be an overgrown rainforest by now, it had been that long since she had bothered with a bikini wax. And she was kicking herself now for not adding it to her treatment time at the Thelasso spa.

'Oh Gina, it's your body, you should celebrate it,' Rosie coaxed, gently, 'and I think you're being very harsh on yourself. You are beautiful, and I'm not seeing that trifle you promised.' And she put her hands on her hips and pulled a comical face as she lifted one eyebrow, making them all laugh again.

'And even if there was a trifle, so what?' Deedee said, and Rosie nodded in agreement. 'Honestly, the feeling of diving into the sea fully naked is one of the most exhilarating things I have ever done... and trust me, I have done some wild things in my time,' Deedee said, patting her still extended hand over Gina's bare back in reassurance. 'Plus, we really do need to get a move on if we want to swim under the sun and see it setting on the sea water.'

'Oh, you two!' Gina shook her head, looking at each of her friends in turn. 'I can't believe I am actually doing this.' And before she could think about it any more, she whipped off her knickers, lifted her arm and lassoed them up high in the air, letting the knickers land on top of the biggest rock.

'Waheyy! Off we go!' And with Gina in the middle now, the three women held hands and ran fast across the sand and into the shimmering sea.

'Ahhh,' Gina gasped, bobbing back up after submerging her whole body into the frothy, white-capped waves. 'It's amazing!' she said, shaking her curls from her face and wiping bubbly sea water from her eyes with cupped hands.

'I told you,' Deedee laughed, swimming towards her. 'The best feeling, isn't it?'

'It so is.' Rosie joined them, rolling onto her back and stretching her arms and legs out like a starfish, paddling gently with her hands and feet to keep herself afloat, the waterproof bumbag bobbing about around her abdomen.

'I can feel salty warm water in places I've never felt it before,' Gina laughed, feeling relaxed now that she was fully immersed in the sea water even though it was crystal clear, her inhibitions from earlier having faded. She felt on top of the world as she flipped on her back too next to Rosie and closed her eyes, letting the moment surround her as the warm sun and sea bathed and soothed her body. For some reason she couldn't fathom, tears trickled from the corners of her eyes. But she didn't feel sad, no it was something else... she felt alive! Vibrant and brand new. And she laughed on considering what she would have thought if she could see herself now, back on that day outside Anne's house when she had been bone-tired and crying in her car after Colin had let her down.

'Hey, there's a woman waving at us,' Rosie said, having resumed an upright position. Gina flipped herself back over too and after tenting her eyes with a hand, looked towards the shore.

'I think I know her,' Gina said on spotting the pink-framed glasses. 'She was on my flight here in the seat next to me.' She waved back, smiling as she saw the woman sitting by herself on the sand, having her Shirley Valentine moment perhaps as she looked so serene in her sundress and straw sun hat, her bare feet crossed, and her face tilted to the sun. The woman was waving again and standing up now and taking off her dress, her glasses and sun hat too. After unclipping her bra and slipping her knickers off as well, which she let fall into a heap at her feet, she stepped out of them and sauntered towards the sea, her ample bosoms bobbing, her own trifle wobbling. Gina and her friends lifted their arms out of the water and up into the air to clap as the woman gathered pace before launching herself into the sea.

'Hope you don't mind me joining you?' the woman said as she surfaced. 'I saw you running in earlier just as I got here and thought you looked like you were all having the time of your lives and I wanted too as well. I'm Angela and—oh, hello again,' she said, smiling on recognising Gina.

'Hello,' Gina grinned, ducking her shoulders back underneath the water. 'We don't mind at all... the more the merrier.'

The four women swam around and chatted for a while until Angela said that she was heading back ashore as she wanted to take some pictures of the sun as it streaked the sky in preparation for setting on the sea.

'I'll take a picture of you all too, if you like, just head and shoulders,' Angela offered, 'unless you want boobs included too.'

'Oh, yes please,' Gina said, thrilled at the thought of another marvellous memory to add to her Instagram grid. 'Head and shoulders only though for me,' she quickly clarified.

'I'll come out too, in that case, after you've taken the picture,' Rosie said, 'I've got the phones so I can give you my number to message the picture on to me and then I can share it with the others.'

'Good plan,' Angela smiled, 'and thanks for letting me join you, it was just what I needed.' She exchanged a knowing smile with Gina and made her way out of the sea. After making it back to her clothes, she slipped her sundress on, found her phone hidden underneath her bra and took several pictures of the three friends in various poses, arms in the air, arms around each other hugging and one of Deedee doing a naked star jump almost right out of the water.

When Angela had finished taking photos, Rosie made her way ashore too, flapping her arms around, presumably to dry off in the sun before she too put her dress back on and gave Angela her number. Deedee and Gina swam around some more, chatting and laughing together for a while until Rosie came back to the water's edge.

'Ladies, I'm going to pop back to the taverna and use the loo, I'll get us some drinks too and wait there for you.'

'Thanks, Rosie,' Gina said, not wanting to leave the soothing cocoon of sea water just yet.

'See you later,' Deedee agreed, and the two of them swam back out.

'This is wonderful,' Gina said, wading boobs-deep into the water before turning, kicking her legs up and letting her body float inland as if riding the waves with outstretched arms.

'I told you, didn't I?' Deedee laughed. 'And look at the sky, just glorious.' The two women turned on their backs to admire the smudge of red and gold clouds as the sun seemed to melt further into the sea turning it into a magical mix of glittering, pearlescent colours.

'You sure did, and you were right that we would have the beach all to ourselves,' Gina said, casting a glance towards the rocks where they had left their clothes. 'Luckily, as I'm going to get out now! I'm starting to get cramp in my foot.'

'OK, I'll be out soon too,' Deedee said, paddling beside Gina, before going in for another swim.

Gina, feeling invigorated and way more comfortable in her own skin than she had been before her first skinny-dipping session, wandered over the sand towards the rocks, relishing the warm breeze on her wet skin. Shaking her curls back, she closed her eyes and tilted her head upwards to feel the last of the day's sun on her face before grinning to herself and opening her eyes.

And froze.

Cristos!

Walking towards her with an easel under one arm and head down looking at his phone. There was nowhere to hide. For a split second she contemplated turning and running back into the sea, but it was too late. He had stopped right in front of her and lifted his head.

'Gina?' Cristos said in surprise upon realising it was her. He quickly and politely glanced away, pushed the phone into the back pocket of his jeans and swept a hand through his hair. 'It's good to see you,' he started, then quickly added, 'here, on the beach... the sunset comes soon, and so, um... Yes, it is very nice.'

'Oh, um... hi, I err... Fancy seeing you here,' she grinned inanely, slinging an arm across her boobs, and simultaneously crossing her legs while slapping a hand over the wild rainforest that she had indeed cultivated down there.

'Yes, I always come here, it's the best spot for painting the sunset,' he said, sounding sort of automated while still keeping his eyes politely focused somewhere on the sand near her toes. But Gina was certain there was a smile on his face as she snuck a look and went to run away, which turned into a hoppity kind of toddle, as she immediately discovered running at any kind of speed was impossible with crossed legs and a crampy foot.

'Lovely!' she squeaked over her shoulder, doing her best to get to the rocks to hide and she had just made it when her foot gave way and she face-planted the sand. Immediately, she launched her wet body back up, which now resembled a crumble-covered cake with sand from her face to her feet. Panicking, she found her dress and slung it over her head, which felt like a furnace, and never mind the map of Australia, she had the whole world, the moon and the flaming galaxy working its way all over her body as she cringed and crouched down behind the biggest rock.

Counting to five, Gina inhaled and held her breath before exhaling and repeating the pattern all over again in an attempt to calm herself down. She didn't even dare to look around the side of the rock to see if Cristos was still there.

'What are you doing?' It was Deedee, standing in front of her with her hands on her hips.

'Hiding!' Gina whispered, 'Cristos is over there. Can you believe it?' She whirled a sandy, and slightly crazed index finger round in circles in the air.

'Oh yes, I know,' Deedee said casually. 'I just saw him on my way over here and he's invited us all to his birthday party at the weekend. Well, what he actually said was, "I want to ask Gina to come to my party, but she ran away so fast there was no time," and so I accepted on your behalf and told him Rosie and I would be delighted to escort you. It's his fortieth, which surprised me as he looks much younger, don't you think?'

'You talked to him?' Gina spluttered, flabbergasted. 'Like that? *Fully naked?*'

'Of course! He's an artist, darling, so it's perfectly normal for him to see naked bodies. In fact, as we were chatting, I remembered my modelling days and so mentioned the life-drawing class I posed for one time. He was very interested,' Deedee said, giving her wet hair a nonchalant flick. 'Anyway, the party sounds fun. It's in his family's clifftop villa. *Fireworks and Fernando* is the theme, after a famous footballer, Cristos said. But he seemed extra happy when I told him what a coincidence it was as 'Fernando' is your favourite Abba song and that a Greek villa with music and fireworks sounds very *Mamma Mia!* to me and the perfect way to end our holiday. So Cristos then promised to ask the DJ to play all the Abba hits, although I doubt Cher will be making an appearance like she did in the film, being a global superstar and all.' Then Deedee wandered over to find her dress, leaving Gina staring after her with a slack jaw, her mind still boggling before remembering she needed to retrieve her knickers from where they'd landed, on top of the tallest rock, so high she might need specialist equipment to climb it.

20

Saturday evening and the three friends had enjoyed a cocktail in Gina's hotel room while they got ready together and were now sharing a taxi to take them to Cristos's birthday party.

'So kind of him to invite us,' Gina said, her eyes twinkling beneath sparkly gold eyeshadow and fluttery false lashes. She was wearing a matching, shimmery gold dress with a deep V-neck and floaty bell sleeves and looked very much like she belonged in a cool Abba tribute band, thanks to Rosie, who had loaned her the gorgeously sexy outfit and had even helped her get the make-up right. Deedee had opted for a chic, cream-coloured jumpsuit with lots of gold layered necklaces and strappy wedge-heeled sandals and Rosie was wearing a red tailored trouser suit with nothing underneath the jacket apart from some tape to stop it from flapping open and exposing her breasts.

'Hmm, Deedee and I are just here to keep you company, Gina, and because Cristos was clearly being polite in extending the invitation to your friends. Just how persuasive were you, Deedee?' Rosie turned to look at her.

'Oh, there was no persuasion involved, darling, he agreed right away. But then I was standing in front of him completely naked,' she laughed.

'I think he would have agreed to anything if it meant having Gina at his party,' Rosie said, nudging Gina.

'Oh, don't start that again,' Gina laughed too, rolling her eyes. 'He's really not as into me as you believe,' she said, remembering what the woman in the art gallery had said about him being a player with an eye for the tourist ladies. 'In fact, he's been avoiding me since that day on the beach and I'm sure it's deliberate. I even saw him turn the other way when he saw me walking into the hotel reception area yesterday.'

'Ah, he was probably being polite, assuming you may feel embarrassed after bumping into him with no clothes on. He's giving you space, which is just so considerate,' Rosie gushed. 'But there's no denying the sexual attraction between you two, we all saw it at the art class, and I know I've said it already but I'm going to say it again, he fancies you and most likely couldn't believe his luck when you appeared like a goddess from the sea. And we've had no luck at all in finding your Nico, despite our best efforts asking all the taxi drivers and visiting practically every cafe and hotel on the island over the last few days. Even showing them the photo of Nico just in case someone recognised him, so a little flirt, a dance together maybe, with Cristos, is just the thing you need to give your holiday a happy ending.' Rosie widened her eyes in anticipation.

'What would you do if Cristos made a move?' Deedee joined in, turning her face to scrutinise Gina. 'Or, indeed, would you make a move on him?' She lifted an eyebrow.

'Hmm, highly unlikely to happen. But, if it did, then I have absolutely no idea!' Gina said, truthfully. 'It's been a long time since I've kissed a man, properly intimately, so will I even remember what to do?' She attempted to laugh it off, but there was no denying her overwhelming physical attraction to Cristos was still there. She had even felt it on the beach when standing naked in front of him, and then in the hotel's reception area even though he had pretended not to see her. The minute she spotted him she had felt that same magnetic pull that she had the first time she had clapped eyes on him when she arrived here, and more intensely so again in the art class. Pure physical attraction.

But she had also been thinking about Nico and the love she'd had for him. She yearned to see him again, to talk, even if it was only to find some sort of closure. Something had awakened in her, and she didn't know if it was being back here on the island, or seeing his face again in the photos, which she now had stored in her phone and admittedly had taken to looking at whenever the fancy took her, but whatever it was, there was no denying that she simply couldn't close down her thoughts and feelings and just carry on never seeing him again. 'Plus, I've only been single for little over a week,' Gina added, thinking of the phone call from Colin. There had been no more calls or messages from him, and she hoped that it would stay that way, at least until she got home and had to start dealing with the divorce proceedings and sort out the house. She was dreading it, to be honest, and wished the holiday could last forever, but knew it was an impossibility, so was trying to make the most of every minute of the time she had left here.

'Nearly *three* weeks, you mean!' Rosie chimed. 'Didn't the trial separation start a week or so before you came on holiday? Now you've been here almost two weeks so that makes three weeks and so practically a whole month.' She beamed.

'The perfect time to treat yourself to a thrilling encounter with an extremely hot guy,' Deedee said, in her typical matter-of-fact way, making them all laugh some more.

It was dark now, the navy sky studded with stars, as the taxi pulled into a circular driveway. A trillion little fire pits on tall stands with flickering flames lit the way to an exquisitely romantic villa on a clifftop that had panoramic views of the twinkling island and the soothing sound of the sea surrounding it.

'This is fantastic! It really is just like walking into a scene in one of the *Mamma Mia!* films,' Rosie gasped. 'See the rooftop terrace up there and the candles and the pergola canopy of glowing lantern lights, and there are lemon and olive trees everywhere! Baskets with pretty pink and red flowers trailing down too. It's stunning and would make the most perfect wedding venue.' She clapped her hands together in delight. 'And such a shame I didn't know about this place for my clients – I wonder if Cristos's family ever make it available to hire – although on second thoughts probably for the best as I'm sure my clients wouldn't thank me for telling them about it now, not when they've signed the contract on the other place.'

'No, definitely not,' said Deedee. 'Now, why don't you forget about work, Rosie darling, and just enjoy this beautiful setting.' She smiled kindly, and Rosie nodded in acceptance.

'It's completely magical,' Gina said in a daze as the three of them walked along a long path under a pink bougainvillea covered pergola following the other guests. She had never seen anything like it, only in films, or in her imagination when reading a book set somewhere exotic and beautiful.

'Champagne?' A waiter appeared at the entrance to a large garden with a central mosaic-tiled courtyard. Traditional Greek music was playing, and people were milling around chatting or dancing, teenagers were splashing around in an infinity pool on the far side and small children were racing around weaving in and out of several long tables laden with every kind of delicious looking Greek food you could ever possibly desire.

'Mmm, yes please,' Deedee said, plucking two flutes full of

bubbles from the waiter's gold tray. She handed one to Gina and then to Rosie, before taking one for herself. 'To us, queenagers!' Deedee added, raising her glass, and grinning widely. Gina and Rosie clinked their glasses in celebration too. 'And here's to an exciting evening full of fun and happy times,' she paused on catching a glimpse of Cristos in the crowd, chatting and mingling with various different groups of guests on the far side of the court-yard. 'And possibility!' she finished with a flourish, winking at Gina who had just taken a sip of the gold liquid that tasted delicious as it tingled and teased on her tongue.

After an hour or so of dancing and people-watching, the three women reconvened by a poseur table to catch their breath and check out where Cristos was now.

'Ooh, there he is, and doesn't he look incredible?' Rosie murmured, leaning into Gina and surreptitiously gesturing with an index finger. 'Some men can just work a crisp, cotton white shirt with black tuxedo trousers, especially tailored ones that comple-ment such physical perfection.' She laughed. 'Not sure it's in keeping with the *Fireworks and Fernando* theme though, or perhaps he's just bringing the fireworks.' Rosie winked. 'But who cares... When it's your birthday party, you can do whatever you want to. And did you see his bottom?'

'Come on, instead of us standing here gawping, let's get closer and actually talk to him,' Deedee said. 'It's pretty obvious all the women, and some of the men too, have eyes on him tonight – see them all gazing, and who can blame them when he's standing there looking like an actual Greek god! So let's get you over there, Gina, and see if we can get you to the fireworks element of the party theme.' And Deedee sashayed right across the centre of the courtyard as if walking a runway with an audience all giving her admiring looks and wondering who she was, the beautiful, striking woman wearing such a sheer – as Gina could see now in the glow of the garden lights – silk jumpsuit. Gina stared after her friend in awe, in her late sixties and stunning, and could only dream of having half as much panache when she was that age.

'I couldn't agree more... Let's go, Gina.' Rosie swiftly chugged a mouthful of champagne, before slipping her clutch bag under her arm and taking Gina's hand so she had no choice but to follow right through the centre of the courtyard too. The gold wedge shoes that Rosie had loaned her were half a size too big and so Gina was having to do a tentative shuffle for fear of stepping out of one of them and doing the comedy stagger routine again.

'Gina, you *are* here, I think I see you arrive and then miss you in the crowd,' Cristos said, immediately excusing himself from the group of people around him, to walk towards her with his arms open wide. 'You look incredible, and thank you for coming,' he said politely, enveloping her in a hug before kissing her cheek and there was no awkwardness at all, no mention of the moment on the beach, in fact it was as if it had never happened. After hugging and kissing Rosie, and then Deedee too, who said something to Cristos that made the pair of them laugh wickedly, he turned again to Gina. 'Come, let me introduce you to my friends.' And he took her hand as if they too were old friends, or dare she think it, fantasise it even... actual lovers! Her hand felt like fire in his and the magnetic pull came hurtling back, only a million times more intense and sending sparks flying up her arm and settling around the top of her thighs as she inhaled his sea salt and sandalwood scent. 'Here she is,' Cristos told his friends – three handsome men of varying ages – before talking some more to them in Greek, to which each man nodded and smiled, making impressive faces as they took it in turns to shake Gina's hand. 'I tell them about you and the sunset painting,' Cristos explained. 'The talented artist... they are art collectors, and saw your work in the gallery, but Nia, who runs the gallery now, told them your painting is not for sale.' He frowned.

'Oh... err, well. I wasn't actually sure it was good enough,' Gina said, instantly wishing she hadn't. Blushing awkwardly, she took a big mouthful of champagne, nodding and shrugging as she swallowed.

'It is more than good enough,' one of the men said in perfect English, 'and if you change your mind then please do get in touch with me.' He plucked a card from the inside pocket of his jacket and handed it to Gina.

'Thank you. I sure will, um, yes, thank you,' she managed, putting her glass on a nearby table so she could slot the card into her clutch bag, willing her body to just try, for once, not to overheat but her cheeks already felt as if they were on fire now and why on earth had she said thank you twice, like some kind of overly grateful, foggy-headed fool? She was utterly flattered, and it was amazing that a proper art collector wanted to buy her painting, but still, she supposed it was just overwhelming, and she wasn't used to it. But she had a plan to remedy this as soon as she got home and had already gone online and enrolled herself on an art course at the local college, which she was very much looking forward to. Plus she was going to get her hair properly cut and styled, maybe try something different and yes it was a cliché, the 'break-up makeover' but wasn't that the point? That it would make her feel brand new! She was excited for her new beginning. And was going to book a call with Deedee's doctor too to get her hormones checked. Yes, a complete overhaul was long overdue. She picked up her glass and took another big mouthful of champagne.

'Let's dance.' Cristos turned to Gina and before she could say anything, Deedee had taken her now empty glass and put it on a nearby table, and Rosie was stashing Gina's clutch bag beside hers in the crook of her elbow. Cristos held out a hand for Gina to join him, his smile softening and encouraging as it reached his chestnut brown eyes.

Gina felt a little shove in the small of her back followed by a whispered, 'Go on, darling,' from Deedee as she breezed past with one of the art collectors in tow.

Soon the mosaic tiles of the courtyard had turned into a dance floor full of party guests of all ages and the music had changed too.

'Dancing Queen'.

'Oh my God... Let's dance and have the time our lives!' Rosie yelled, dumping both clutch bags on a nearby table and clapping her hands in the air as she danced her way over to join Gina and Deedee. Cristos and the art collector were clapping too now and standing back to admire Gina, Deedee and Rosie who were all singing at the top of their lungs while dancing and most definitely having the time of their lives. Gina glanced around at all the happy faces, people feeling pure joy, vibrant and alive, celebrating life, and she loved it. Absolutely loved it. It felt like a moment, a proper turning-point moment, the one she had been waiting a very long time for. It dawned on her too that she had no need to worry about saying the wrong thing... It didn't seem like anyone had even noticed. No, it was good vibes only here, and so she tossed away her inhibitions from earlier and just danced like she meant it. Deedee and Rosie sang along to the song as Gina kicked off the wedge shoes, so they slid under the nearest food table and ran back to join her friends, raising her arms in the air as she shook her hips like Shakira and sang the song she knew all the words to from her favourite film, only she wasn't drunk this time. She was completely sober and savouring every second.

As the music changed and the three of them hugged in celebration of the brilliant time they were having, Cristos came over and took Gina's hands in his and moved in close. The rousing strum of 'Fernando' played now, and the younger guests drifted away to dive back in the swimming pool or to help themselves to more baclava. Gina glanced over and saw Rosie by the table where she had left the bags, now with her hands clasped together up underneath her chin as if watching her like a proud parent. Deedee beside her gave Gina a double thumbs-up.

'I see you are having a good time,' Cristos said, leaning in closer to Gina so she could hear him over the music.

'Yes, the best time, Cristos. Thank you for inviting me,' she said, going on tiptoes to reach his ear. Wobbling when her ankle twisted slightly, Gina instinctively placed one hand on his shoulder, and the other on his firm chest to stop herself from falling over. 'Sorry, I—'

'Gina, please... No need to say sorry again,' Cristos smiled gently, his arms moving around her waist. 'I've got you.'

'Oh,' she breathed, her whole body melting into his as the music slowed, and they danced together up close, her face against his chest where she could hear his heartbeat – considerably slower than hers, which was hammering almost right out of her body. No words were necessary as the lights lowered and the warm evening air wrapped around them like their own private bubble.

'Do you feel OK?' Cristos said, dipping his lips to her left ear, which felt as if it was on fire now.

'Yes, it's incredible. I love it here. Are you OK?' she replied in a rush of hedonism, the music, the lights, and the incredibly sexy man holding her and making her feel like the only woman in the world all over again. She knew that he most likely schmoozed all the tourist women this way but right now, right here, she was going to enjoy every moment of it.

'I love it here too, dancing with you,' Cristos said. 'And it's my turn to say sorry,' he added, his mouth nuzzling the side of her neck as they swayed together to the music.

'Oh, what for?' Gina asked.

'When you fell on the sand and I didn't come to help you,' he said, his breath warm and teasing on her skin. 'But I think you feel embarrassed to see me, so I not want to make you more uncomfortable.'

'You saw that?' Gina lifted her head to see into his eyes. Her cheeks flushing as the realisation sunk in that he had seen her bare bottom, the clumsy toddle and her body slamming the sand.

'Yes, I see it. I can't take my eyes off you, Gina. I tell you this... You are beautiful, but I think you do not believe me?'

'Um. Oh,' Gina said, trying to think of something to say before settling on the truth. 'You're right, Cristos, I'm not sure I do believe you.'

'And why is that?'

'Well, look at you, Cristos. You're gorgeous and could have your pick of any woman here.'

'I do not want to pick any woman here,' Cristos said, a look of hurt flicking through his eyes that were fixed on hers. 'I like to pick you. And please believe me, Gina, you are beautiful, a sexy woman and a very talented artist too.'

Silence followed. Gina didn't know what to say until eventually she muttered, 'Nobody has ever said these things to me before,' as if thinking aloud.

'Then they should have,' Cristos said, and with his thumb and index finger, he gently lifted her chin until her lips met his for a kiss. A short, but very, *very* sensual kiss. His hand moved to the nape of her neck sending a shiver all the way down her spine as he pulled her body even closer to his so she could melt into his embrace with her arms wrapped around his muscular back.

They carried on chatting and moving in time to the music, with Cristos smiling and lifting a hand away from her occasionally to shake hands or wave at other guests as they arrived, but always bringing his attention back to Gina. She let herself fully focus on the moment, swaying and twirling together, talking, and laughing and revelling in the mutual physical attraction, even daring herself to wonder where tonight might take them and if her fantasy could become reality. Gina stole a glance over Cristos's shoulder to see Deedee smiling and Rosie do a much less subtle clap as she bobbed her head up and down in glee. Gina smiled and subtly shook her head, pretending to be telling them off for being too obvious, but the truth was that she couldn't actually believe her luck and was relishing every second of dancing up close with Cristos. But then he lifted his head from hers and after saying something in Greek, he waved to someone standing at the top of a small flight of steps on the other side of the courtyard near the entrance.

'My cousin from Athens.'

Gina turned to take a look and then everything seemed to move into slow motion as she saw Deedee and Rosie turn their heads at the same time.

Surely not.

It couldn't be.

But it was.

It definitely was.

Her Nico. Older and broader. The same cheekbones and jawline and smile, right up to his long-lashed eyes. The messy black curls still there too. He looked directly at her. She caught her breath in a gasp on seeing his face changing to one of incredulity, delight, joy, surprise, or was it hurt or regret maybe? She couldn't tell for sure, but now as his eyes darkened and moved from her to Cristos, she wasn't mistaken when she saw Nico's face cloud over in confusion. His waving hand went down, and he turned and swiftly walked away. 'I go to find him,' Cristos said, suddenly dropping his arms from around her trembling body to go after his cousin… Gina's first love.

21

Gina stood motionless, stunned, wondering what to do. Her face smarting from the humiliation of being abandoned on the dance floor as all the other guests stared at her, wondering, no doubt, what on earth had happened to make their handsome host, Cristos, drop his arms from around her body and practically race from the room. She could see people gesticulating as they spoke in rapid Greek, motioning with their heads and flicking their eyes at the tourist lady taken in by his charm and pity for her. *What was I thinking? I should have paid attention to the elderly woman in the gallery. Of course he was playing with me. And what about Nico, taking one look at me and leaving like that!*

'Gina! GINA!' She heard Rosie bellow over the music that was still playing, and then felt Deedee's hand in hers, instantly bringing her back to attention.

'What should I do?' Gina managed, her mind still working overtime to process the horrible jumble of negative thoughts and feelings of rejection and mortification. She tugged awkwardly at the gold dress which suddenly felt suffocating and silly, and she could feel one of the false lashes flapping precariously at the corner of her eye.

'No time to talk. Come on. Let's go.' Deedee clasped Gina's hand tighter and with Rosie steering her from behind, Gina found herself swiftly putting the wedges back on and being propelled through the throng of people across the dance floor and up the stone steps.

Soon the three women were outside on the circular driveway, the trillion or so firepits still flickering as a frame around the scene playing out next to a red sports car in the distance. Cristos was waving his arms around, remonstrating and yelling something in Greek. Nico was pacing up and down with his hands shoved deep into his trouser pockets, his shoulders hunched. Gina couldn't see either of the men's faces clearly in the dark night sky but it was obvious they were arguing and so she went to walk towards them, desperate to try to fix things and to see Nico again. But Deedee still had hold of her hand and she didn't let go.

'Gina, wait, please... I don't think now is a good time to reunite with Nico,' she said, moving an arm around Gina's shoulders. Rosie appeared on her other side and squeezed Gina's free hand.

'I agree,' Rosie said softly. 'Let's just hold back and see what happens. The reunion is supposed to be a happy, joyous occasion. Not awkward and angry. Come on, maybe we should go back inside and wait for them to sort out whatever this is and then I'm sure they'll return to the party.'

'But what if Nico doesn't come back? I'll have missed my chance to talk to him,' Gina said quietly, scanning in the dark to see what the two men were doing now. But Cristos was still yelling, and Nico was waving a dismissive hand in the air. And then her heart sank even further as he was now pulling open the door of the sports car. Cristos went to close the door as if to stop Nico from getting in the car, but it was no use as Nico pushed his cousin's hand away, jumped in and started the engine up with a loud roar. 'Please, I need to go after him,' Gina said, wriggling free from her friends, but she was too late. Nico's red sports car reversed and then thundered away so fast it was out of sight almost immediately.

Gina felt tears stinging in her eyes and the lashes grazing her left cheek, so she pulled the strip free and pushed it inside a pocket. She turned to her friends to gauge what to do next, should she go and talk to Cristos? Try to explain about her love for Nico, their enduring friendship from all those years ago? Or, and then it struck her, did Cristos already know? Was this why he had played her? Was it some sort of stupid game? Gina inhaled hard through her nostrils and out through her mouth in a desperate bid to gain some clarity.

'We should go,' she said, staring at the ground.

'Are you sure?' Rosie asked, glancing over to where Cristos was still standing. Gina hesitated. But then the decision was made for her as Cristos ran towards a silver Mercedes, grabbed open the door, got into the driver's seat and drove off in the same direction that Nico had.

'Yes, I'm definitely sure,' Gina said. 'The dancing queen party mood has evaporated. Plus, I'm sure I look completely ridiculous now with wonky eyelashes,' and she attempted a grin as a cover for the confusion she was feeling inside.

'You look gorgeous as always, Gina,' Deedee started, 'but I agree, this party is over. Let's go back to the hotel and have our own little party with plenty of raspbouzos while we work out a plan of where we go from here.'

22

The last day of the holiday and the hot Greek sun sizzled high in a cloudless blue sky as the three women stepped onto the deck of the yacht.

'Gina, Rosie, this is my dear friend, Yiannis,' Deedee said, slipping her arm around the back of a very distinguished looking Greek man.

'Welcome aboard,' Yiannis said, stepping forward to shake their hands in turn. 'What can I get you to drink?' he asked in an American accent as he led them across the deck towards a cream leather, cushioned, circular seating area. Gina glanced around the yacht, taking it all in, and smiling inwardly on seeing that Deedee had surprised her yet again. She had assumed Yiannis's 'boat' was a sailboat similar to the ones she had seen bobbing around in the shallow water on lengths of rope in the harbour. But no, this was an actual yacht! A proper Sunseeker, with polished teak-panelled flooring, and bedrooms, a kitchen, a dining area and several lounges that Deedee had mentioned mere minutes ago as they arrived and were walking along the jetty. It was bigger than Gina's whole house!

'Lovely to meet you, Yiannis,' Rosie smiled, 'I'll have one of the soft drinks please, I'm still recovering from our little after-party in the hotel last night.'

'I'll have the same please, Yiannis, and so nice to meet you too,' Gina said, delighted to be coming on the sailing trip that Deedee had talked about at the start of the holiday. And perfect timing as she needed the distraction after the shock of seeing Nico and everything that had happened at the party last night.

'Yes, Deedee told me you had several after-party cocktails,' Yiannis laughed, 'so time to relax and recover now.' He gestured to the mini pool, the blue water enticing as it glistened in the Greek sun. 'Make yourself at home, ladies, while we sail around this beautiful bay.'

'Thank you darling.' Deedee gave Yiannis a kiss on his cheek before exchanging a glance, Gina noticed, smiling to herself, wondering if he was the lover that Deedee had told them about at the start of the holiday. She hoped so. Deedee deserved happiness, after the loss of her husband, and Yiannis seemed like a really nice guy and clearly adored her, if the way he gazed at her before kissing her right back, was anything to go by.

'Who will join me?' Deedee asked, having already slipped off her silk kaftan, revealing a stunning turquoise bikini. After setting her drink down in one of the holders, she stepped into the pool. Gina took a sip of the ice-cold orange juice and, after taking off her dress and adjusting the straps of her red swimsuit, went to join Deedee, closely followed by Rosie.

'Mmm, this is amazing.' Gina lowered herself into the perfectly temperature-controlled refreshing water. Stretching out her legs, she picked up her drink and took another sip.

'So how are you feeling after last night, darling?' Deedee asked Gina, stirring her tomato concoction with a large celery stick. 'Sure I can't tempt you with a Bloody Mary to take the edge off?'

'Err... no!' Gina and Rosie said in unison, giving each other a look.

Gina took another sip of orange juice and answered Deedee. 'My head is all over the place, to be honest,' she started. 'I still don't understand why Nico left like that. I know we talked about it a million times over last night, but still...' She paused to contemplate all over again if it was as she had feared: that he was shocked by the change in her. Or he had actually forgotten about her all those years ago, moved on and didn't want reminding of the past.

'And don't be doing that again, Gina,' Rosie said.

'Do what?'

'That self-doubt thing. Devaluing yourself. I know you're thinking that's why he ran away. You looked stunning last night, completely beautiful, and you need to remember that!' Rosie said, sharply, which was unlike her.

'OK.' Gina looked away, grateful that she was wearing shades to hide behind.

'Sorry, Gina,' Rosie immediately said, 'I'm just a little tired today and it's making me grouchy. Plus, I so wanted the romantic reunion for you. But you're right, it doesn't make sense that Nico would just speed off in his car like that. Unless of course he's just rude with no manners at all.'

'He was shocked,' Deedee said, quickly, followed by, 'well, that's my theory... he saw his cousin kissing you and most likely reacted in the moment.'

'Hopefully we can find him before we go home tomorrow,' Rosie said, turning her head to look at Deedee.

'I'm not sure how we can do that,' Gina said, 'with nobody knowing where Cristos is. I even asked at the reception desk this morning, and they said he's not due to come back to work for another two weeks. He's having a holiday in Italy to celebrate his birthday apparently. I could go to his family's villa to see if Nico is there, but it doesn't feel appropriate after both men literally ran away from me last night. Plus, Nico could have already gone back to Athens, for all we know.'

'Hmm, so what will you do, Gina?' Deedee lifted an eyebrow.

'I thought I might leave a letter with the reception staff to give to Cristos when he returns and ask if he can pass on my details to Nico, with my phone number, Instagram, that kind of thing in the hope that Nico will make contact and want to talk to me. Although I'm not holding out much hope after the way he left so swiftly last night.'

'Oh, you mustn't give up hope, Gina,' Rosie said, 'you never know what might happen in the future.'

'True,' Deedee said, smiling at Rosie. Gina managed a smile too as she fell silent and thought about what she could write in the letter to Nico.

Several hours later, having enjoyed a delicious lunch of grilled shrimp and Greek salad in the shaded dining area, followed by plenty of sunbathing with intermittent cool-down soaks in the pool and admiring the breathtaking view of the Greek island coastline, the yacht had sailed in, close to the shore of a small cove.

'I recognise this beach,' Gina said, sitting up and lifting her shades to get a better look. 'We are at the other end of the beach, not far from where we went skinny-dipping. Yes, Toula's is over the dunes there on the other side to the right.' She pointed towards the grassy-topped mounds of sands on the horizon. 'And over there to the left is where I used to come and sit as a teenager to sketch.' She fell silent.

Yiannis appeared. 'You can swim ashore, if you like. I can ask the crew to set up the ladder over the side. Or you can just jump into the sea... it's perfectly safe here, the water is rock free.'

'Oh, yes please, could we? I'd love to take a look,' Gina said.

'And I have the waterproof bumbag in my tote,' Rosie remembered. 'So we can bring phones to take pictures.'

'Good idea,' Gina said, excited to be going back to the beach where she had spent so many summers snorkelling, shell collecting, horse riding on wet sand and sitting on the rocks with Nico, sketching and chatting and then, later on, making love under that velvety moonlit sky.

'That's settled then,' Deedee said, 'let's swim ashore.'

The sea water sparkled and lapped gently around Gina's bare feet as she stood up in the shallows to walk across the wet sand. The sun glistening as it dried her skin and curly hair which she scooped up into a bun secured with a scrunchie from her wrist.

'I recognise those rocks over there.' Gina pointed to a cluster of granite mounds on the far left of the beach, shaded by grassy cliffs and tamarisk trees. 'That's where Nico and I used to come to chat and sketch the view.'

'Let's head over there then,' Deedee said, walking alongside Gina, with Rosie on her other side.

'This beach is beautiful,' Rosie said. 'No wonder you two young love birds used to hang out here, it's a perfect place to fall in love.'

'Yes,' Gina said quietly. 'It was.'

The three women walked across the sand until they reached the rocks.

'Oh, someone has beat us to it.' Gina spotted a couple of blue and white striped towels on the flat of one of the rocks, a silver bucket beside it packed with ice around several cans of drink. 'It's Fanta Orange! Why would someone leave this here?' she said vaguely, surveying the scene and seeing the beach was deserted. 'Do you think they've forgotten?'

Gina turned around to see Deedee and Rosie looking over to the grassy dunes and then back to her with wide smiles wreathed on their faces.

'No darling, I don't think they've forgotten!' Deedee looked again towards the dunes behind the rocks. Gina followed her friend's eyeline and saw a man wearing dark shades, a white T-shirt and faded jean shorts walking through the dunes towards them with a parasol under one arm.

'Oh Gina, I can't contain the surprise any longer. It's Nico! He's here for you. He never did forget you. Deedee went back to the villa early this morning to see if she could find him and, well... Nico is here now.' Rosie clapped her hands together and did a little dance on the sand.

'*Rosie.*' Deedee nudged her. 'Remember what we agreed?' She motioned with her head towards Nico who had almost reached the beach.

'Yes, yes, I know, but let's at least get a picture of the moment they reunite,' Rosie pleaded, hurriedly going to unzip her bumbag.

'We can do that later, maybe... but for now, let's leave them be.' Deedee turned to Gina who was rooted to the spot, her heart racing so hard there was a very real danger she might keel over and cover herself in sand all over again. She felt Deedee's hand, reassuringly on her back, as she went to leave. 'Good luck, Gina, it's time to fly,' she whispered. 'We'll be waiting on the boat for you.'

23

Nico reached the rock as Gina still stood rooted to the spot. She opened her mouth to say something, but the words wouldn't come out. He was here, so that must mean he hadn't forgotten about their romance completely, and he had brought Fanta Orange so he must remember the good times too. It was a nice touch, she thought, but still, he had literally raced away from her last night and so she went apprehensively towards the rock where Nico was standing. Her heart was still hammering, and she wished she was wearing something more than the red swimsuit that made her feel exposed, vulnerable. Seeming to sense this, Nico lifted one of the towels from the rock and handed it to her without saying a word.

'Thank you.' She wrapped the towel around her waist as Nico flipped open the parasol and lodged the pole into a crevice, so it rested at an angle to shade them. He sat down on the other towel and, following his cue, Gina sat too. Reaching into the ice bucket, Nico lifted a can of Fanta and gave it to her. 'You remembered,' she managed, conscious that he still hadn't said a word. Taking a can for himself, he flipped the tab and took a big mouthful.

'Of course, and still as good as it tasted then,' Nico said, in perfect English with the hint of a Greek accent, looking at the can and then shifting his gaze directly ahead towards the sea. Gina opened her can and took a few small swigs, the taste transporting her back in time to her teenage self. Silence followed as they sat side by side. Gina could feel the skin on her bare arm tingling from the close proximity of his tanned arm, mere millimetres away. His scent the same as it always was, spicy and woody and so very evocative, nostalgic even, of happier times where there had been no awkwardness, only joy and laughter and good moments sketching and kissing and making love. She drew a big breath in and then out, in an attempt to calm herself, to focus. She needed to find out what had happened to him since they last sat here together thirty years ago because he seemed sad, angry even.

'Nico, it's good to see you,' she started, wishing she could say so much more, but instinct told her to tread carefully. He seemed a million miles away. Or maybe it was just too late, and they were strangers now and he was merely here to be polite after Deedee had somehow persuaded him to come to the beach and meet her.

'My cousin will hurt you; you know.' Nico glanced at her briefly before staring out to sea again. 'He always does.'

'Um... We are not together,' Gina found herself saying.

'You like him though?'

'I don't know him,' she answered truthfully. 'He's attractive, yes, but—' She paused and took another mouthful of Fanta. 'Nico, I had no idea you were going to be at the party last night, if I had then—' she paused again. 'It's such a coincidence.'

'Not really,' he said.

'What do you mean?' Gina loosened the towel and stretched out her legs.

'An old friend from the market told me about an English woman looking for someone called Nico.' He fell silent again before adding a few seconds later, 'Her first love.'

'I see,' Gina said. 'My friend, Rosie, was trying to help.'

Nico shrugged. 'And when my cousin talks about a beautiful, but shy, English woman called Gina, an incredible artist, he invites to his party, and I wonder if it's the same woman I used to know. Could it be possible that you had returned to the island? So, I came right away hoping you'd still be here, but it seems I'm too late. You have moved on again.' Nico shook his head.

'Again?'

'Like you did before, Gina. And I get it, you fell in love with another man and married him, but it wasn't the same for me. I didn't ever really move on. I couldn't get you out of my head or heart in fact, and it was hard. It ruined my own marriage in the end.' He stopped talking and put the can of Fanta down to push a hand through his dark curls. After inhaling and letting out a long puff of air, he carried on, as if unburdening himself of feelings he had harboured for a very long time. 'And that was all my fault, I should have made myself wait until I was really over you, before I rushed into another relationship, but like a fool... I know that now,' he smiled wryly. 'I thought I could transfer my love to someone else. But it doesn't work that way. "Leftover love" my wife called it. Yes, my biggest regret. It was a sad marriage and she deserved better. Delphine died three years ago.' He lowered his head.

'Nico, I'm so sorry.' Gina instinctively went to touch the back of his hand but as her fingertips reached his warm skin, he pulled away. 'Sorry,' she added again in a quiet voice, trying to work out what was going on. More silence followed. 'So why did you come back here?'

'I don't know.' He shook his head. 'Curiosity perhaps? To see if I still felt the same way, or if it would be different; that I could finally forget and let you go. I know you never really loved me, but Gina, I loved you with all my heart and I never forgot about you.'

'What do you mean? Why do you say that? I did really love

you,' Gina said, her voice catching. 'With all my heart too. You were my first love.'

'I thought so but then when you stopped writing...'

'I know... and I'm sorry, things changed when my mum died and—'

'I remember Shirley so well; she was fun and kind.' He nodded, and a small knot caught in Gina's throat. He remembered, a shared history, and she wanted to hear more, she wanted to talk about the good times, the happy holidays with him and the memories he had of her mum, but not right now. In this moment she needed to know why he'd thought she had never really loved him.

'And then I met my husband,' she continued, 'and I did stop writing to you for a while but then sent more letters later on to explain and to see if we could continue our friendship. It was wonderful to keep that connection, to remember the brilliant times we had here, it was an escape of sorts, a way to cope with the grief by blocking it out almost and just focusing on the memories. But in the end, it became painful when I didn't hear back from you, and I just couldn't carry on.'

Silence followed.

'I don't understand.' Nico turned to her; his forehead creased. 'I only heard from you once again, after that summer when I asked if you'd come island-hopping. Did you move to a new house?' He lifted an eyebrow. 'Because I sent letters. But nothing came back.'

'No.' She shook her head, a swirling feeling building in the pit of her stomach. 'I remember the postcard that came out of the blue on my birthday... I still have it, the last time I heard from you.'

'And I remember the letter you sent in return. I didn't keep that one though,' he said solemnly. 'I didn't need to, every word of it has stayed with me.' He finished the last of his Fanta and crushed the can before dropping it back in the ice bucket.

And then Gina knew. She hadn't been able to find the memory

box with Nico's address inside and it wasn't on the postcard, so she
hadn't been able to send a reply! The swirling feeling turned to
nausea, and she stood up, resting her hands on her hips, she paced
around, taking deep breaths to settle herself. Nico was on his feet
now too and standing opposite her.

'What did the letter say?' she said, her voice soft and low.

'Gina, please... The words were painful to read,' he paused, and
she pushed up her shades to look him in the eye, pleading, as she
had to be sure. He lifted his shades away too and the same, velvety
brown eyes she remembered looking into, as they'd made love on
this very sand, met hers. 'OK, the letter was cold, hard and unlike
you.' He glanced away. 'It was typed too, which was different, but I
guess you wanted to make sure I knew how serious you were. You
said our relationship was only ever a bit of holiday fun, that it was
nothing serious, forgettable in fact, and that you wished for me to
stop bothering you now that you were married and in love with
another man. So I respected your wishes and kept my distance, but
I never stopped thinking about you or loving you. I figured if you
truly love someone then you have to let them go...' He put his
shades back on and pushed his hands into the pockets of his jean
shorts.

'Oh Nico.' Gina stepped forward, but he took a step back. 'I
didn't write that letter. I promise you, but I know who did! What
you and I had was special and I know it changed when I didn't
come here on holiday any more, but I thought our love had deepened in those letters to one of a true, everlasting friendship, even if
we couldn't be together romantically.' Tears slid down Gina's face –
hot, angry, and then sad – pooling in the dip at her collarbones.
She lifted her shaking hands to wipe them away, but it was no use,
the tears turned into a torrent trickling over the backs of her hands
and couldn't be stemmed. She crouched down on the towel as if to
comfort herself as she used a corner of it to clean the salty tears

away, starkly aware of Colin's cruelty cutting her off from her past and causing unnecessary hurt for Nico.

Nico was next to her now, crouched down beside her, pulling her into his arms until somehow, they were tangled together on the rock, sitting silent and still. Holding one another as the rhythm of the waves tumbling over the sand and the warm breeze soothed them. As the tears subsided and Gina's swell of emotion steadied, she turned her face towards Nico.

'My ex-husband sent that typed letter, I'm sure of it. And he must have intercepted your mail to me because it never reached me, only the postcard on my birthday when I was home alone.' Gina shook her head. 'And I used to leave my letters to you on the hall table for posting as Colin works in an office so said he could easily drop them off in their mail room. I'm assuming they never even made it that far.'

Silence followed.

'Shuuuuuush,' Nico soothed gently, reaching for a towel which he draped around her shoulders. 'You're shaking,' he murmured, the heel of his hand moving in circles over her back before he lifted it to her shoulder and held her tightly.

'I'm so sorry, Nico. I truly am, and sad that you were led to believe our relationship meant nothing to me for all these years.' She dipped her head onto his shoulder. 'I've often wondered what would have happened if I had accepted your invitation and taken the trip to go island-hopping. It seems that we both could have had very different lives if I had...' Gina's voice faded as she contemplated that alternative path, if only she'd had the courage to take it. But instead, she had chosen safety and security. And, although she didn't regret those early years of her marriage, recent revelations meant the memory of that time would always be tainted.

'The past is gone,' Nico said, 'and we are here now.' He reached into his pocket and then lifted her hand to place something within it. 'The future can be ours.' And Gina gasped as she saw the friend-ship bracelet that she had given him all those years ago.

'You kept it!'

'Always... to "Bring Me Sunshine",' he smiled, remembering *their* song as she touched a finger to the now fading letter beads that she had threaded onto the string before tying the two ends into a heart knot.

'"In your smile",' she sang softly, turning her face to his for a kiss... the sweet tang of Fanta still there on his lips.

EPILOGUE
KALOSIROS, GREECE... ONE YEAR LATER

Gina swirled her paintbrush in the water jug and stood back to admire the now familiar scene. Seven easels, dotted around the garden to give each artist a breathtakingly beautiful view of the beach at the bottom of the hill, rugged and wild with grass-topped cliffs turning into rows of olive trees and grape vineyards. A red and purple winged butterfly fluttered from a nearby arch of pink bougainvillea to land on the romance book on the wooden table beside her. She loved this part of the day, the golden hour, when the light was perfect for painting or sitting back and reading. Only these days it felt as though she was actually living inside one of the gloriously escapist romance novels she adored reading – as many as she could lay her hands on.

When the holiday ended last summer and Gina had returned to England to kick off the divorce process, she had immersed herself in the art course at the local college but had yearned to be back here on the island. So when Colin had said he and Pam would only move out if the house was sold, she had jumped at the chance and got the estate agent round the next morning. She had been staggered at how much the cottage was now worth. A cash buyer came along, so the sale was swift and after giving Colin a fair share of the proceeds, as advised by her solicitor, to reflect his 'interest' over the years and allow Gina to feel fully free from him, she had just enough money left to put her plan into action; to help Meryl by buying the dilapidated holiday apartment complex. But the best part of packing up to leave was finding the memory box that had been hidden under a wonky floorboard, along with all of Nico's letters to her that she had never received, and the ones she had written to him, revealed when a rug was rolled up to go in the container to be shipped over here. All the photos of Gina with her mum from those happy holidays were now on the wall in the office, making Gina smile every time they caught her eye. She adored being here, feeling that same happiness and contentment. It was where she felt closest to her mum, who Gina was convinced would have wanted her to sell their house and move to the place where she always felt happiest, to truly live her life the way she wanted to.

The last six months had been hard work, cleaning the apartments and clearing the grounds but so worth it to see so many happy artists from around the world coming here for the various art workshops and holidays. Gina provided all the tools, easels, paints and of course the perfect view, and thanked her lucky stars every day that she got to do this. Meryl was over the moon too to be able to take a step back now and enjoy a well-earned retirement at last. Although she still liked pottering around the place, petting Kip and folding the washing in the garden or making coffee for Gina when she had a rare break from running the holiday home business, that was now thriving again.

'There she is!' Gina heard voices behind her and so turned around.

'We've been looking all over for you. This place is enormous... The grounds are exquisite and would be perfect for hosting wedding receptions. Have you thought about that at all?'

'Oh Rosie, I've missed you.' Gina put the paintbrush and jug down on the grass and hugged her dear friend. They messaged every day in their WhatsApp group – aptly called 'Come Away With Me', the profile picture of the three of them skinny-dipping – after they had made a pact to meet up as often as they could for more fantastic holidays together. But it wasn't the same as seeing each other in real life. 'And Deedee, you look even more sensational, if that's even possible.'

'It's the se—'

'Sex!' The three friends yelled at the same time, laughing and looping arms as Gina steered them over to the main house where she lived now.

'Let me take these for you.' Gina went to pull Deedee's and Rosie's wheelie suitcases, one in each hand.

'You will not!' Deedee said, pretending to be cross.

'But you're my guests. And paying to stay here... Even though I told you a trillion times at least that it really wasn't necessary.'

'And we are your best friends who want to support your brilliant new business venture, so we will take our own luggage,' Deedee told her firmly.

'But I wouldn't say no to a nice cool shower... My new HRT is taking a while to kick in,' Rosie added, fanning herself dramatically.

'I can do better than that,' Gina said, pointing to where the pool was, cleared of debris and fully restored to how it had been when she'd holidayed here as a child. 'Or if you follow this path, it will take you down to the beach, if you fancy a sunset skinny-dip instead?' She lifted one eyebrow, looking in Deedee's direction.

'Ooh, maybe later. First, I can't wait to shower and get dressed up for your birthday party,' Rosie said, her eyes twinkling.

'So how does it feel to be fifty, darling?' Deedee asked, turning to Gina as they reached the apartment Gina had reserved for them.

'Pretty good, actually,' she said, pushing her now long brown curls, honeyed from being in the sun, away from her face.

'Well, you're obviously thriving if the twinkle in your eyes is anything to go by.' Rosie nudged her.

Later, having showered and done their hair and make-up together in Gina's bedroom, the three women went to the garden to join the other guests who were mingling and chatting and laughing together. Music was playing; a special party mix of mostly Abba and uplifting happy house music that Rosie's son, Tom, had made especially for the party.

'Dr Nico, and Pavlos,' Gina smiled, 'I'm so pleased you could make it.' She gave them each a hug before Rosie and Deedee did too and then went to mingle. 'And Anne! Oh my God, you came.' Gina couldn't believe it, secretly thinking that Anne might have so many far more important engagements to attend than her ex-cleaner's fiftieth birthday party. They had kept in touch after Gina handed in her notice, with the occasional email or Instagram comment.

'I wasn't going to miss this for the world, my dear,' Anne said, gently placing a hand on each of Gina's arms to give her a kiss on the cheek, not once or twice, but three alternating times.

'Oh, um... thank you,' Gina said a little awkwardly, smiling and doing her best to reciprocate the sophisticated greeting that she wasn't used to.

'Yes, it's a pleasure to be here, and I've taken a leaf out of your book and travelled here solo. Harold is holding the fort at home,' Anne explained, lifting her glass to take a sip of prosecco.

'Well, good for you,' Gina nodded, her smile widening. 'But he was very welcome to join us here for the party too.'

'I know, and that was very kind of you, but I'm a firm believer in having a little holiday by myself from time to time and so far, this one is proving to be a marvellous tonic. Anyway, I shan't hold you up, I can see someone else who is looking keen to talk to you over there.' Anne pointed through the crowd towards the stone steps leading up to a veranda that Gina had discovered disguised by undergrowth one day while clearing the garden. 'But before you go, I'm so delighted for you, Gina, what you've created here is incredible. You're truly an inspiration and most *certainly* a woman of substance.'

'Thanks to you,' Gina said. 'I won't ever forget that day you helped me.'

'My dear, you helped yourself! And good for you, having the courage to free yourself and turn your life around... You're now living your dream, it seems.'

'Oh Anne, you are so kind. And welcome here any time.' Gina pulled her friend in for a proper hug before making her way over to the veranda.

'Hello.' Gina beamed as she lifted her long, silky, satin silver skirt and carefully walked up the stone steps.

'Hello you.' Nico turned around and with his back to the breathtakingly beautiful view of the Greek island with the sparkling sea and the golden sun on the horizon dazzling around him, he rested his hands either side of him on the top of the veranda's curved brick wall. Gina caught her breath on seeing his handsome, tanned face, the stubbled chin and thick, messy black hair. The crinkles at the corners of his eyes the only change from the young man he'd been when they first fell in love. Moving closer, Gina slipped her arms around his waist.

'I'm so pleased you're here,' she breathed, drawing in his delicious scent. She hadn't seen him for over a week which felt like a lifetime these days, now they were trying to make up for lost time. Nico still lived in Athens and worked as an eminent paediatrician and so having time away from the hospital was a rarity and something that Gina fully appreciated as it made their precious time together even more special.

Soon after they had reunited on the rock that day, Nico had been invited to deliver a keynote speech at a medical conference in London and so had managed to extend the trip so they could spend some time together getting to know each other again. Gina had been delighted to show him the sights, at last, in person, and yes, he'd 'had his way with her'... several times, and it was glorious and sexy and every bit as special as the first time they had made love on the beach under a velvety moonlit sky. They had soon fallen in love all over again and their relationship had deepened further over the last year with many phone calls and online conversations in the first month or so while she had still been in England. She loved the memories of catching her breath every time he had appeared on the screen, looking ridiculously hot in his doctor scrubs, but had also found the whole 'see but not touch' experience extremely frustrating. But now that she lived on the island, only forty minutes' sailing time to Piraeus Port near Athens, it was always thrilling to hop on a boat and sail over to see him, if only for a few precious hours while he was on call.

'You look sensational, Gina.' Nico gently took her hands in his and held her at arm's length to fully see her before enveloping her in a hug. 'Happy birthday, my darling,' he whispered, his warm breath nuzzling the side of her neck and sending shivers down her spine before turning into a tantalising swirl of longing between her thighs.

'Oh Nico, this is so much better than a postcard,' she laughed, remembering a brief glimpse of the memory of that birthday before, when his postcard with the bobbing sailboat had landed on her doormat. If only she had known then what the future would hold. The life she lived right now, here in this moment with the Greek sun burning gold, copper and amber as it streaked the sky like an exquisite painting, behind the man that she truly loved. His lips reached hers, his mouth hot as they kissed passionately, the longing intensifying and turning into a trilogy of sparkling fireworks as she held him tight, knowing she would never let him go again. And knowing too, that everything had worked out the way it is supposed to and that sometimes you have to revisit the past to figure out the future. Gina's future was here, with her first love, her everlasting love, and her friends, and it was so much more than she had ever dreamed it would be. She was having the time of her life.

ACKNOWLEDGEMENTS

My first thank you is to Rowan Lawton for her generous guidance, support, kindness, friendship, and wise counsel as always; I'm so grateful for the comfort and reassurance this gave me as I wrote this book while navigating the adoption process. Thanks to my talented editor, Isobel Akenhead, whose passion for publishing, intuitive editing, and love for our GIRLS right from the start means the world to me.

Thanks to the brilliantly dynamic publishing team at Boldwood for the warm, and very exciting welcome and for sharing my ambitions for the future. Thanks as always to the inspiring, wise and funny women in my life; my dear friends Dr Caroline Cauchi, Tracey Capelett, Rachel Noble-Forbes and my Saturday Ladies, I'm so happy and thankful for your friendship. Thank you to Carmel Harrington for the treasure hunt idea, and for your kind-hearted friendship. To my other author friends, Lola Jaye, Sarah Morgan, Samantha Tonge, Veronica Henry, Milly Johnson and Cathy Bramley, your generosity is so very much appreciated.

My biggest thanks goes to you, my readers, from all around the world. I love chatting to you on social media and reading your emails and messages, and I feel very humbled on hearing you've chosen one of my books to read in your precious holiday time, and by the trust you place in me when you share personal accounts of how my books have been a comfort or a welcome escape during a difficult time in your lives. Especially now when I know many of you are enduring extremely challenging times in the countries where you live, I send love and solidarity to you. You mean the world to me and make it all worthwhile. Thank you so very much for loving my books as much as I love writing them for you.

And lastly, but definitely not least, a very special thank you to my family. As a young girl going through an unhappy childhood I used to dream of having a happy family one day and so it fills my heart with joy to have the continuous love and unwavering support of my husband, Paul, aka Cheeks, my daughter and new son who all bring me sunshine every day.